ʃ *β*

It seemed Julia Tennant was always slipping away from him

Max watched her slim figure walk swiftly down the sidewalk to the bus stop, her shoulders hunched. He felt a chill spread through him.

She loved her child. The anguish he'd heard in her voice had been wrenchingly real. Yet her daughter was supposed to have been on the flight with Julia's husband the night he was killed. For Julia to be guilty, she'd have to have been willing to kill not just her husband, but her child, as well.

The floor beneath his feet seemed to buckle. "She didn't do it," he breathed.

And suddenly he was sprinting toward her, calling her name, knowing he had to stop her from walking out of his life again.

Dear Reader,

We have a fabulous fall lineup for you this month and throughout the season, starting with a new Navajo miniseries by Aimée Thurlo called SIGN OF THE GRAY WOLF. Two loners are called to action in the Four Corners area of New Mexico to take care of two women in jeopardy. Look for Daniel "Lightning" Eagle's story in *When Lightning Strikes* and Burke Silentman's next month in *Navajo Justice*.

The explosive CHICAGO CONFIDENTIAL continuity series concludes with Adrianne Lee's *Prince Under Cover*. We just know you are going to love this international story of intrigue and the drama of a royal marriage—to a familiar stranger.... Don't forget: a new Confidential branch will be added to the network next year!

Also this month—another compelling book from newcomer Delores Fossen. In *A Man Worth Remembering*, she reunites an estranged couple after amnesia strikes. Together, can they find the strength to face their enduring love—and find their kidnapped secret child? And can a woman on the edge recover the life and child she lost when she was framed for murder, in Harper Allen's *The Night in Quesiton*? She can if she has the help of the man who put her away.

Pulse pounding, mind-blowing and always breathtaking—that's Harlequin Intrigue.

Enjoy,

Denise O'Sullivan
Associate Senior Editor
Harlequin Intrigue

THE NIGHT IN QUESTION

HARPER ALLEN

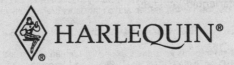

HARLEQUIN®

TORONTO • NEW YORK • LONDON
AMSTERDAM • PARIS • SYDNEY • HAMBURG
STOCKHOLM • ATHENS • TOKYO • MILAN • MADRID
PRAGUE • WARSAW • BUDAPEST • AUCKLAND

ISBN 0-373-22680-2

THE NIGHT IN QUESTION

Copyright © 2002 by Sandra Hill

This edition published by arrangement with Harlequin Books S.A.

® and TM are trademarks of the publisher. Trademarks indicated with ® are registered in the United States Patent and Trademark Office, the Canadian Trade Marks Office and in other countries.

Visit us at www.eHarlequin.com

Printed in U.S.A.

ABOUT THE AUTHOR

Harper Allen lives in the country in the middle of a hundred acres of maple trees with her husband, Wayne, six cats, four dogs—and a very nervous cockatiel at the bottom of the food chain. For excitement she and Wayne drive to the nearest village and buy jumbo bags of pet food. She believes in love at first sight, because it happened to her.

Books by Harper Allen

HARLEQUIN INTRIGUE
468—THE MAN THAT GOT AWAY
547—TWICE TEMPTED
599—WOMAN MOST WANTED
628—GUARDING JANE DOE*
632—SULLIVAN'S LAST STAND*
663—THE BRIDE AND THE MERCENARY*
680—THE NIGHT IN QUESTION

*The Avengers

Don't miss any of our special offers. Write to us at the following address for information on our newest releases.

Harlequin Reader Service
U.S.: 3010 Walden Ave., P.O. Box 1325, Buffalo, NY 14269
Canadian: P.O. Box 609, Fort Erie, Ont. L2A 5X3

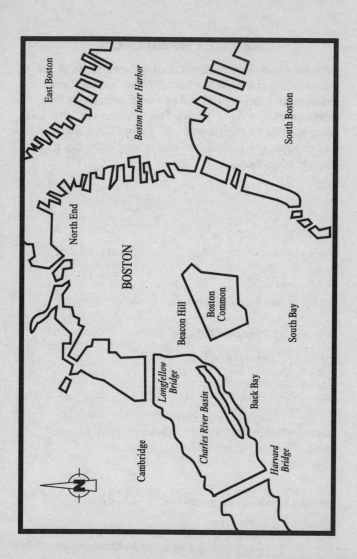

CAST OF CHARACTERS

Julia Tennant—She's spent the past two years in prison. Now she's out and determined to find her child—with the help of the man who once tore her world apart.

Max Ross—The FBI agent had Julia convicted of a crime she didn't commit. Falling in love with her was an even bigger mistake.

Willa—Four years old when she was taken from her mother, Willa now seems to be the target of a killer—and her mother is in a race against time to find her and save her.

Noel Tennant—He lost a corporate battle against his brother Kenneth. Did he seek his revenge in a murder plot?

Barbara Van Hale—Kenneth's sister, Barbara lost her own husband when the bomb went off. After fearfully testifying against Julia, Babs was put into a witness protection program along with the little girl she now has custody of—Julia's daughter, Willa.

Olivia Tennant—The Tennant family matriarch, she's destroyed each of her children's lives one by one. But did she arrange to have her own son eliminated?

Peter Symington—Blind since birth, Noel's friend may be the only one who sees the truth.

To Ann Leslie, with thanks and appreciation.

Chapter One

She looked nothing like he remembered.

Max Ross studied the unnaturally still figure of the woman sitting across from him while their waitress carelessly slapped down a couple of cups of coffee on the stained tabletop.

"Anything else?" The waitress's nametag said, Hi! I'm Cherie—Have a Great Day! There was a smear of ketchup on the collar of her uniform, and her mouth was bracketed with two dissatisfied lines. Max doubted if she could make anyone's day great. Certainly she wasn't having an uplifting effect on the silent woman across from him. Except for pulling the thick cup and saucer closer toward her with one finger, Julia hadn't given the slightest indication that she was taking any notice of either him or the incongruously named Cherie. It was as if there was an invisible shell around her, a shell that nothing was allowed to penetrate.

So what? He didn't give a damn if Julia Tennant never had a good day the rest of her life, he thought coldly. Just walking around Boston as a free woman was way more than she deserved.

"That's all, thanks." Without raising his eyes he held

out a twenty. "Keep the table next to us empty for half an hour."

The twenty was plucked out of his hand, but the waitress didn't move. "No guarantees, mister. If one of my tables is free then I lose out on tips. Making a living is tough these days, right, girlfriend?"

This last was addressed to Julia in an attempt at female solidarity. When Max saw the chipped red nails rest lightly on Julia's shoulder he started to say something.

He was too late.

"Get the hand off. *Now!*"

She was still staring down at her coffee cup and he could swear those pale lips hadn't moved, but the words had hissed out in a shockingly threatening undertone and the spoon she'd been using to stir her coffee was clenched in her fist. Before he could intervene, Julia lifted her eyes to the frozen waitress.

"I'm not your girlfriend, honey. And I don't like being touched." A lank strand of hair fell into her eyes but she ignored it. "If you want to sweeten the deal you can probably get ten bucks more out of him, but don't push your luck."

No one else in the place seemed to have noticed the incident, and Max wanted to keep it that way. He handed the shaken Cherie another bill. "Half an hour. This is private, okay?"

"Okay." The white-faced woman flicked a frightened glance at Julia, now hunched over her coffee again as if nothing at all had occurred. "Private. Sure, mister."

She turned and made a beeline for the swinging doors to the kitchen, ignoring the disgruntled looks of other customers who were trying to get her attention.

"Lousy coffee." Julia patted the breast pocket of the cheap windbreaker she was wearing and pulled out a battered pack of cigarettes. Sticking one in her mouth, she lit a match with the economical movements he was beginning to associate with her, squinting against the smoke. She didn't leave the pack on the table, Max noticed, instead tucking it securely back into the pocket it had come from.

"You didn't smoke before, did you?" he asked. As soon as the words were out of his mouth he felt stupid. She glanced up as if sensing his discomfiture.

"No, Mr. Ross, I didn't smoke before," she said flatly. "I've picked up a few bad habits in the last two years. And I've lost a few too—like pretending I give a damn about small talk." The corners of her lips lifted humorlessly, but her eyes were opaque, giving no clue to her real feelings. "What do you want from me?"

The Boston papers had called her The Porcelain Doll, and the name had been apt, Max recalled. Her skin had had the pearlescent glow of delicate china, her fair hair had brushed like a swath of spun silk against the shoulders of the discreetly expensive black suits she'd worn and her eyes had been the bluest he'd ever seen, fringed with thick dark lashes. Much of the time they'd been spilling over with tears, and that had reminded him of a doll too.

God, she'd been able to turn on the waterworks at a second's notice, he remembered with sudden anger—trembling, crystalline drops that hadn't been real enough to smudge her mascara. At the time of her trial he'd been thirty-one, and no gullible FBI probationer but a ten-year veteran of the Agency. But even he had found himself wondering once or twice if there was any way he'd made a mistake about her. Julia Tennant had been on the stand for three gruelling days, and at the end of the third she'd looked as breathtakingly beautiful as if she'd just choked up watching a particularly emotional rendition of *La Boheme,* rather than being mercilessly cross-examined on multiple murder charges.

Actually, her nickname had been The Porcelain Doll Bomber. Those slim and still-delicate fingers had handed over a gift-wrapped package to her husband, Kenneth Tennant, just minutes before he'd boarded his executive jet. Those blue eyes had probably widened in well-rehearsed horror as, only seconds after takeoff, the resulting explosion had rained flaming debris through the night sky.

But in the end, despite her tears and the protestations of innocence that even days of grilling couldn't shake, the twenty-three-year-old widow had been found guilty of the murders of her husband and the three other unfortunate souls who'd been on the aircraft with him that night. Justice had been done, Max thought with grim satisfaction. His only regret at her sentencing had been that she didn't have four lifetimes to spend in prison—one for each victim she'd callously snuffed out.

A few days ago he'd been told she was about to be released. Considering the date, he'd thought it was a bad April fool's joke at first.

"If we're just going to sit here gazing into each other's eyes I've got better things to do, Mr. Ross." Julia ground the butt of her cigarette out in an ashtray and pushed her coffee cup away from her as she started to rise from her chair. "It's my first night of freedom. You're not how I planned to spend it."

"Sit down." His voice revealed nothing of the outrage simmering inside him, but for a moment he saw a flicker of apprehension behind that blank gaze. Tucking a stray strand of lusterless hair behind her ear in the first extraneous gesture he'd seen her make, she sank back into her seat.

From the tables around them came a buzz of noisy conversation. Cherie hadn't reappeared, but the two other waitresses working the floor called out their orders to the short-order cook at the counter and exchanged sarcastic banter with the customers. Max hardly noticed. Under the harsh lighting Julia's skin was unhealthily pale and the smudges beneath her eyes looked like bruises. Her fingers were laced tightly together on the table.

She still looked like a doll. The unwanted thought darted through his mind. Except now she looked like a doll that someone had discarded a long time ago—the expensive paint chipped away, the pretty dresses lost over the years, the glamor gone. The sapphire eyes that had once sparkled with diamond tears stared at him expressionlessly. Julia Tennant didn't cry anymore, he realized with sudden certainty.

There was no reason why that should bother him. When he spoke his voice was harsher than he'd intended.

"You're never going to see her again. You understand that?"

"Don't worry." She looked away. "They told me."

He continued as if she hadn't spoken. "If you think that anything's changed just because you manipulated the system, forget it. If there was any real justice in this world, you'd still be upstate making mailbags with the rest of the twenty-five-to-life sewing circle instead of being handed a get-out-of-jail-free card. You got away with murder, Julia." He kept his voice even with an effort. "But if I even suspect that you're trying to find her—"

"Back off. I said I understood the situation." She lifted her chin slightly, her shoulders tense under the thin nylon of the windbreaker, and for a moment the ghost of the former Julia flitted across her features. He'd seen a newspaper photo of her at an arts gala once; her hair swept up and held back with jewelled combs, those delicate eyebrows arched in polite detachment, that same slight tilt to her chin.

Kenneth Tennant, his thick dark hair a distinguished silver at his temples, had been in the photo too. A proprietary arm had been around his beautiful trophy wife, and he'd been smiling at another couple in the picture— his sister Barbara and her new husband, Robert Van Hale.

Tennant and Van Hale had been doomed even then, he thought. Both of them had been on the jet when Julia Tennant's exquisitely wrapped package had been opened.

"You couldn't stop staring at me throughout the trial. I see you haven't been able to break the habit." Her voice held a thread of anger. "You must be attracted to dangerous women, Mr. Ross—or is it that girls-behind-bars fantasy that some men have?"

"Get one thing very clear, Julia," he said, leaning forward slightly. When she automatically moved away he reached over and grabbed both of her clasped hands in one of his, holding her there. "You're not my fantasy. You're a black widow spider, as far as I'm concerned— a cold-blooded murderer who killed the father of your child, the husband of your best friend and two other people you didn't even know."

"Yeah, that's right," Julia said tightly. "I walked into prison that first day with quite a reputation to defend. You know how it is when you're the new kid on the cell block."

"I'm sure you held your own." He didn't loosen his grip on her. "You're the type who always lands on her feet. Your overturned conviction proved that."

"Too bad the court takes pesky little details like constitutional rights so seriously. Now let go of my hands. You're hurting me.''

Despite the lack of expression on her face, her voice had risen enough to attract attention, and Max released her fingers in reluctant frustration. What the hell had he expected? he asked himself. Some show of remorse? Some acknowledgement, however belated, of guilt?

A part of him had never been able to believe that she was exactly what she appeared—devoid of any real emotion, unmoved by the lives she'd destroyed. He wasn't naive enough to think that her all-too-brief incarceration would have worked any miracle of rehabilitation, but he'd held to the faint hope that her time in prison might have made her face up to what she'd done. He'd been a fool. Nothing touched Julia Tennant.

Not even the loss of her child.

He'd done what he'd come here to do, he thought heavily. He'd delivered the message, although from her reaction it hadn't been necessary. Like a phoenix, Julia had risen from the funeral pyre of her old life and was ready to start a new one—unburdened by any inconvenient baggage from her past. He pushed his chair back, unwilling to spend even a moment longer with her, and then he stopped.

''What's that?'' His gaze was on the back of her hand, and when she followed his glance her own wavered. Then she gave him a cold smile.

''You don't want to know, Ross. It might upset your preconceptions about me landing on my feet.'' She held her hand up and studied the odd marks on the back of it, slowly turning it so that her palm faced outward at him.

The same four red scars showed, a mirror image of the other side, but Max wasn't looking at them. Her eyes were steady and there was a tiny mocking hitch at the corner of her mouth, and all of a sudden he saw her coolness for what it was.

Behind the mask was a woman just barely holding herself together. Julia Tennant had been through hell.

Wrong tense. She was still there.

He felt as if he'd just been kicked in the solar plexus. The stale air of the restaurant pressed in on him, making it hard to breathe, but he knew it wasn't the haze of smoke drifting from a nearby table or the unpleasant odor of frying grease that was creating the suffocating miasma. The air around Julia was thick with despair. It was an almost palpable thing.

"What was it—some kind of homemade weapon?" he asked, his throat dry and his voice a harsh rasp.

"It was a fork, Max." Her outspread fingers trembled, and she instantly stilled them. "They got the new girl in a corner one day, and they nailed my hand to a table with a fork. I guess it was an initiation rite or something."

She held her hand out a moment longer, in much the same pose as she might once have held it to admire the green fire of an emerald on her finger. Then she wrapped it around the coffee cup so that the wound wasn't visible to him, drained the last of her coffee and set the cup back down on the table with an audible click.

"I'm leaving now," she said offhandedly. "I have to find a place to stay for tonight, and since I don't have reservations at the Ritz I'd better start looking for a room. If you ever approach me again, Ross, I'm putting you in a world of pain that you'll never crawl out of. Do *you* understand *that?*"

The woman was threatening him. Compassion fled, and Max narrowed his gaze. "What are you planning, Julia—another gift-wrapped bomb?"

"No. A gift-wrapped attempted rape charge," she said,

her tone as cold as his. "You come near me and I'll have my blouse ripped so fast you won't have time to pull your damn ID from your wallet before the cops come. The charge won't stick, but that's the kind of thing that stays on your personnel file. Think about it."

"And you think about this." He'd passed the point where he could hide his anger and he knew it. "I'm never going to stop watching you. I'm making it my personal mission in life to ensure you don't ever find her, Tennant, so keep that in mind if you get the urge to play mommy someday in the future and decide to go looking for her. She's doing fine without you. She's starting to get back to normal, and I won't let you rip her world apart a second time."

"You—you've seen her?" Julia had already started to turn away. Now she froze. Slowly she turned back to face him, her shoulders rigidly set and what little color there'd been in her face ebbing away. "When did you see her? Is she all right? Has anything *happened* to her?"

The questions tumbled from her bloodless lips too rapidly for him to answer, and the previously dull eyes blazed with sudden urgency. She looked down at him, and for a moment she seemed to be holding her breath.

Then she let it out. One corner of her mouth lifted in a mocking grin, and she shrugged carelessly. Reaching into her windbreaker, she pulled out the pack of cigarettes, shook one free and tossed the pack on the table. From the front pocket of her worn jeans she extracted a box of wooden matches, and one-handedly she snapped a thumbnail against the head of a match and peered at him through the flaring flame.

"Isn't that what you wanted from me, Max?" There was a jeering note in the husky voice. She put the cigarette between her lips, raked back a limp strand of blond hair and brought the flame closer. "Isn't that why you mentioned her—because you wanted to see if I would crack, just a little?"

"You didn't crack when you watched your husband's plane go down. You didn't crack on the stand." Max ignored the tendril of smoke that curled down at him and kept his tone even. "I hear you didn't crack in prison, Julia. No, I didn't expect the mention of her would upset you. But tell me one thing—why can't you bring yourself to say her name?"

The shadow he thought he saw pass behind her eyes was gone so quickly that he realized it had to have been a distortion from the cigarette's smoke. She was still holding the burning match in her right hand. With a deliberate movement she brought the fingers of her left to the flame, her gaze locked on his. Slowly she let her thumb and her index finger get closer, until he knew it had to be burning her. Then she pinched the flame out, her eyes still not leaving his face.

"Willa," she said flatly. "Her name's Willa, and she used to be my daughter, before you people took her away from me. I can say it, Max. There's just no reason to, since I'm never going to see her again."

She held his gaze for a moment longer. Then her lashes dipped briefly to her cheekbones, as if she was suddenly weary of the conversation. He didn't know what prompted him to utter his next words.

"I saw her the day before yesterday. She's fine. Nothing's happened to her."

Julia's eyes were still closed, and he saw her lips tighten. The burning end of the cigarette trembled slightly. When the dark lashes lifted, the fabulous sapphire gaze that had disturbed his dreams for the last two years rested on him.

"Thank you," she said in an undertone so low that he barely caught it. A wisp of smoke drifted between them, and she looked down at the cigarette in her hand as if she'd forgotten it was there.

"Cherie's on her break. Did you folks want anything else?"

An older waitress had approached their table, and, disconcerted, Max wrenched his gaze from Julia. "No." He shook his head. "We're just about to leave."

As he turned back to the slender figure in the windbreaker and jeans, Julia bent swiftly forward and stubbed out her cigarette in the ashtray. Once again she was under control, he realized. Any vulnerability she might have inadvertently revealed a moment ago was gone, and her eyes were no longer sapphire-like, but a hard, opaque blue.

"Don't ever try to push my buttons like that again, Ross," she said quietly. "You of all people should know what a cheap shot that was."

He stared at her, taken off-guard. Then he frowned. "Look, lady, I wasn't trying to push—" he began, but she cut him off.

"I know more about you than you think I do. I made it my business to find out all I could about the man who ripped my life away from me." Her gaze darkened. "You lost a child yourself, didn't you?"

The door to the coffee shop opened and a blast of chilled air blew in. There was a chorus of half-joking shouts from the table of construction workers nearest the door, but Max heard nothing except for the crashing roar that was suddenly filling his ears.

How had she known? He felt violated. She'd dug into his background—how in hell she'd managed it, he didn't know, but somehow she'd learned more about him during her two years in prison than his closest acquaintances at work knew. She'd had no *right* to—

"You don't like having your personal life pored over by a stranger, do you?" Julia said thinly. "Mine was on the front pages, Max—courtesy of you and your associates. Like I said, I don't ever want to see you around me again."

This time when she turned away he let her take a few steps before he called out her name. She looked over her shoulder at him, a flicker of anger crossing her features.

"What the hell is it now, Ross?" she asked, not disguising the impatience in her tone.

He shoved the cardboard package to the edge of the table. "You forgot your cigarettes, Julia," he said, his own voice barbed. "I don't want them. I don't smoke."

She took a half step toward him. Then she checked herself. "Neither do I, Max. I just quit." Her grin was tight. "I'm going to be a model citizen from now on."

The next moment she was gone. Across from him her coffee cup and the battered pack of cigarettes were the only proof that she had been there at all.

She'd been taunting him, he thought with sudden anger. Even her last remark had held a hidden message she'd known he would understand. She'd been telling him that she had the strength and the willpower to do whatever she had to do.

She'd been taunting him and she'd been lying to him.

Julia Tennant fully intended to go looking for her child.

Chapter Two

"You smell like a party, Mommy..."

Julia felt Willa's hair brushing against her neck as her small daughter gustily breathed in the scent of Dior. She tightened her hold on her, praying that the tears she could feel prickling behind her eyelids would remain unshed for these final few moments. But Willa's attention was on something else, she noted thankfully. She felt tiny fingers touch the luminous pearl studs she'd defiantly fastened to her ears earlier that morning.

"You look like a princess, Mommy."

"Do I, kitten-paws?" Even as she used the endearment her throat closed in pain. She couldn't do this, she thought desperately—she couldn't go through with it. If she packed a bag for Willa right now they could be at the airport before anyone started looking for her. She could get them on the first flight leaving the country— she could find a job, change their names, make a new life for the two of them—

Except that she didn't have a passport. And within minutes of her non-appearance at court, all airport and border crossing personnel would be on the lookout for a woman and a little girl.

She couldn't do this. But she had no choice.

She opened her eyes as Maria stifled a sob a few feet away, and the housekeeper's tearful gaze met hers. Thomas, the chauffeur who'd driven her on countless shopping trips and frivolous outings, stood by the door awkwardly twisting his cap between his hands.

It was time to go. And even though it felt as if her heart was being ripped from her body, she had to make this final parting as normal as possible for her child's sake.

Julia pressed a desperate kiss to the flaxen head, gave Willa one last too-tight hug and set her back on her feet. Round blue eyes looked up at her in slight alarm as Maria came forward and placed her work-worn palms on the small, OshKosh-clad shoulders.

"Why are you crying, Mommy?"

Because when I walk into court today I'm pretty sure I'm not going to walk out, honey. Because twelve people who don't even know me are probably going to find me guilty of doing a terrible thing. Because you're my life—my sun and my moon and my stars—and I'm so very, very afraid I'm never going to see you again.

She forced a smile and saw the worry in her daughter's eyes disappear. "Because pearls are for tears, silly. It's the rule. Now, go back into the kitchen with Maria and finish your toast, okay? See you then, red hen."

"See you later, alligator," Willa giggled. "Love you trillions."

Before the rest of their ritual could be completed, the sturdy little legs were skipping down the hall to the breakfast room with Willa's usual exuberance.

Julia said it anyway.

"Love you trillions," she whispered, the tears finally spilling over completely as her hungry gaze imprinted this last precious image of her daughter on her memory. Willa reached the end of the hall and turned the corner.

"Trillions and jillions," Julia breathed hoarsely to the empty hallway. "And forever and ever, kitten-paws."

Slowly she turned to where Thomas was waiting for her, and the endless pain began....

JULIA HUGGED the damp pillow tightly, willing herself not to awaken. Sometimes the dream would repeat itself. And despite the wrenching anguish she relived night after night at the end of it, it was worth it to hold, even in her imagination, that small wriggling body, press her face against that silky topknot of blond hair, breathe in the sweet, milky, little-girl scent of Willa's skin. But this time it was no good. Tiredly, she opened her eyes to the unfamiliar room around her.

The next moment she was sitting up abruptly, her heart crashing against her ribs as full consciousness returned.

She wasn't in prison anymore. She was free. She was *free!*

Swiftly flipping back the thin blanket that had been covering her, she swung her legs over the side of the bed, her bare feet impervious to the chill of the linoleum floor. Joy so pure it felt like a physical element tore through her. No matter that she was in the cheapest room of the cheapest flophouse she'd been able to find last night— she was *free,* she thought, trembling with excitement. There had been times that she'd thought this moment would never come.

Free meant she could start looking for Willa. She could hardly believe it was true, she thought faintly. No wonder she was shaking like a leaf. She let her breath out in a ragged exhalation.

"You got out," she whispered. Across the room her

reflection wavered at her from a smeared dresser mirror, and she met her own gaze.

"There were times in there you weren't sure you were going to make it, but you did," she told the woman staring back at her. "They said you were too pampered, that you'd never survive. They were *wrong*. They didn't know how much you had to live for."

Slowly she got to her feet. Drawing closer to the mirror, she stared at her reflection in it, her palms flat on the dresser's surface, her arms braced.

She'd slept in the cotton bra and the utilitarian briefs that were all the underwear she owned. Against the pallor of her skin the bra straps looked dingy from too many washings, and she felt a brief flicker of humiliation.

She'd gone into that place wearing a teal-blue designer suit, handmade Italian heels, satin and lace lingerie. She'd come out almost two years later in a shapeless polyester smock, her own clothes somehow having been mislaid, she'd been told. In the smock she'd felt as conspicuous as if she'd had her inmate number stencilled across her back, and the first thing she'd done when she'd gotten out yesterday was to spend a few of her precious dollars in a secondhand clothing store.

She'd left the hated smock balled up on the floor of a change room, and for an hour or so she'd just walked aimlessly down one street after another, not noticing the April chill but finding herself trembling instead with nervous exhilaration. Around her streetlamps and neon signs and car headlights had begun to come on, piercing the blue Boston dusk, and gradually she'd started to feel at ease among the stream of humanity flowing around her on the sidewalks.

Then a tall figure had detached himself from the passers-by and had stepped in front of her, blocking her path.

As easily as that, Max Ross had ripped away any delusions she might have had of putting her past behind her. At the sight of him she'd felt immediately exposed, as if everyone around them knew what she was and where she'd spent the last twenty-three months.

He'd *meant* her to feel that way.

But he'd made one vital miscalculation, she thought with a spark of cold anger. He'd thought he'd been dealing with Julia Tennant—the Julia Tennant she'd seen two years ago, the Julia Tennant he'd helped put behind bars. That woman might have accepted his warning.

That woman didn't exist any longer.

She raked her hair straight back from her forehead, and narrowed her gaze at her reflection in the mirror. "You tipped your hand, Ross. That wasn't smart," she said softly. "You shouldn't have let me know how much you hated me, because now I'll be watching out for you."

Despite her words, a sudden tremor ran through her as she recalled their briefly antagonistic meeting the night before and saw again the hostile implacability in his expression.

He would do anything he could to stop her. Sick fear washed through her. In the mirror, her reflection swayed slightly, and she squeezed her eyes shut.

Sometimes the dream went on, the rest of the memories, less vivid but still unforgettable, tumbling through her mind like a collection of spilled photographs. The faces of the jury members as they'd filed back that final time into the courtroom, the electric excitement from the press section as the verdict had been delivered, the blank expressions of the court officers as they'd moved toward her after she'd been found guilty. Her own confused hesitation as to what was expected of her until she'd seen the handcuffs one of them was unfastening from his belt.

And just as she was escorted out, the flash of pity, instantly erased, that had crossed Max Ross's features while he'd watched from a few feet away.

Abruptly she straightened, blocking out the images in her mind. She'd imagined that, she told herself. Pity wasn't in Ross's repertoire. If the man had any humanity at all, he certainly didn't intend to waste it on the woman he thought of as a black widow spider.

As she'd learned over the past few weeks, he wasn't alone in that attitude.

"Your sister-in-law only testified against you after the authorities guaranteed her safety," Lynn Erikson had told her in prison. "Do I think you've got a good chance of having your conviction overturned with what we've found out about the search of your summer home? Absolutely."

Lynn had shrugged, and in the small gesture it had been possible to see a ghost of the arrogant and high-powered attorney she'd once been before a cocaine addiction had raged out of control, destroying her life and robbing her of her freedom.

"They didn't need a search warrant for the house that had been your husband's, but the summer place on Cape Ann had always been in your name only. The wiring and the chemicals they found there should never have been allowed into evidence, and without them, all the state has is Barbara's testimony of seeing you hand the package over to Kenneth just before his flight. That's not enough to prove you knew what was in it."

She'd shaken her head wearily, as if to forestall Julia's hopes. "But it doesn't change the deal Barbara got, or the fact that permanent custody of Willa was given to her when you got sent here. Oh, maybe after a lengthy court battle you might win your daughter back, but I doubt it. Even if your sister-in-law didn't have the Tennant fortune backing her, she'd still have the sympathy of any judge. Her own husband was on that private jet— who's going to take a child from the arms of a victimized widow and find in favor of the woman who got away with killing both her husband and her brother-in-law?'' Lynn's husky voice had softened. ''You say Barbara always adored Willa. At least you know your little girl's being raised by someone who loves her, Julia. A lot of the women in here don't even have that to hold on to.''

She owed her freedom to Lynn, Julia thought, turning from the dresser mirror and staring unseeingly out of the grimy window. Maybe the sensible course of action would be to take the disbarred but still brilliant attorney's advice and accept that Willa was lost to her forever.

But she didn't accept that. Because if she ever did, there would be no reason to go on living.

The teal-blue suit she'd worn that last morning when she'd said goodbye to Willa hadn't been found when she'd signed for her belongings upon leaving prison. Her heart had been in her mouth as she'd waited for the rest of her possessions. When the clerk had brusquely told her that her leather handbag had also gone missing, and would be forwarded on to her if and when it was found, she'd feared the worst.

''There was a pair of costume earrings,'' she'd told the woman, forcing a meek note into her voice. ''They weren't worth much, but they had sentimental value. Are they still here?''

The clerk had exchanged a dry look with the guard behind her. ''Sentimental value?'' She'd snorted disbelievingly. ''Were they a present from your late husband, honey? Here they are.''

Carelessly she'd rolled the huge pearls across the

counter, her hostility barely veiled. But Julia was used to it. Most of the prison personnel had made it clear they disagreed with her release. She'd said nothing as the woman went on.

"Honestly, I've seen less tacky fakes in a gumball machine. I've heard you rich bitches never wear the real thing, but couldn't you at least have bought decent copies?"

Through the grime of the hotel room's window Julia could see a knot of pedestrians waiting for the light to change on the street below. For a moment she thought she recognized Max Ross standing a few feet away from the group, and she froze. Tall. Broad shoulders. Dark hair. Then the man glanced impatiently up at the red traffic light and she relaxed as she saw his face. It wasn't him. She was safe for the time being.

Her jeans were slung across the back of a chair, and she went to them. Feeling inside the front pocket, she withdrew two tissue-wrapped objects. Carefully she nudged aside the nest of tissue and stared at the pair of earrings in her palm.

Willa had called them her princess earrings. Kenneth had bought them for her as a wedding present, and had insisted she wear them whenever they were out in public together. He'd told her once that he enjoyed displaying his impeccable taste—in jewelry as in women.

Appearances had been vitally important to him. She hadn't known until too late that his gifts and attentions to her were as empty as their marriage had soon become, and it was even later that she'd realized his daughter meant just as little to Kenneth Tennant. She and Willa both had existed only as accoutrements to him—part of the background that he'd felt necessary for a man of his station in life.

He'd been the coldest human being she'd ever known—as emotionless in his personal life as he was in his business dealings. She'd always been privately convinced that the latter had led to his death. Some rival he'd destroyed, some executive he'd ruined—it had to have been someone like that who'd found a way to kill him and make it look as though she'd been responsible. But even though that unknown enemy had robbed her of two years of her life, she had no intention of trying to discover his identity. She was only interested in one thing, and it wasn't revenge.

If Kenneth had still been alive, the wife he'd thought of as a possession would no longer have attracted him, Julia thought without self-pity. But the baubles she'd once been adorned with had kept their value. They were South Sea pearls, exquisitely matched and rimmed with diamonds. They were going to get her back her child.

"I'm going to find her, Ross," she said softly to the empty room. "I want what your people took from me— my daughter, my life, my freedom—and I'm going to get it. And when I do, we're going to disappear so completely that you'll *never* see us again."

"YOU WHAT?"

Julia stared at the overweight young man sitting in front of her. He hit a key and spoke over his shoulder at her.

"I said it only took me a couple of hours to do the job after you left on Tuesday. You should have given me a number where I could reach you." He tucked a greasy strand of hair behind his ear. "So you've been in the joint, huh? What for—dealing?"

There was absent curiosity in his tone, but most of his attention was focused on the computer screen in front of him. He typed in another command without waiting for her reply. She wasn't about to tell him the truth anyway, Julia thought wryly.

She'd gotten his name from one of the women in prison.

Since the morning she'd sold her pearls to yet another shady connection she'd learned of in prison she'd been on tenterhooks, wondering desperately if Melvin Dobbs would be able to find Barbara's and Willa's whereabouts with the medical data she'd given him.

It had been three days of knowing that Max would be on her trail, three days of looking over her shoulder and half expecting to see him there, even though she'd stayed in a different place every night.

"You said the kid and the woman both had a rare allergy to wasp stings, so I ran a cross-check on prescriptions for the antidote that had been ordered in adult and child strength from the same pharmacist." Dobbs hit the Enter key and sat back as the glowing blue screen in front of him rapidly filled up with lines of type. "There were several matches, but only one where both the adult and the child were females. By the way, they're still in the state."

For a moment Julia wondered if she'd heard him correctly. "They're still in *this* state?" she repeated stupidly.

At his casual nod her hand flew to her mouth, stifling a choked-off sob. She felt the hot prickle of tears in her eyes, but thankfully Dobbs's attention wasn't on her.

Dear God—they were still in Massachusetts! For two years she'd imagined Willa as being thousands of miles away from her, had ached with the certainty that between her and her daughter were rivers, mountains, countless cities as barriers—and all the time only a few hours at most had kept them apart.

She could see her *today*, Julia thought, her mind racing. She wouldn't do anything rash or foolish—she wouldn't do *anything* that might jeopardize her goal— but if she was careful she might be able to catch a glimpse of Willa in a park or a playground. Just one quick look. Surely that would be safe enough.

And then I'll figure out a way to have you with me forever, sweetheart, she thought tremulously. *I still don't know how I'm going to do it, but we'll be a family again, you and me.*

She fixed her burning gaze on Dobbs's computer screen as the lines of type scrolled downward and then stopped.

"That's the one." He grunted and reached over to a nearby printer. "I'll run off a copy for you to—"

"She was in prison for killing the girl's father and the woman's husband, Dobbs. And unless you shut down that computer right now, you're looking at hard time yourself."

Shocked, Julia spun around at the sound of the harsh voice coming from the doorway. Her appalled gaze met the coldly assessing glance of the man standing there.

"Hullo, Tennant," Max said with a tight smile. "Looking for something?"

"This is harassment, Ross." She dragged in a constricted breath, and willed her voice to remain steady. "I warned you to leave me alone, and I meant it. You're interrupting a private business transaction here, so get the hell—"

"I said shut down the computer, Dobbs. Do it," Max ordered, not taking his eyes from Julia. "Right off the top of my head I can come up with at least two charges that can be laid against you unless you cooperate. Endangering the life of a child is the first one. Being an accessory to kidnapping is the second. Shut it down.''

But Melvin's fingers were already flying over the keys, and even as Max delivered his ultimatum and Julia turned back to the computer, she saw the lines of type flicker and disappear from the screen. Her eyes opened wide in denial.

''Bring it back up, Dobbs,'' she commanded unsteadily. ''I *paid* you for that information. He's got no authority to—''

''He's a fed.'' Flicking a switch at the side of his computer, the hacker jerked his head at the open ID wallet that Max was negligently displaying. ''That's authority enough for me.'' Dismissively he turned away from Julia to the man behind her. ''I didn't know why she wanted it. Just get her out of here and let's pretend this whole thing never happened, okay?''

''No! No, it's *not* okay, dammit!'' Her hands balled into fists at her sides, Julia looked wildly first at Dobbs, and then Max. ''Damn *both* of you—that's my daughter's address you're keeping from me. I have the *right* to know where she is!''

''No, Julia, you don't.'' Max had been standing a few feet away, but now he took two swift strides toward her. Behind the coolness of his gaze heat flared, and was immediately extinguished. ''And if I even suspect that you've persuaded our venal friend here to change his mind and tell you where she is, I'll have her relocated so fast you won't get within a hundred miles of her. For a while after she was moved she was a sad and lonely little girl, but now she's started to adjust. She's in kindergarten now. Do you really want to be responsible for uprooting her all over again?''

''She was sad and lonely because her mother was

taken away from her, for God's sake!'' Julia hissed at the implacable face only inches from hers. ''*You* were responsible for that, Ross!''

''And I'd do it all over again in a heartbeat.'' His voice was ice. ''She's got a shot at a normal life. She wouldn't have that, growing up with the woman who killed her father, her uncle and two innocent bystanders.''

''You keep forgetting something.'' He was so close she could feel the warmth of his breath on her parted lips, and she realized with a small shock that it had been years since there had been this little distance between her and a man. Julia thrust the thought aside and continued. ''They had to let me go, Max. They couldn't prove their case. I'm an innocent woman.''

''You got off on a *technicality*, Tennant!'' As if she'd goaded him into action, he grasped her arms just above her elbows, and pulled her closer, obliterating the last few inches of space between them. His jaw was set and his grip on her felt like steel. ''You got off, but that doesn't mean you're not guilty. The only innocent one in this whole damn mess is that little girl, and I intend to keep her safe—from *you*. Do we understand each other?''

She was vaguely aware of Melvin Dobbs, sitting frozenly a few feet away from them. But on a deeper, more visceral level, she suddenly felt as if nothing and no one had any solid reality except the man in front of her.

His grasp on her arms was tight enough that it should have been uncomfortable. Instead she felt ridiculously as if it was all that was keeping her from falling into a terrible void and plummeting to her own destruction. He was strong, she thought disjointedly, but his strength wasn't merely a matter of muscle and sinew. It was a strength made up of conviction and a bedrock foundation of personal honor. He meant what he said. He cared enough about a child he hardly knew that he would go the limit to keep her safe.

Under different circumstances, she and Max Ross might have found themselves on the same side, she realized with a small shock. She would have liked that. He was a man a woman could count on.

And if she were honest with herself, in those alternate circumstances there might well have been more than just cooperation between them. Even now, facing each other as enemies, there was a suppressed undercurrent flowing beneath the surface of their anger and antagonism.

She distinctly remembered the first time she'd noticed him, although, as she'd learned during her trial, he'd been involved in the investigation from the first and had actually spoken with her an hour or so after the explosion on the night it had happened. She didn't recall the encounter, but that was understandable. She'd been in shock those first few days, and then had come the nightmarish realization that the authorities saw her as their prime suspect. From then on her world had unravelled so swiftly she hadn't taken in much of anything.

Besides, Max was the original invisible man. Obviously that was an asset in his line of work, and she supposed he'd cultivated that ability he had of unobtrusively melting into the background, but she still didn't know how he did it. Granted, there was nothing about him that was jarringly noticeable, unless the casual observer happened to look directly into his eyes. They were a dark, clear green, and in the tan of his face they looked like chips of arctic ice. But his hair, dark brown and cut fairly short, was ordinary enough, and his features, although harder than the average, were regular.

Still, it seemed impossible that a big man with such a—she searched for the word—such a *solid* presence could go unnoticed in a crowd whenever he wanted to. Which meant that at her first remembered meeting with him, he'd wanted her to know he was there.

It had been on the first day of her trial, and she'd been walking into the courtroom when she'd become aware of him standing a few feet away. His gaze had been steady and assessing, his expression carefully blank, and she'd suddenly known that the privileged shield of wealth and beauty and social status that had protected her for so long had been ripped away from her. She hadn't realized who he was at that point, but she knew that the man watching her didn't see her as Julia Tennant, the attractive young widow of a wealthy and powerful man. Those green eyes had seemed to be looking straight through her, as if they were trying to read her very soul.

And even as he'd continued to stare at her, his attitude impersonally professional, she'd seen a hard edge of color rise up under the tan of his cheekbones. He'd turned away immediately, and during the rest of the trial he'd been careful not to meet her eyes again.

But as she'd told him in the coffee shop, she'd known he'd been watching her. And, if she were honest with herself, the undercurrent she was feeling right now had been there from the start, on her side as well as his.

Except that wouldn't make any difference to him, she thought with renewed despair. Max Ross might have his alternate realities just as she did, and his might even be more urgent than hers, but even if they included sweat-soaked sheets, total satiation, and every dark desire he'd ever had, he would never let them interfere with real life.

He was the law. She was an ex-convict. They weren't on the same side and never would be, as far as he was concerned.

She gave it one last try, knowing it was futile.

"She's my daughter, Max." Her voice was husky. Her gaze on his, she tried desperately to make him see it her way. "I love her—surely you believe that? Even if everything else you thought about me was true, you must know that I love her too much to ever put her in danger. I'm her mother. She *needs* me."

Just for a second she thought she saw him waver, and her heart leapt. Then he shook his head and the irrational hope died.

"If you love her you'll give her up, Julia." His voice was as low as hers had been, and it had lost its edge. "What kind of a life could you give her, even if you did find her? Her aunt has legal custody of her now, and that would make you a fugitive. You and Willa would be on the run, never putting down roots, never being able to give her a secure home. Is that what you want for her?"

He stared at her for a long moment. Then he let go of her arms, and his own dropped to his sides. His eyes darkened with something that could have been compassion. "I think you'll do the right thing, Julia. I think you'll let her go."

And looking at him, she knew with sudden despair that he was right.

Chapter Three

She was soaked to the skin, but that didn't matter. Hunching her shoulders against the downpour, Julia dimly realized that she was shivering, but that too was unimportant. She kept walking. Despite having no real destination in mind, somehow it seemed to her that she was heading in the right direction.

Damn Max Ross. The unspoken epithet was automatic, with no heat behind it. Damn him for showing up, damn him for making sure she hadn't gotten the information she'd wanted and damn him for what he'd said.

But most of all, damn him for knowing her better than she'd known herself.

"...on the run, never putting down roots, never being able to give her a secure home...is that what you want for her?"

She'd wanted to scream at him that he was wrong, that it wouldn't be that way. She'd wanted to tell him that no matter what difficulties faced her, she could give her daughter a stable life, a happy childhood. She'd wanted to tell him all the lies she'd been telling herself. She'd looked into his eyes and she hadn't been able to say any of it, because she knew she didn't believe it.

She'd been holding on to a dream that had died the

day she'd been convicted, and Max was right—no one would ever believe she hadn't done what she'd been accused of. Although no reporters had tracked her down, in the last few days a newspaper or two had covered her surprising release. The gist of the stories was that she'd made a mockery of the legal system.

No, there had never been any chance of getting Willa back again—not really. Max had known that from the start. Now she did too.

There was no reason to go on anymore.

The thought slipped into her mind as if it had been lurking there and waiting for the right opportunity to reveal itself. She was dead already, Julia thought distantly. Her body might go on for years, but it was only a shell. Everything that had been good, everything that had been real, everything that had been *life* to her had been held in a tiny pair of hands that had once clutched hers, had shone out of a pair of eyes that had gazed at her with absolute trust, had been encompassed by a love so perfect she could give nothing less in return.

Max was right. If she persisted in trying to get Willa back, ultimately she would tear her daughter apart. Did he understand, even a little, what he was forcing her to face?

He had to. He'd lost a child himself. And although the few details she'd garnered about that loss had been scant, the impact it had had on him was visible. Oh, he'd managed to continue functioning. He'd kept his job, and even performed it with a kind of automatic zealousness—her own case was proof of that. But there was an almost two-dimensional quality to him, as if when his workday was over, and he was finally alone with only himself for company, he simply...shut down. Maybe his ability to fade into the background wasn't simply a tool of his trade, she thought with sudden insight. Was it possible for a man to turn into a ghost one day at a time?

Dead man walking. How much sheer strength of will did he have, that he could force himself to get up every morning and face an empty world, day after day?

More than she had. More than she cared to have, she thought numbly.

She stepped off the curb onto the street with barely a glance at the traffic lights. Her face was wet with rain, her hair plastered to her skull as if she'd just surfaced from a dive and suddenly she didn't feel as if she could take another step. She squeezed her eyes tightly shut, wanting to blot out the present, wanting to bring back the past...and just for a moment, it worked.

She was holding Willa again, and feeling those tiny fingers delicately touching her ears.

"Why are you crying, Mommy?"

"Because pearls are for tears," Julia said out loud, forcing a shaky smile to her lips and stopping stock-still in the middle of the road as the rain came down and the scars on her heart finally gave way and tore asunder. Her vision of Willa faded slowly away, and her voice sank to a raw whisper. "Everyone knows that, kitten-paws. Even I know that now."

Her head bowed, her shoulders shaking with soundless sobs, she didn't hear the hoarse voice calling out her name until it was too late. Blindly she looked up and saw the bus bearing down on her.

HE'D ALMOST BEEN too late. Max rubbed his jaw wearily and looked down at the still figure tucked under two comforters and a wool blanket in his bed. Her hair was still damp, and just below the hairline and above her closed eyes was a raw-looking graze. He'd given her that when he'd managed a fair imitation of the high-school football player he'd once been and had knocked her out of harm's way with a flying tackle in the intersection. He realized he was gingerly rotating his shoulder, and he winced just as the doctor he'd called in looked up.

"There's nothing physically wrong with her except for exhaustion and a bad chill. Now that she's fallen asleep, I'd prefer not to wake her." The older man lifted an eyebrow. "Even if I could get her admitted, hospital beds are in short supply. She'd be released tomorrow."

"She refused to let me take her to one, anyway." Max met his quizzical gaze and shook his head firmly. "And no, Doctor—there's nothing here you have to worry about. I'll let her get a decent night's rest and then send her on her way in the morning. My interest in her is professional, not personal."

One-handedly he fumbled his ID wallet out of his jacket pocket—his torn jacket pocket, he realized with little surprise—and displayed it briefly. The doctor grunted.

"I didn't peg you as the type. But doesn't she have anywhere else to stay?"

"She's a transient." Max's reply was more curt than he'd meant it to be. "And I'm not sure she didn't deliberately step out in front of that bus, Doctor. I'd given her some bad news earlier, and..." He paused uncomfortably. "Hell, who knows. Maybe I should have handled it differently."

"I see. Well, if you're still worried about her emotional state tomorrow, give me a call and I'll arrange to have her put under observation for a few days, although I'm sure she won't thank me for that." There was shrewd assessment in the physician's faded gaze as he got to his feet and walked to the door with Max. "She's recently been a guest of the state, am I right?"

At Max's quick glance he gave a wintry smile. "Please, Mr. Ross—she's got a prison pallor, a wound from some kind of homemade weapon on her hand, and she's obviously been living on sheer nerve for far too long. And you're FBI, which raises a whole passel of awkward questions I don't think I'll ask."

"Like I said, the relationship between us isn't personal," Max said evenly. "I was the one who put her behind bars. If I had my way, she'd still be there."

They'd reached the front door, and the older man took the lightweight topcoat that Max was holding out to him and shrugged into it. He pursed his lips thoughtfully, patted his pockets for his keys and picked up his medical bag.

"Then it's all the more interesting that you unhesitatingly risked your own life tonight to save hers, wouldn't you say?" He tucked an umbrella under the arm that held his bag, and grasped Ross's hand with the other. "Call me if you need to. But Mr. Ross, don't forget that old Chinese saying—if you save someone's life, you're responsible for them forever."

"My forebears were hardheaded Scots Presbyterians, Doctor." Max didn't smile as he opened the door and stepped aside. "That philosophy would have struck them as annoyingly fanciful."

He waited until he saw the other man get into his car. Then he closed the door against the still-wet night and snapped off the porch light. A few steps along the short hall, he stopped to unlatch and slide open the pocket doors that led to the living room.

"Sorry, buddy. You can come in now."

At his words, the big black dog that had been lying on

the living room floor got heavily to his feet, his tail beating in acknowledgement. Stiffly the animal walked over to him and stopped, looking up inquiringly.

"Yeah, we've got a guest, Boomer." Max dropped a hand to the dog's head and idly scratched the folded ear, frowning. "I'm damned if I know what I was thinking, bringing her here, but we've got a guest. I'd better go check on her."

The house was quiet as he passed through the kitchen, the only sounds the ticking of the clock on the wall and the irregular dripping of the faucet. He'd been meaning to fix that, he thought, pausing to tighten the loose tap. Maybe tomorrow he'd stop by the hardware store and get some washers after he sent Julia Tennant on her way.

Julia Tennant. Julia Tennant in his house—no, in his bed. What exactly *had* he been thinking, for God's sake?

He'd told the good doctor his interest in her wasn't personal. That might have been true at some point, but even two years ago he'd been in danger of crossing over the line between professional and personal. Now there was no doubt about it. His involvement with her in the last few days hadn't been any part of his official duties.

In fact, if anyone found out just how involved he'd let himself become with Julia Tennant, Max told himself with calm certainty, he could end up losing his job.

He'd had a whack of vacation time due him. Other agents might plan a trip to Disneyland with the wife and kids, a wild and crazy jaunt to Vegas, a fishing trip with a few good buddies. He'd taken a week off three years ago, mainly because his director had insisted on it, and for the whole seven days he and Boomer had sat on the couch in front of the television, watching old movies and the afternoon soaps.

But when the word had gotten out that Julia Tennant's

conviction had been overturned and she was due to be released, he'd immediately asked for time off. He just hadn't told anyone that he intended to spend his vacation making sure that she didn't get within a hundred miles of her daughter and the woman who had once been her friend and sister-in-law.

So, yeah—this whole thing was emotional, Max admitted, staring out of his kitchen window into the night. But despite what Julia probably thought, the emotion driving him wasn't hatred of her. She was a murderer, and he'd put plenty of them behind bars without giving them a second thought. On the Tennant case, however, he'd had to watch a little girl's world be torn apart by the cold-blooded actions of her mother, and Willa Tennant's innocence had broken through the wall of detachment he tried to keep between him and his work.

She hadn't deserved to have her father killed, her life turned upside down, and everything familiar taken from her. He'd vowed her mother wasn't going to do it to her a second time.

But this afternoon when he'd seen Julia standing in that intersection as if she had no desire to go on living, his blood had turned to ice. And a few seconds later, when he'd been cradling her suddenly fragile-seeming body beneath him on the pavement, he hadn't been thinking of Julia Tennant as the enemy at all. Oblivious to the shaky anger of the bus driver who'd stopped a few feet past them and the surge of bystanders who'd gathered around, his attention had been fixed on her hair, dark with rain under his hand, on the vulnerable line of her throat, on the delicate fanning of her lashes against her cheeks. Then her eyes had opened.

They really were sapphire. For a moment they'd simply gazed at him as if waking up and finding him close to her wasn't anything out of the ordinary. For that same crazy moment, he'd felt exactly the same way.

He was losing his goddamn mind, Max thought flatly, turning away from the sink and just barely concealing his disconcertion as he met those sapphire eyes once again. This time they were staring expressionlessly at him from a few feet away.

"If you'll tell me how much I owe you for the doctor, I'll be on my way."

Her posture was ramrod straight and the shoulder-length blond hair was pulled tightly back from her face in a low ponytail. The graze on her temple had been cleaned by the doctor, but pinpricks of blood had welled up on it again.

She looked about as vulnerable as an electric fence. She was looking at him the way she always had—as if breathing the same damned air as he did was an ordeal. Max felt a muscle in his jaw twitch.

"Don't worry about it." His tone was deliberately dismissive, and with a flicker of satisfaction he saw her stiffen. "It was my decision to call him in. He gave you a fairly clean bill of health, by the way."

"So barring any more encounters with the Boston transit system, I should live to a ripe old age. That's good to hear."

If he hadn't been watching her closely he would have missed the total despair that flashed over her features. She bent her head, holding out her hand to Boomer as the dog sniffed her leg with canine formality. After a moment the heavy black tail gave a slow wag of acceptance.

"You stepped out in front of that bus deliberately, didn't you?" He hadn't intended to ask her the question, but as soon as the words were out he knew he needed to hear her answer. Julia's head remained bowed.

"I don't know, Max," she said finally. "I honestly don't know. Anyway, what happens with me isn't your problem now, so don't worry about it." She gave Boomer one last pat and straightened, meeting his gaze directly. "I want to thank you for opening my eyes. You were right—Willa's better off without me. I won't be looking for her anymore."

The smile that lifted her lips was brittle, as if she was one small muscle movement away from cracking. The least impulsive of men, with difficulty Max curbed the impulse to reach out to her. There was nothing he could say, he told himself harshly. He'd accomplished what he'd set out to do.

All that was left was to let her walk away. In silence he preceded her down the short hallway. He unlatched the front door and opened it, seeing with obscure relief that at least the rain had stopped.

The woman before him was a stone-cold killer, he reminded himself sharply. Forty days and forty nights of rain wouldn't wash away the enormity of her crime.

"There's a bus stop at the corner." He didn't meet her eyes. "There should be one coming by in a few minutes."

"I'll wait for it on the curb this time." There was a touch of wryness in her tone. "Goodbye, Max."

He saw the slight movement as she began to extend her hand to him. Before she could complete the action, he bent down to grasp Boomer's collar. Her expression went very still.

"I'll hold him while you leave," he said shortly. "Sometimes the old boy forgets he's not a pup anymore, and tries to make a dash for freedom."

"Tell him it's not worth it." Julia's words were clipped. She put her hand on the aluminum handle of the outer door and then paused, looking down at the two of them. "The answer to your question is yes, Max. Some part of me couldn't bear the thought of going on without her. But even while I was lying there on the pavement a second later, I thanked God that I'd been prevented from doing it—because one day, maybe years from now or decades from now, my daughter might want to meet the mother she can't remember. And even if that meeting only lasts long enough for her to satisfy her curiosity, it'll be something to hold on to for the rest of my life."

She turned back to the door, averting her face from him, but not before he saw the terrible bleakness that shadowed her features, the raw glaze of desolation in her eyes. Before he could speak she went on, her voice a whisper and her words no longer directed at him.

"In *kindergarten* already. Oh, precious—I wish I'd been there to hear about your first day."

For a heartbeat she rested her forehead against the glass of the door, her eyes tightly closed and her teeth catching at her bottom lip. Then she raised her head and took a deep breath.

The next moment she'd pushed open the door and was gone, so quietly and quickly that by the time Max released his hold on Boomer's collar he could just make out her slim figure swiftly walking down the sidewalk, her shoulders hunched against the night air, her hands jammed into the front pockets of her jeans.

It seemed that Julia Tennant was always slipping away from him, he thought with illogical frustration. She'd walked out on him at the coffee shop, she'd walked out on him this afternoon at Dobbs's place and now she was gone for good—from his life, and her daughter's.

And something about that just didn't make sense.

Still standing at the door, he felt a chill spread through him. Julia had reached the corner, and the harsh street lighting gave her face and her hair an even paler hue. A block or two past her he could see the bus approaching.

She loved her child. The anguish he'd just heard in her voice had been wrenchingly real. She loved her daughter more than life itself, and that love was so total she was willing to give Willa up rather than bring any harm to her.

When he sat in on a trial, Max had a habit of focusing on one jury member out of the twelve, using his or her reactions as a gauge for the others. At Julia's trial, he'd chosen a middle-aged woman as his barometer, and he'd been able to pinpoint the exact moment when Julia's fate had been sealed. The prosecutor had brought out the fact that Willa had been supposed to be on the flight with her father the night he was killed. The little girl had actually boarded the private jet with him and the others, and only the fact that she had promptly gotten sick as soon as she'd been buckled into her seat had saved her life. Kenneth had apparently insisted on having her taken off the plane, rather than cope with her nausea.

Max had seen the middle-aged juror, probably a mother herself, turn appalled eyes on Julia as the implication had set in—that the woman they called The Porcelain Doll had been willing to kill not only her husband, but her child as well. The rest of the trial had been merely a formality.

The worn parquet flooring beneath his feet seemed suddenly insubstantial, as if it was about to buckle and splinter. Max clutched at the door frame as everything he'd thought was real was swept away.

"She didn't *do* it," he breathed, his frozen gaze fixed

on the lonely figure standing under the streetlight. He saw the bus slow as it approached her, saw her waiting for it to stop so she could get on. "If she'd known there was a bomb in that package she would have gotten on that plane herself before she'd ever put Willa in danger. She didn't *do* it, dammit!"

He pushed open the door, sprinting toward her and calling out her name in a hoarse shout as he saw her step up onto the platform of the waiting bus. He *had* to stop her, he thought desperately.

Because if Julia Tennant was an innocent woman, then someone else had gotten away with murder.

Chapter Four

"When did you last eat?" Before Julia could reply, Max pulled two flat packages from the freezer compartment of his refrigerator. "It looks like you've got a choice of He-Man Beef or He-Man Chicken. Both have some kind of apple crisp dessert and mashed potatoes."

"I'm not hungry." Julia saw that her hands were trembling slightly on the tabletop. She slipped them onto her lap out of sight. "How are you going to persuade the Agency to reopen the case? Would they do that on your say-so alone?"

"No." Carefully he folded back a square of foil from the corner of each aluminum rectangle before sliding the dinners into the oven. He set a timer on the counter and took his place at the table across from her. "The Agency doesn't operate on gut feelings and instinct. As far as they're concerned, they got the right person, whether you were released from prison or not. Your file's officially closed."

"So you'd be looking into this on your own time?" She shook her head. "You don't strike me as the type to operate on gut feelings either. What's in this for you?"

The woman she'd once been would have approached the question more obliquely, would have softened its bluntness with a social padding of courtesy. As she'd told him in the coffee shop, Julia reflected, she seemed to have lost that knack. She flushed slightly as his gaze met hers.

"Does there have to be something in it for me?"

The black Labrador on the braided rug in front of the sink heaved himself to his feet with difficulty and padded over to his master's side. Max let his hand drop absently to the dog's head before he continued.

"I guess I can't blame you for thinking that way." He shrugged. "Let's say I'm looking to clear my conscience, Julia. I screwed up and you paid for my mistake with two years of your life. I want to put things right again—not only for you, but for Willa."

His tone was steady, but she thought she could hear a trace of self-recrimination in his words. She searched his face.

"You think she's in danger, don't you?" Under the table her fingers laced together tightly. "Dear God—you don't think *Barbara* planted that bomb?"

He frowned. "It's a possibility. But it doesn't really make sense when you look at the lifestyle your sister-in-law's adopted since the tragedy."

"Her lifestyle?" Julia's brows drew together in confusion. "Maybe she doesn't take off to Europe at the drop of a hat or go to parties every night of the week, but she's never thought anything of snapping up a Picasso lithograph without even asking the cost, because it happens to catch her eye. She keeps a floral designer on staff, for heaven's sake, and the flower arrangements in her house are changed twice a week."

"That's my point. These days she's more likely to cram a handful of cornflowers and daisies into a jelly jar, and instead of Picassos, she's got Willa's drawings stuck up on the refrigerator. She's handed control of Tenn-Chem over to her mother, and, as far as I know, she refuses to have anything to do with any of the other Tennant businesses.''

He shook his head. "Like I said, it doesn't fit. And she'd never let any harm come to Willa, Julia. She's been a good mother to her."

He hadn't meant his words as an accusation, she knew. But at them she felt as if a ball of ice had settled in her stomach. "My daughter has a mother, Max," she said sharply. "Or she did, before you put me behind bars."

"I just meant—" he began, but she cut him off, her voice rising.

"*I'm* the one who should be picking wildflowers with my little girl. *I'm* the one who should be admiring her artwork, taking her to kindergarten, tucking her in at night. I don't want to hear how well another woman is fulfilling my role, Max—I want my daughter *back*." She held his gaze stonily. "How are you going to do that for me, when you don't even have the backing of the Agency?"

She pushed her chair back from the table. "So you finally believe I didn't do it. Big deal. Am I supposed to be grateful that you don't think I'm a black widow spider anymore?"

She kept her tone deliberately flat. It wasn't hard, she thought tightly. Prison had taught her how to hide her real thoughts behind a mask of indifference, but even without that training she doubted whether there would have been any inflection in her voice. She didn't care what Max Ross thought of her, she told herself. In fact, she didn't even know why she'd come back here to his house when he'd caught up to her at the bus stop.

"No, Julia, you're not supposed to be grateful." A

muscle moved in his jaw. "But maybe you could set aside that chip on your shoulder long enough to see that I want to help you."

"The only way you can help me is to make the last two years go away. That's not about to happen." She smiled thinly at him. "Nothing's changed from this afternoon just because the agent who ripped my life apart now wishes he could paste it back together again. It's too bad you didn't have this change of heart before you built your airtight case against me, but you didn't. Now it's too late."

She started to get up from the table, but a heavy warmth at her knee stopped her. Looking down, she saw Boomer had planted himself solidly beside her, and was looking up at his master expectantly.

"Sorry." Max took in the situation at a glance. "It's time for his heart medicine and his biscuit, and he's capable of sitting there all night until he gets them. I'll shut him in the living room in a minute."

Frustration tightened her lips, but as Max turned to the cupboard and took down a bottle of pills and a bag of dog treats she let her hand drop to the old Lab's glossy head. His ears felt like worn velvet under her fingers, and unexpectedly she felt the edginess inside her ease a little. She shrugged, speaking before she thought.

"He's not really bothering me. I used to have a golden retriever when I was a little girl."

Immediately she regretted revealing even that much of herself to the big man in front of her. *This isn't show-and-tell, Tennant,* she told herself harshly. *Ross isn't interested in your childhood, and even if he were, you're not interested in sharing it with him. Why don't you just step over his damn dog and get out of here?*

But somehow she couldn't. The Labrador's tail beat

once, slowly, against the floor, and when she began to take her hand away from his head he laid his muzzle on her knee and looked soulfully up at her. She gave in and resumed stroking the silky ears.

"Lady." Max looked over his shoulder at her as he tipped a capsule into his palm. "Isn't that what her name was? You got her for Christmas when you were six?"

Her hand stilled. She narrowed her eyes at him. "That's right. How did you know?"

His face was expressionless, but as he bent to Boomer and deftly slipped the capsule down the dog's throat she thought she saw a flash of apology behind the green gaze. He palmed the biscuit in front of the salt-and-pepper muzzle and Boomer took it with more enthusiasm than he had the pill.

"I read the psychological profile on you." Straightening to his full height, he turned to the sink and washed his hands before drying them on a nearby dishtowel. He faced her, and if there had been any apology in his gaze before, it was no longer visible. "It was comprehensive."

Boomer had settled down on the floor with difficulty to crunch his biscuit. This time when Julia stood she was able to step over him without disturbing him, and she did, her legs feeling suddenly shaky.

She should have been used to it by now, she thought, tamping down the spark of dull outrage that threatened to flare inside her. She should have been used to having her whole life and personality laid out for any stranger to comb over, looking for some clue as to why Julia Tennant, née Weston, with her cosseted, albeit somewhat unconventional upbringing, should have strayed so far from the norm of human behavior as she had. She'd read op-ed pieces in the papers that had laid the blame for her actions on everything from her mother's peripatetic lifestyle to what one writer had called the "Grace Kelly syndrome"—society's adulation of the kind of cool blond beauty she'd once been told she possessed.

She'd reminded herself that the authors of those articles hadn't known her. But this was different.

She was in the man's *home,* for God's sake. She was only inches away from him. She felt suddenly as if she was standing there without any clothes on, powerless to prevent him from looking his fill of her.

Prison had taught her to keep her mouth shut. But she wasn't in prison anymore. The spark inside her ignited into a cold flame.

"It must have made for some interesting bedtime reading." She allowed a note of husky amusement to creep into her voice and widened her eyes at him. "Is it still tucked away in a drawer somewhere to pull out on those restless nights when you can't fall asleep? Did it feed a fantasy or two?"

His mouth tightened. He shook his head. "I told you, Julia—you weren't my fantasy. Learning everything I could about you was part of the job."

Leaning back against the counter, he crossed his forearms over his chest and met her eyes. "Maybe we should get this straight right now. Even if we hadn't met under these circumstances, you're not my type. I don't go for high-maintenance blondes who were born clutching a charge card. Sure, when I first saw you I realized you were probably the most beautiful woman I'd ever seen, but you're a little too rich for my blood, honey. I live in the real world."

"I didn't think you were considering taking me home to meet Mom and Pop, Ross." Julia returned his gaze steadily. "That's why I used the term *fantasy.* And no matter how hard you try to deny it, I know you indulged once in a while.'' Her smile was cynical. ''What exactly are you hoping this will lead to?''

She saw the flash of anger, quickly veiled, in his eyes and knew her arrow had found its mark. But the next moment he proved that his aim was at least as good as hers.

''The same thing you want it to lead to, Julia.'' Casually he pushed himself from the counter he'd been leaning against and took a step toward her. In the less-than-spacious room that one step brought him close enough to touch her, but he merely unfolded his arms and let them hang by his sides, his manner relaxed. ''Maybe you're right. Maybe all this hostility between us is a front for something else. Why don't we test your theory?''

The suit jacket he'd been wearing earlier had been thrown over the back of a nearby chair, and he'd rolled back the cuffs of the plain white shirt he was wearing. Against the skin of his wrist glinted the steel of a utilitarian watch. Everything about him was unobtrusive, as she'd noted before, Julia thought. Everything about him was almost boringly ordinary. She should have been able to let her gaze sweep over and by him without feeling the slightest twinge of interest, and for one moment, she almost made it.

Then her eyes met his, and suddenly it seemed as if the air around them had thickened, making it hard for her to breathe.

Ordinary? she thought faintly. How had she gotten *that* impression? Maybe feature by feature there was nothing about him that grabbed attention. The dark brown hair was a little too long to conform to current style, a little too short to be sexily shaggy. The even features were bluntly masculine, but not memorable. He was tall, but not more than an inch or two over six feet, and although his shoulders were broad enough to strain the seams of the white shirt, they didn't have the obsessive muscularity of a bodybuilder.

And none of that was important, because emanating from him like an almost physical force was an aura of pure maleness.

An insane vision of tangled sheets, sweat-sheened skin, intertwined limbs fogged her mind for a second, and for that second it was so real that she could almost feel his hands spread wide on her hips, feel him thrusting into her. It wasn't her fault, she thought disjointedly. Any woman would sense what she was sensing. Line Max Ross up with three other men, men with movie-star good looks, men who knew and used all the tricks to make a female heart turn over, and without even exerting himself he would be the one that a woman would pick out, maybe without even knowing why she'd done so.

She felt a spreading heat radiate through her, and let herself sway infinitesimally toward him.

Trillions and jillions, Mommy. And forever and ever…

Julia jerked back, sanity flooding through her. The man in front of her had taken her *child* away from her. The man in front of her had destroyed her whole life. How could she have seen him, even for a moment, as anything but her enemy?

The heat she'd thought she'd felt was anger, she told herself unsteadily. *Rage.* She just hadn't recognized it, because for too long now that emotion had been forbidden her.

"Forget it, Ross." Her tone was ice. "Maybe if I thought you really could help me get my daughter back I might go for your deal, but you can't and we both know

it. So I guess it's just you and your fantasies again tonight.''

She took a step away from him, expecting him to react
in some way and not knowing what she would do if he
did. She didn't want to get into it with him, she thought
in sudden weariness. She didn't have the energy to indulge in any more skirmishes with the man, especially
since there was absolutely nothing to be gained from
them. What she really wanted to do was to find some
anonymous place to lay her head for the night, blot out
the last few hours from her mind and wait for sleep to
claim her. Maybe she would dream of Willa, she thought
without much hope. Tomorrow she would have to start
planning how she was going to spend the rest of her life,
but maybe just for tonight she could linger in the past a
while longer.

''It wasn't a quid pro quo.'' Behind her he spoke, his
voice harsh in the silence. ''But okay, there's been a
fantasy or two, Julia. I don't know why, but I can't deny
it. If that makes me a bastard, then go ahead and pin the
label on me. Just don't insinuate that I'd put conditions
on helping you. No matter what you think of me, I'm
going to do my damnedest to bring your daughter home
to you.''

She paused at the doorway of the kitchen. ''The
woman I used to be might have believed you, Max,'' she
said tonelessly. ''I used to be able to fool myself about
nearly everything. But you told me yourself how it would
be for Willa if I managed to find her. I won't do that to
her.''

A few minutes ago she'd told herself she didn't know
why she'd come back here with him, she thought. But
like so much in her life, that had been a lie too. She'd
come here hoping he would save her, hoping she could

dump all her problems in his lap and let him solve them for her.

Like Sylvia used to. The comparison brought the usual conflicting mixture of love and regret that thinking of her mother unfailingly stirred in her. *You always told yourself you'd never grow up to be like her, but in the end you turned out exactly the same. Admit it—some part of you really did think he could wipe out the past for you.*

But life, no matter what the impulsive and beautiful Sylvia Weston had believed right up until the end, wasn't a fairy tale. There were no knights in shining armor, there were no magic solutions, there weren't any guaranteed happy endings. And sometimes the only choice left was the hardest one of all.

Whether or not Max managed to pull off the impossible and clear her name wasn't the point. Willa didn't need her. Barbara was a born mother—the kind of mother that Willa should have had from the start.

Babs always wanted children. You forfeited your right to Willa before she was even born, and you know it.

The truth was so ugly. No wonder it had taken her this long to gather up the courage to face it. Now all she had to do was to speak it out loud, so that never again would she be tempted into thinking it had been any other way than how it had really been.

She turned. He'd come up behind her and was standing only a foot or so away, as if he knew she had one last thing to say. Her eyes met his.

"I married him for the money, you know," she said unevenly. "He married me for my looks. I knew I was a trophy wife, and I didn't see anything wrong with the bargain we'd struck. It wasn't until the maternity nurse put Willa into my arms for the very first time that I realized what I'd done."

Her gaze went past him to the kitchen window. Frilled Priscilla curtains were held back on each side of it, and beyond the fussy eyelet lace the night outside seemed empty and black. She closed her eyes for a second, and opened them again to find him still watching her.

"It was a bad marriage." Her teeth caught at her bottom lip, and she shook her head. "No—it was a hellish marriage. There'd never been any love there, on Kenneth's part or mine, and a month or so after the wedding I realized that I didn't even like him. He was the coldest, most ruthless person I'd ever known."

She smiled bleakly at the silent man in front of her. "But like you said, I'd been born with a charge card in my hand. I'd been raised to believe that marrying for love was unthinkably naive, and as long as I made myself available to him when he needed me—whether it was to accompany him to some social function, to host a dinner party or to provide him with an heir to take over the Tennant empire one day—Kenneth paid for anything I wanted without question."

"You were his wife, for God's sake." Max broke his silence as if he couldn't help himself. His jaw tightened. "Maybe you married for all the wrong reasons, but you wouldn't be the first to make that mistake."

"It wasn't a mistake. I put a price on myself, and Kenneth met that price." Her voice didn't waver. "But when Willa was born, I took one look at her and fell completely and totally in love—and I knew I'd already done the most terrible thing to her I could do. I'd had no business making a child with a man I didn't love, Max. I'd had no right to bring a life into the world to fulfill my end of a bargain. And to Kenneth, all that was important was that she was the wrong sex. He wanted a boy to carry on in his footsteps, not a daughter."

"That was his problem, not yours." Max's voice was edged. He took a step closer to her. "Why didn't you leave?"

"Because I wouldn't have been allowed to take Willa with me," she said, looking away. "Kenneth saw both of us as possessions, and even if he couldn't stop me from walking out of the marriage he would have made sure I never saw her again. I'd wanted a rich man. I got one. He had enough money to buy anything, even sole custody of his daughter. I think if I'd given him the son he'd wanted he might have made some kind of deal, but after Willa was born I vowed to myself I wouldn't bring another child into that marriage."

Her smile was crooked. "You know what's funny, Max? Once or twice I really did daydream about how life would be if he wasn't there anymore. I never actually considered murder, but when I saw his plane explode I couldn't find it in my heart to mourn for him. I felt more grief over the deaths of Buddy Simpson and Ian Carstairs than I did over my own husband's."

"The Tenn-Chem pilot and Kenneth's personal secretary." He nodded. "Yeah, they left families too. And then there was Van Hale."

"I hadn't really known Robert long. He and Babs had only been married for a short time when he died, but losing him like that devastated her. Until I was arrested and charged with planting the bomb, I stayed with her as much as I could. I was afraid of what she might do to herself."

"She was your best friend, wasn't she?" He took in a tense breath. "And now she's the woman keeping your daughter from you. That's my fault too, Julia. But whatever it takes, I'm—"

"It's not your fault. That's what I've been trying to tell you."

It was ironic, she thought. For over two years now the man in front of her had been convinced she was guilty of the one crime she hadn't committed. Now he seemed just as determined to find her innocent on all counts—and some part of her was more than willing to let him keep his good opinion of her.

But that was why she'd needed to confess to him in the first place, she told herself coldly. Because she had to make him see that she didn't deserve absolution.

He could get Willa back for you. He said it himself—if your name was completely cleared, no court would keep her from you. That's what you've wanted, isn't it?

The small voice inside her head didn't belong to her anymore. It was the voice of the woman she'd once been, Julia thought dully—Sylvia's daughter, who, if she'd learned nothing else from her beautiful mother, had been taught that her golden looks and an ability to tell the number of carats in a diamond at a glance entitled her to glide through life without taking any responsibility. And there was still enough of Sylvia left in her that she'd shirked from telling him the whole truth, even yet.

She raised her gaze to his, schooling her features into a frozen impassivity.

"I thought you would have come across it during your investigation, but I guess Kenneth's lawyers must have figured it made him look almost as bad as it did me." Despite herself, her voice shook. "But it exists, Max. I wish to heaven it didn't but it does, and my signature's on it."

"What exists, dammit?" Obliterating the last few inches between them, he took her by the shoulders, his grip firm. He shook his head in confusion. "Did Tennant get you to sign some kind of prenuptial agreement or something? Whatever it was, it won't have any bearing on whether you're given custody of Willa. You're her *mother,* for God's sake—no one can take that away from you.''

''That's just it—it *wasn't* taken away from me!''

Wrenching out of his grasp, Julia felt the tremors start to spread. She wrapped her arms tightly around herself, as if to hold them in, but it was no use. She stared back at him, her vision glazing in pain.

''It wasn't taken away from me, Max—I gave it up.'' Her voice cracked hoarsely. ''I gave *Willa* up.''

She saw the incomprehension in his eyes and suddenly the guilt and shame that had been dammed up in her for so long spilled over in a corrosive wave.

''You still don't *get* it, do you?'' she said, her tone rising thinly. ''I signed all rights to my daughter away two days before I got married, Max! She's the most precious thing in my life—and nothing can wipe out the fact that I traded her away before she was even *born.*''

Chapter Five

He'd been wrong, Max thought grimly.

When he'd met with her in the coffee shop, he'd told himself that Julia had been through hell. He'd assumed that the internal demons that drove her had appeared the day she'd been put behind bars, never to see her child again.

But some part of Julia's soul had been in torment even when she'd been living as Kenneth's wife.

And her tough facade had been just that—a facade. She'd reached her breaking point. Even as the thought went through his mind, he saw what little color there had been in her cheeks drain away. With one swift movement he caught her just as her limbs began to crumple.

"I know you don't like being touched, Julia," he said shortly as her eyes widened in instant consternation and her body stiffened. "But I don't like letting women fall face-first onto my kitchen floor."

"For God's sake, put me down." Her lips were still bloodlessly white, but her eyes lasered blue fire at him as he carried her into the living room. "I'm perfectly all right, Max. Put me *down*." Her tone was tight with tension.

"You're not perfectly all right."

A strand of hair that had escaped the rubber band curved toward the corner of her mouth, and he resisted the insane impulse to stroke it back off her face. He lowered her to the overstuffed sofa and deposited her on it without ceremony.

"Dammit, Julia, do you have to fight me every inch of the way?" he ground out. His own nerves were stretched taut, he realized, disconcerted. The woman was scrawny, prickly, and pretty damn close to a breakdown. So why did he look at her and see delicate, vulnerable and haunted?

He sighed. Pulling up a worn leatherette hassock he sat, leaning forward until his face was only a foot or so away from hers, his forearms braced on his knees and his hands hanging down between them in what he hoped the woman in front of him would take as a non-threatening pose.

"So what was it Tennant had you sign before your marriage?" He saw the light behind those sapphire eyes flare to pained brilliance and then extinguish, leaving her gaze dull and hopeless.

"It was an addendum to the financial agreement I'd signed when our engagement had been announced." Julia looked down at her hands. Following her glance, Max saw her fold her left palm closed, swiftly hiding the scars on it from his view. She went on, her tone leaden. "It stated Kenneth would have uncontested custody of any child of our marriage if we divorced or separated. I didn't even think twice about signing it."

She looked up at him, her expression frozen. "He'd just given me the earrings he wanted me to wear on our wedding day. They were South Sea pearls, perfectly matched, and I told myself they proved he was crazy about me." Her lips stretched into a smile. "My mother had taught me it was a whole lot easier to fall in love with a rich man than with a poor one, and even though I didn't love Kenneth, it never occurred to me I'd ever have any reason to leave a man who could afford to buy me presents like that. And since I'd never met a man I couldn't wrap around my little finger, I couldn't imagine that his adoration of *me* was anything less than genuine. So I signed.''

She looked away from him, as if she could no longer meet his gaze. ''You were right in your assessment of me, Max. I was spoiled, shallow and vain. But then I found out I was pregnant.''

''You gave birth to Willa in the first year of your marriage.'' He didn't have to pause to remember. As she'd said, Max thought uncomfortably, he'd read her file until he knew it by heart. ''You must have gotten pregnant within months of the honeymoon.''

She nodded tightly, her eyes still averted. ''Believe me, that wasn't my plan at all. I was horrified.'' She shrugged tensely. ''By then I knew Kenneth had only married me because he'd come to the conclusion it was time for him to be married, and because I looked decorative on his arm at social functions. But I filled my days with shopping and my evenings with parties, and I still thought I'd made a good deal. Pregnancy would end all that, and I knew it.'' She turned to him suddenly, her gaze glittering with unshed tears. ''Do you know what I did the afternoon the doctor confirmed my suspicions, Max? Was *that* in my file?''

He shook his head, keeping his eyes on hers. ''No. What did you do?''

Even if it had been in the damned file he would have wanted to hear it from her, he realized slowly. The reports on her—the reports he'd read and reread until he thought he knew everything about Julia, including what made her tick—were *crap*, he thought in sudden anger. The subject of them bore no relation at all to the guilt-ridden woman sitting here in front of him and turning a merciless spotlight on her soul.

How many people had the courage to examine their innermost selves as unflinchingly? *Not you, Ross,* he told himself heavily. *The only way you can live with yourself is by keeping to the shadows.*

"I went out and bought a skintight sequined dress with practically no back and a slit up one thigh. It looked like I'd been poured into it." Her laugh was uneven. "I tried on shoes until I found the perfect pair of Blahnik stilettos, and I had my hair done. Kenneth was out of the country on a business trip, but that didn't matter. I went to a party and danced until dawn with one man after another, and I told myself I was having a fabulous time." She smiled tightly at him. "I'd never felt so alone in my whole life. When I finally got home that night I peeled off that ridiculously uncomfortable dress, kicked off those heels and stood in front of the mirror absolutely naked. I persuaded myself that I could already see a curve to my belly that hadn't been there before. I put my hands on my stomach, and suddenly it hit me—there was a baby growing inside me. *My* baby. A child who needed *me.* And all at once everything I'd always thought I'd wanted meant nothing at all anymore."

An imperious *ding* sounded from the direction of the kitchen as the oven timer went off. Max ignored it.

"And then you recalled the agreement you'd signed?"

Julia shook her head, her smile unsteady and her gaze lit with remembered joy. She drew her legs up to her chest and wrapped her arms around them in an oddly protective gesture, as if there was still a child inside her to shield.

"Don't forget I was the queen of self-deception, Max. I didn't let myself think about the agreement, I just was happy—supremely *happy*—for the first time in my life. Even Kenneth's reaction when the ultrasound revealed we were going to have a girl instead of the boy he'd wanted didn't change the way I felt. The first time Willa kicked inside me I nearly went crazy with excitement." Her smile faltered. "But yes, eventually I remembered. I remembered when they put her into my arms after she was born. She was so perfect and so innocent—and already the person she depended on to keep her safe had let her down. I—I didn't deserve her, Max. I didn't deserve her, and I knew it."

She swung her legs off the sofa. Placing her hands on her jeans-clad thighs, she pushed herself to her feet. Julia Tennant had fallen a long way down, Max thought, standing himself and taking in the windbreaker she was wearing, the graze on her forehead, the scraped-back hair. He'd helped with that fall. Maybe her self-assessment had been partly right. Maybe the girl she'd once been had been frivolous and foolish and shallow, and maybe it had been inevitable that life would teach her a lesson or two along the way. But whatever she thought about herself, there was a forlorn gallantry in her that must have always been there.

She'd never had a *chance,* he thought, the anger catching and flaring within him. There were details that hadn't made it into the public file, that the press had never learned, that Julia herself had probably shoved into the furthest recesses of her mind. Details like her playboy father, Sylvia's first husband, whose penchant for thrills and experimentation had ended in a Paris hotel room

when Julia had been seven, with the official cause of his
death being listed as a tragically allergic reaction to some
prescribed medication he'd been on. Sylvia herself,
who'd found that her blue-blooded and extravagant
young husband's trust fund had ceased with his death,
had spent the rest of her life snaring and discarding
wealthy husbands until her latest *amour* had killed both
of them by taking a curve too fast with three times the
legal limit of alcohol in his bloodstream. Details like the
men Sylvia had taken between husbands, including a certain wealthy European industrialist who'd been attracted
more to a teenaged Julia than to her mother and whose
attentions had come to light only after Julia had been
caught trying to steal a handgun from the locked desk of
the father of one of her schoolfriends.

And Kenneth Tennant himself, who'd had no interest
in his beautiful young wife beyond the flawless image
she projected and the heir she could provide him with.

Max felt a surge of self-dislike. Finally, there was the
agent who'd been assigned to her case. He himself had
looked at Julia and seen only the golden facade, completely missing the essence of the woman, her one defin-
ing characteristic. Because of his blindness, she'd lost her
very reason for living.

He couldn't make everything right for her. But he
could try to give her back that.

"You probably didn't deserve her." She'd already
taken a step away from him, but at his words she turned,
her expression stricken. He went on, his voice not entirely steady. "Nobody deserves the total love and trust
of a child. Nobody ever truly earns it. But children are
too young to know that, and they give it anyway. Willa
did, didn't she?"

"Yes." She squeezed her eyes shut, as if riding out a

wave of pain. She opened them again, and Max saw the crystalline tears that had once struck him as impossibly contrived trembling at the corners of her lashes. "She gave me total love, Max. I was the center of her world, and she was the center of mine. But as you said, children are too young to know who's worth their love and who's not."

There was a finality in her tone. She really believed it, he thought slowly. She really believed she wasn't worthy of the love of her own child because of a single thoughtless act she'd regretted ever since.

Or did it go deeper than that? Sudden comprehension tore through him, and with it came a swift stab of appalled compassion.

"It wasn't the agreement you signed, was it? That's got nothing to do with letting her go." He crossed the space between them before she could turn away again, and took her by the shoulders.

Her expression closed down. "It has everything to do with it. For God's sake, Max—what more proof do I need to convince myself that I'm not the mother Willa deserves?"

"But that's just it—you never needed *any* proof," he said forcefully, tightening his grip on her as she tried to pull away. "Because you learned a long time ago that you didn't deserve to be loved. That's why you told yourself you weren't looking for it in a marriage, and that's why when you finally found it with Willa you wouldn't allow yourself to have it."

Her gaze was dark with denial, but behind the denial Max thought he could see another, stronger emotion. Her response was automatic. "That's *crazy*, Agent Ross. Maybe it's time you chose something else to read before bedtime. It's obvious that poring over my biography is starting to get to you."

"It would get to anyone who cared to read between the lines," he agreed promptly. "I thought I was the one who put you in prison. But you were already there— you've been there for a long, long time. Who was it who put the final brick in that wall that surrounds you, Julia? Was it your father, who never seemed to know he even had a daughter? Sylvia, picking you up and depositing you in one new home after another as if you were a monogrammed piece of luggage she had to remind herself not to leave behind? Or was it left to Kenneth to finally teach you that there was nothing worthwhile about you except the way you looked?" He gave her a small shake. "Whoever it was, they were *wrong*. The only one who was right was Willa."

"If she was so right then how come her mother ended up leaving her, Max? If she was so right, then why was I punished?" Julia twisted out of his grasp, her voice rising as she flung the questions at him like accusations. "Twelve strangers sat in judgment on me and found me *guilty,* dammit—and even if I didn't commit the crime they convicted me for, I must have deserved that verdict for *some* reason!"

She held up her left hand. It was shaking so badly that the obscene marks on it were a red blur against the white of her skin. "*This* is the proof, Max! The way you looked at me the night I was released proves what kind of person I am! All my life I've been terrified that someone will find out what the real Julia Tennant looks like, and now the whole *world* knows. She's not pretty at all, is she? There's *nothing* worth loving about her—and she doesn't deserve to keep her child!"

She stared up at him, the skin stretched so tautly over

her features that her bones stood out in sharp relief. She was still holding her hand out, and at the sight of it Max felt something inside him give way painfully. His own touch unsteady, he caught her fingers lightly.

"No, she's not pretty anymore," he said hoarsely. "Pretty is for girls. Pretty is on the surface. She used to be just pretty, but now she's beautiful." He bent his head to her hand. His eyes never leaving her suddenly wide and fearful gaze, gently he pressed a kiss to the wounded palm. He felt the shudder that ran through her. "Willa's mother is a beautiful woman who walked through fire and survived, Julia. *Everything* about her is proof of that."

For the space of a heartbeat she simply stared at him, her face a frozen mask. Then her mouth opened in a silent rictus of grief, tears flooding her eyes and spilling over, those perfect features contorting in overwhelming anguish. Two years ago with her freedom at stake, the woman he'd eventually put behind bars had taken the stand at her trial and cried so exquisitely that her mascara hadn't even run, Max remembered. Now Julia's face was free of any makeup, and there was nothing delicate at all about her sorrow. It blazed, naked and raw, from the red-rimmed eyes, and when her voice finally burst from her throat it came out in an almost inarticulate sob.

"I want her *back,* Max! Sometimes I pretend she's just behind me, or she's in the next room, or she's waiting for me around the corner. But then I turn the corner and she's not there, and I have to start pretending all over again."

She didn't protest when he pulled her roughly to his chest and wrapped his arms around the shaking shoulders. He could feel the hot wetness of her tears soaking through his shirt as she went on, her voice muffled.

"Barbara always wanted children. She only got married because she didn't want to wait any longer to start a family of her own. When Willa was a baby Babs knew exactly what to do when she had a stomach upset, and the toys she bought her were always the ones the child-care books recommended. She used to babysit when I had to attend some gathering or another with Kenneth in the evenings, and once when I went in to kiss Willa good-night before going out I had on a beaded dress. One of the beads must have come off and fallen into her crib when I tucked her in. Barbara found it just as Willa was trying to put it into her *mouth*."

She looked up at him, her face blotchy and stray strands of her hair sticking wetly to her cheeks. "You're wrong, Max. I'm not the best mother for her—Barbara is. She won't make any mistakes. She won't let her down. Willa needs a mother like Babs, not someone like me!"

He hadn't wanted to let her know, Max thought in frustration. But Julia *was* strong—strong enough to give up the most precious thing in her world if she thought it was the right decision. Brutal or not, he had to show her it wasn't.

"She thinks you left because you didn't want her," he said harshly. "Your sister-in-law's tried everything—told her you didn't want to go, told her you'll always love her even if you can't be with her, taken her to counsellors for professional therapy. It's helped a little. Most of the time she's happy enough. But she still thinks it was something she did that sent you away. She still thinks that if you love her, you'll come back for her. I do too."

"She—she thinks it was *her* fault?" Clutching twin handfuls of his shirt, Julia stared at him in shock. "She thinks I left because I didn't *love* her anymore? Oh, *no*, Max! No—she *can't* believe that! I can't *let* her believe that! If she grows up thinking that she'll end up just like—''

She stopped in midsentence, her hands flying to her mouth in an oddly childlike gesture as if for a split second she was once again the little girl she'd been and was appalled at how close she'd come to telling her most closely guarded secret. Her eyes widened painfully.

''She'll end up just like *me*,'' she whispered. ''How soon can you take me to her, Max?''

Chapter Six

"*This* is what you meant when you said you'd take me to see my daughter?" Julia stared at the man in front of her in disbelief, and then across the wooded valley below them to a barely visible path skirting the edge of a gorge. She could just make out the sparkle of early-morning sunlight on the wide ribbon of water cutting between the far-off cliffs. "What the hell am I supposed to be using—binoculars?"

"They're Agency issue. We use them for surveillance all the time. Trust me, you'll be able to see every freckle on her nose." Unslinging the canvas duffel bag he'd worn over his shoulder since they'd left the car half an hour ago, Max reached inside and pulled out a light-weight pair of field glasses. She didn't take them from him.

"I don't get it, Max." With difficulty she regulated the timbre of her voice. "Last night you said Willa needed to have me back in her life. Catching a glimpse of her on a nature walk with ten other children and their parents without being able to let her know I'm here isn't being back in her life. How is spying on her through the trees from half a mile away going to reassure her about *anything?*"

"It's not." He met her glare steadily. "I brought you here today to reassure *you*."

He flicked a glance at his watch and then gestured to a nearby rock. "We've got at least an hour before they come into sight. Sit down, Julia."

What choice did she have? she thought in frustration, complying with ill grace and lowering herself stiffly onto one of the lichen-covered boulders that seemed to be a feature of the hilly, cliff-carved landscape. They were out here in the middle of nowhere—well, not nowhere, she admitted with grudging honesty, but certainly this wild little nature preserve on the edge of the Berkshires was a world away from Boston—and according to Max, soon Willa would appear, accompanied by Babs and a group of like-minded parents who made a habit of these Saturday-morning walks with their children. It wasn't what she'd hoped for, but seeing her daughter, even at a distance and even for only a few seconds, overrode everything else.

But she still felt as if she'd been tricked. Hunching her shoulders against the brisk breeze and wishing she had something more substantial than the flimsy windbreaker she was wearing, she lifted her chin at him.

"Reassure me about what? And why couldn't we have approached Babs directly? You were the agent in charge of this case, Max—why couldn't you have contacted her and told her you no longer believed I was guilty?"

He didn't answer her immediately. Instead, he gave her a sharp glance, taking in the shivers she was trying to suppress, and the next minute he was stripping his sweatshirt over his head and tossing it her way. Julia caught it one-handedly and in turn narrowed her gaze at his T-shirt-clad torso.

"Cut the Sir Galahad stuff, Ross," she snapped. "If

I'm not wearing appropriate clothing that's my fault, not yours. I'm not taking your clothes.''

About to toss the sweatshirt back to him, she saw a flash of expression cross his features. She paused in disconcertion, her grip tightening on the heavy cotton garment. Had that been embarrassment she'd seen appear and disappear so quickly in his eyes? she wondered incredulously. Had she made Max Ross, the king of no emotion at all, feel ill at ease?

Suddenly she felt embarrassed herself—embarrassed, and ashamed of her churlish response. She'd been out of the normal world too long if this was the way she reacted to a simple kindness, she told herself edgily. She flushed, and jammed her arms into the oversize sleeves.

"Sorry," she muttered, thankful for the brief moment of invisibility as she dragged the top, still warm from his body, over her head. "I seem to have mislaid my party manners."

"I'm not much of a party guy, so don't worry about it." A corner of Max's mouth lifted wryly. His smile, slight as it was, changed his whole countenance.

Obviously it had been way too long since a lot of things, Julia told herself faintly. That had to be why her heart was suddenly crashing against her ribs like a jackhammer and her knees felt suddenly so weak. So what if under the suits and shirts she'd always seen him in, the man had been hiding smoothly muscled biceps and that solid expanse of broad chest, now clearly delineated under the navy T-shirt? So what if in the instant his mouth had quirked up, those cat-green eyes of his had been momentarily veiled by dark lashes as thick as any girl's, providing an erotic contrast to the hard planes and angles of that masculine, but in no way startlingly handsome, face? That still wasn't any reason to gape at him as if she'd never seen a man before.

"I may have been the agent in charge, but I don't have any authority to change the deal your sister-in-law made." The smile was gone, she saw with vague relief. "What I'm doing right now is grounds enough to get me dismissed from the Agency, but I figure the risk is worth it. I wanted you to reassure yourself that she's all right— because after today, it might be a while before you see Willa again. Just having your conviction overturned wasn't enough, Jules."

He'd called her that once before, she remembered. At the time she'd thought it was a slip of the tongue, but hearing him use the nickname again sparked a tiny flame of warmth inside her that had nothing to do with the sweatshirt he'd loaned her.

She needed all the warmth she could get.

"Because to the rest of the world I'm still The Porcelain Doll Bomber," she said flatly. "Remind me again how we're going to change that, Max."

She could hear the antagonism creeping into her voice once more, but she couldn't seem to control it. "I never knew much about the business, but I know that while Kenneth was at the helm of Tenn-Chem he buried a lot of bodies. He used to tell me it was a dog-eat-dog world, but it looks as though in the end there was a faster and more ruthless dog out there than my husband. After all this time he'll have covered his tracks completely. Face facts, Max—no one else will ever go to trial for those murders."

Even before she'd finished speaking she saw he was shaking his head in disagreement. "I know you always thought that Kenneth was killed by a business competitor or maybe someone he'd ruined in a takeover bid. I never bought that theory. Now I like it even less."

"But that's just it—it doesn't matter what you or I think." Her tone sharpened further. "If I'm wrong, and my husband was killed for personal reasons, then whoever wanted him dead accomplished what he set out to do and I took the fall for it. We're still left with nothing, unless you know something I don't."

"I know that the case against you was damning enough to put you in prison." Max's tone took on the same edge as hers. He jammed his hands in the back pockets of the chinos he was wearing and looked down at her impatiently. "I know if you hadn't been taken out of the picture, control of the Tennant business empire would have been in your hands until Willa reached the age of majority and took over the company as her father's only heir. Instead, Barbara's the one who's holding it in trust for her—and Barbara's disinterest in the business was always a given."

He shrugged tightly, the muscles of his shoulders shifting under the navy cotton. "You didn't exactly marry into the Waltons. There's no love lost between any of them, and Kenneth himself wrested control from his mother and shunted aside his brother Noel when he took over. I think there's a good possibility that his murder was a family affair—and if I'm right, then Willa's living on borrowed time."

Julia hardly realized she had risen to her feet. She took a swift step toward him, her hands clenched at her sides. "I asked you *yesterday* if you thought my daughter was in danger! Why didn't you tell me what you suspected then, dammit?"

She darted a glance across the valley to the little clearing by the fenced-off gorge, but even without the binoculars she could see that it was still peacefully empty. She looked back at Max.

"Olivia Tennant's her grandmother, for God's sake! She has to be well aware of Willa's whereabouts—and now you're telling me you think it's possible she arranged her own son's death and might be contemplating a second murder? Or Willa's uncle, Noel? If your theory's right and he planted that bomb, what's to stop him from eliminating his niece whenever he feels like it?" She bit off the question furiously and continued without giving him a chance to answer.

"Last night I began to *trust* you, Max. Last night I started to let myself think there was still a spark of humanity in you that hadn't been totally burned out by your past, that some small part of you wasn't as mechanical and sealed-off as you wanted everyone to believe. I was wrong. You just see this as a case you screwed up, don't you? All you care about is bringing in the real killer— and the fact that my daughter could be in danger right now doesn't mean a *thing* to you! What the hell runs through those veins of yours, anyway—ice water?"

"So I'm told." As she began to turn away, Max's hand shot out and grabbed her by the arm. He jerked her around to face him again, and her outraged gaze met his.

"Get your freakin' hands *off* me, Ross," she hissed furiously. "I'm going back to my original plan, dammit—I'm going to get my daughter back myself and disappear with her. That's the only way she'll ever be safe. And if you're thinking of blowing the whistle on me, don't forget that the Agency is going to want to know how I located her so quickly. I know you well enough to guess you don't want them learning that their own man led me to her."

"You don't know the first thing about me, honey. You

don't even know the first thing about yourself, for God's sake," he ground out. "Number one, as long as Willa's with Barbara she's not in danger. If I thought there was any possibility of her being harmed I would have snatched her myself. And number two is this crap about you not liking being touched. You like it from me, all right. You like it a lot."

"Do I, Ross?" Without attempting to twist out of his grasp, Julia smiled humorlessly at him, her right hand going to the back pocket of her jeans to withdraw the object she'd purchased and carried since the day she'd been given back her freedom. In a blur of movement her hand came up. "Then how come I've got a knife to your throat, *honey?*" she whispered hoarsely.

Max froze as she pressed the flat of the blade to the hard line of his jaw. His gaze, dark green and unreadable, slanted down at her.

Two years ago the notion of carrying any kind of a weapon would never have occurred to her, but, along with everything else, she'd lost that complacent sense of security as well, Julia thought bitterly. Even before replacing the hated prison smock with the secondhand jeans and windbreaker, she'd approached a group of working girls standing in a cluster by an alleyway and had traded a few of her precious dollars for the switchblade she was now holding.

"Hell, I don't know, Jules." Despite the stillness of his posture, there was a thread of wryness in his voice, and as her disbelieving gaze met his she saw that one-sided smile reappear at the corner of his mouth. "Maybe you think I like it rough. And maybe you're right. Would you really do it?"

"I think so, Ross." Her throat felt suddenly dry, which was strange, since the hand holding the knife seemed just as suddenly damp with nerves. She tried to swallow and found she couldn't. "But there's only one way to find out for sure. You don't want to push me that far."

"Like I said, you don't know the first thing about me." He bent his head toward her a fraction. She felt the unshaven prickle of his skin chafe slightly against the knuckles of her clenched hand. "I do want to find out for sure. I'm just that crazy."

Seemingly oblivious to the cold steel poised so dangerously near to the tanned column of his throat, slowly he lessened the distance between them until she could feel the warmth of his breath on her own parted lips, see her own startled gaze reflected in the brilliant green of those darkly lashed eyes.

She'd read him wrong right from the start, Julia thought incredulously. The emotionless demeanor, the blandly conservative suits and ties he usually wore, the impassive and by-the-book manner that she remembered from the investigation and the trial—they were all an *act*.

The man was a loaded gun. And for some reason, being around her switched off his safety mechanism.

"You're not a straight arrow at all, are you?" Even to her own ears her voice sounded tremulous with shock. "You let everybody think you are, but you're really a damn *cowboy*. How the hell have you managed to get away with it?"

"Did I get away with it?" There was a touch of real curiosity in his tone. "I always figured you saw through me just a little, Jules. After all, you're the one who kept bringing up the subject of fantasies."

There was no space between them at all now. Her grip tightened convulsively on the weapon in her hand even as his lips brushed against hers.

He was going to go through with it, she thought disjointedly. She held all the cards and he knew it, and still the man was willing to go through with this. He *was* crazy.

"You're taking one hell of a chance, Agent Ross." The ball of her thumb was pressed firmly against the pulse-point of his neck, and she felt his heartbeat begin to speed up. "Maybe your ideas about me are just as wrong as mine were about you. Are you so sure you want to put them to the test?"

"You do what you have to do, Julia." His words were whispered against her parted lips, and as he spoke his lashes drifted completely down, cutting off that electric gaze. "I won't stop you."

He was handing the situation over to her, she thought with a surge of anger. After pushing the envelope as far as he could, now he was leaving it up to her to take the last step—and he wasn't even giving her the opportunity to let him see the fury in her eyes.

To hell with him, Julia thought tightly. She let her own lashes sweep down, and opened her mouth fully against his.

Instantly she felt his tongue enter her, and just as instantaneously a white-hot flame tore through her, racing along every last nerve ending in her body like a runaway bolt of lightning. His mouth covered hers and he went deeper, as if he was deliberately discarding whatever vestige of self-regulation he'd been holding on to until now.

He wasn't one of the good guys. Even when they'd been on opposite sides of the fence, even when she'd told herself he was the enemy, she'd thought of him as being on the side of law and order, but at some basic level Max Ross stood for the exact opposite. Law and order? Julia thought faintly. Anarchy and disorder were more like it.

The man was insane. The situation was insane. Worst of all, she was going crazy here too.

She'd told herself it had been too long. That wasn't strictly true. She'd *never* had anything like this before.

She could taste him—taste his inner lip, taste his tongue, taste the slightly salty tang of his skin. She had the irresponsible impulse to bite him, and a part of her that she hadn't even known existed urged her to act on the impulse.

She nipped his lower lip and felt the sudden shudder, instantly stilled, that ran through him. He spoke without taking his mouth from hers.

"Drop the knife, Jules. You're dangerous enough without it."

Her eyes flew open in consternation at his ironic reminder. Appalled, she started to pull away from him, but before she could, he reached up with his left hand and uncurled her fingers. She heard a tiny metallic clink as metal struck rock at their feet.

"Remember what a goddamn gentleman I was last night?"

His voice was barely audible. Casting her gaze up through her lashes, Julia saw that his eyes were still closed. She nodded anyway, the movement little more than an awkward jerk of her head. He exhaled.

"I came into the spare room after you'd fallen asleep. I stood in the doorway for about an hour, just watching you. Then I went to my own bed and—" He stopped. His eyes opened and met hers calmly. "Anyway, this morning I decided that from now on I was going to keep to the straight and narrow where you were concerned. I don't think it's working, so screw that plan."

His left hand was still loosely clasped around her fingers. He brought his right palm up and traced the curve of her lower lip with the side of his thumb before sliding his open hand along her cheekbone to her temple.

It was time to say something, Julia thought stupidly. It was time to say something—*anything*—to break up this irrational feeling of lassitude that seemed to be gripping her. His fingers slid into her hair. She caught her breath and closed her eyes, and immediately it was as if she was standing in the middle of a field on the Fourth of July, the black velvet of a summer night lapping against her skin, a skein of sparks from the fireworks directly above her falling and sizzling onto her lips, her eyelids, her breasts. His voice, lower and rougher than a whisper, was in her ear.

"You can have me any way you want, Jules. You can have me any way you want, anytime you want, and you can do any damn thing you want to do to me. Every dark dream that ever went through your sleep, everything you never dared demand from anyone before, I'll give to you." He released her hand, and she felt his fingertips touch her lips. "Like you said, honey, I'm not a straight arrow. I can drive you out of your mind, and you can bring me to my knees. All you have to do is say the word."

With no warning at all his mouth was on hers, hard and urgent, and this time it wasn't like lightning at all. She felt him inside her, felt slow fire surging through her limbs, her thighs, the pit of her stomach. He could make her *dissolve* with desire, she thought hazily—that stroking tongue, those strong hands, that husky voice. And all he'd done so far was kiss her. What would it be like to have that sure mouth everywhere on her body, feel those hands around her hips maneuvering her into any position she asked for, hear that sex-roughened murmur beside her in the darkness putting into erotic words every secret fantasy she'd ever forbidden herself to think about?

You can find out what it would be like. You can find out anytime you want. The small voice inside her head was compellingly persuasive. *Who knows why or how, but for some reason the man's yours whenever you want to take him. It could be as soon as tonight, if that's what you—*

His mouth left hers. His hands slid down to her shoulders. Startled, she opened her eyes to meet his.

At first glance he looked the same as he always did. Taking in the expressionless features, the rigidly motionless posture of the man facing her, Julia felt as if she had just been doused with a bucket of cold water. Then his gaze wavered.

All of a sudden she could see the differences. Under the tan of his cheekbones ran a faint ridge of color. Those dark eyes were still glazed and slightly unfocused. Beneath the thin cotton of the T-shirt his chest rose and fell unsteadily, and his bottom lip was swollen.

"Yeah, Jules, that's right." His voice held a lingering huskiness. "With me what you see isn't necessarily what you get. You and I are going to have to work together to find out who really planted that bomb on your husband's plane, and you might start thinking that the man in the suit and tie standing beside you asking questions of strangers and taking notes is the real Max Ross. I don't give a damn if everyone else thinks that. But I want you to know that whatever I'm saying or doing at any given moment, underneath it all is the man you saw just now, waiting for one word from you."

He was still gripping her shoulders. Without letting go of her he twisted his wrist just enough to glance at his watch. Then he did release her.

"If they're on schedule, Willa's group should be showing up soon. I'll get the binoculars focused and ready, Jules, but first—" He bent down easily and picked up the fallen knife, one-handedly levering the small but wicked-looking blade into its handle before holding it out to her. A corner of his mouth lifted. "You know, I'm pretty sure you nicked me, honey. But I didn't feel a thing at the time."

Numbly she allowed him to deposit the small weapon into her palm. As he turned away to retrieve the binoculars she slipped the switchblade into her back pocket with trembling fingers, her thoughts chaotic.

What had just happened between them? she thought shakily. If they'd been here under any other circumstances, right now he wouldn't be calmly adjusting a pair of binoculars a few feet away and she wouldn't be standing around like a statue. Under any other circumstances what he'd told her would already be happening—he'd be driving her out of her mind and she would have brought him to his knees.

She felt the hot color mount her cheeks and turned almost angrily away, grateful for the brisk hilltop breeze that had chilled her earlier. Except they *weren't* here under any other circumstances, she told herself sharply. There would never be any other circumstances between them. He was the man who could help her get her daughter back, and that was where her interest in him began and ended. For some reason, although she doubted almost everything else he'd said, she found herself trusting in his estimation of the situation—that for now, and while she was with Barbara, Willa was safe. And some part of her accepted the rest of his theory too, she admitted unwillingly.

While she'd been in prison, it had been more bearable

to hold on to the conviction that Kenneth's murderer had been a faceless stranger than to allow herself to consider that someone close to her could have claimed four victims. She couldn't let herself think that that someone was still out there, perhaps a part of her daughter's life, because in prison she'd been powerless to protect Willa. But she wasn't in prison anymore. She wasn't powerless anymore. And this time Max Ross was working with her, not against her.

But that was as far as it went, Julia thought edgily. That was as far as she could afford to let it go.

"I think I hear them." He was beside her, and as she turned he dropped the strap of the binoculars over her neck, lifting her hair out of the way as he did. "Train the glasses on that clearing. They usually take a play break there before heading back."

"You—you've watched them from here before?"

Julia raised the lenses to her eyes, her mouth suddenly dry and her stomach seemingly alive with butterflies. Any minute now she would *see* her, she thought tremulously.

A terrible possibility occurred to her, and she wondered why she hadn't thought of it before. The binoculars slipped in her damp hands, and Max reached around from behind her to steady them.

"I've kept an eye on her. I made it my business to know their routine, and at least once a week I ran a surveillance on her, just to make sure everything was still okay. Don't worry, Jules, you'll recognize her. She looks like her mom, only tougher."

A weak bubble of laughter escaped her. He'd known what she'd been fearing, Julia thought in surprise—he'd known, and he'd even managed to make her see how unlikely her fears were. She felt a quick rush of thankfulness that he was here with her, and then she forgot everything and everyone as she too caught the sound of children's voices drifting faintly upward and she trained the binoculars on the far-off clearing.

But it wasn't a child that burst into sight first.

Like a small golden bomb, a puppy exploded out of the woods and tore into the clearing, the leash he was dragging behind him clearly visible. The laughter got louder, and the next moment the previously deserted little picnic area was suddenly filled with children of all ages and sizes, their shouts of excitement and their out-stretched hands only encouraging the small canine run-away to speed even more quickly around the fenced-off clearing, as if he was enjoying the chase as much as they were.

But amid the tangle of flying arms and short, pumping legs, Julia's eyes saw only one small figure.

"Willa," she breathed. "Oh, kitten-paws, is it really *you*?"

Max had been right—through the magnifying lenses the little girl seemed as close as if only a few feet sep-arated them, instead of half a mile or so of hilly terrain. She was wearing a bright pink T-shirt and a pair of baggy dungarees that she kept impatiently hitching up at the waist, and two flaxen plaits flew around her head as she raced after the puppy with the others, her blue eyes alight with excitement.

Julia felt the tears streaming down her face. She'd grown so *big,* she thought with a pang. When she'd last seen her, Willa had been four years old and only just emerging from babyhood. There'd been a round chubbiness to her limbs and her cheeks that had made her seem at times like a puppy herself. Now her legs had a tough wiriness, and her eyes seemed to fill her whole face.

Was it her imagination, or was there a shadow dimming the exuberance of that cornflower-blue gaze? she wondered anxiously.

She was being foolish, she knew. *It's just that you've got two years of worrying to catch up on,* she told herself in shaky remonstration. *Two years of your heart stopping every time she took a tumble, two years of imagining the worst when you couldn't hear her moving around at night, two years of bandages and warm milk and kisses on scraped elbows.*

"Two years of not being there for you, precious," she whispered, keeping her burning gaze on the pink-clad figure reaching out for the trailing leash. "But I never stopped loving you. Don't *ever* think that, kitten-paws. I was in a place where I couldn't see the sky, but you were my sun every morning when I got up and my moon every evening when I fell asleep. I *never* stopped loving you. I never will."

She was dimly aware of the group of four or five adults who had entered the clearing and were calling to the still-tumbling children with more indulgence than admonition in their voices. But even the slim, laughing figure of Barbara didn't take her attention away from the child her heart had hungered for for so long. Willa was healthy and loved, Julia told herself. She was a normal little girl, living a normal life. The shadow she'd thought she'd seen in those blue eyes was a trick of the light, a product of her own feverish need to get her child back. For now, as Max had said, Willa was perfectly safe....

Except that wasn't true, she thought slowly. No matter what had happened, she was still Willa's mother, and she *knew* that wasn't true. Icy dread washed over her, and the premonition she'd been trying to ignore for the past few minutes rose up, nightmarish and immediate, to the forefront of her consciousness.

Willa was in terrible danger. Her daughter was in danger right *now*.

She swung around to Max, the binoculars falling from her nerveless fingers and slamming against her chest. She saw the incomprehension in his eyes as she started to push past him, felt his hand on her arm holding her back. She looked up at him frantically, and knew that the burgeoning terror inside her was plainly visible on her face.

"Jules, what's the matter?" There was sharp concern in his voice. He glanced across the treetops to the far-off clearing by the gorge, and then back at her. His tone softened. "She'll be with you again one day soon, Julia. I know it's hard—"

"She's in *danger*, Max!" She attempted to wrench away from him, but he held her fast. "Let go of me, for God's sake! Willa's in danger right *now*—and I have to *get* to her!"

Chapter Seven

"How do you know she's in danger?" Max's eyes darkened in confusion. "Did you see something?"

"I don't *know* how I know!" The helpless words burst from her in agitated frustration. "But I'm her *mother!* I just know. Damn you, Max, I have to go to her!"

"You'd never get there in time." A muscle in his jaw jumped, as if some of her fear had transferred itself to him. "For God's sake, it's an hour's hike from here to there even without crossing the river. By the time we arrive they'll all be back in their cars and on their way home. She's perfectly *safe,* Julia. They come on this outing every weekend and nothing's ever happened—"

A thin, far-off scream ripped across the rest of his words. Julia whirled around, bringing the binoculars up to her eyes so convulsively that they jarred against her cheekbones.

She didn't feel them. She didn't feel Max's arm around her, or hear his sharply indrawn breath. She stood on the edge of the hill and watched in terror as her world shattered into a thousand slicing pieces around her.

"Dear God—*no!*" The unconscious prayer came from her numb lips in an agonized moan.

Again, the chilling tableau she was looking at seemed

to be taking place only a stone's throw away—the renegade puppy, trembling and abject now, held firmly in the arms of an older child, the stark terror on the face of a mother herding the group of children over to a nearby picnic table, the gaping emptiness in the wooden fence at the edge of the gorge where it had given way.

Julia inched the binoculars downward. Her heart stopped beating.

About ten feet below the crumbling edge of the steep cliff—the edge that the fence had been erected to cordon off—a pink-and-denim-clad figure hung suspended over the gorge. Even as Julia's fingers gripped the twin barrels of the binoculars Willa suddenly seemed to lurch downward a foot or so before jerking to a halt. Blue eyes fluttered closed in the small white face.

One of the shoulder straps of her overalls was caught on a massive root that protruded from the sheer face of the cliff. Far below her, creamy rapids tumbled and spilled over jagged rock.

"Someone's going to have to rappel down to her." Max's voice was terse. "They've got that extendable dog lead. It should be long enough."

Julia didn't take her eyes from the scene. A movement at the edge of the cliff drew her attention. It had been two years since she'd seen her sister-in-law, but unlike Willa Barbara hadn't changed much at all. The silky dark hair was still held back at either side of the delicate face with plain silver clips, and she was wearing the same kind of pastel twinset with a heathery tweed skirt that Julia remembered as her preferred mode of dress. But right now her hands were bunched into fists at her mouth, and the soft brown eyes were wide with terror as she looked frantically around at the small group of parents surrounding her.

In disbelief Julia saw them, one by one, uncomfortably avert their eyes from Barbara's beseeching gaze. The only man in the group turned away stiffly, grabbing the hand of a small boy and moving farther from the broken fence.

"No one's *moving!*" she gasped. "No one's *doing* anything!"

"I can see that." His words were clipped with anger. "And your sister-in-law looks as if she's about to faint."

"Babs has a phobia about heights," Julia said automatically. "She can't even climb up a stepladder without passing out from fear. But why isn't anyone else even *trying?*" She wrenched the glasses from her face. "Max, I've got to get over there—"

He was no longer beside her. A few feet away from her, he was slinging the duffel bag over his shoulder, his features tight. Even as she looked at him she saw him draw an implement from it, his jaw set with determination. He unsheathed the tool in his hand with one grimly swift motion, revealing a shining blade.

"Machete," he said briefly, meeting her eyes. "I'm going to take the straightest line I can, and this might help with the undergrowth. I only pray I'm in time."

"I'm coming with you." Julia took a quick step toward him, but before she could take a second he was in front of her.

"No. I need you here." He looked out over the trees below. "I don't have a compass. Whenever I come out into a clearing I'll look for your signal. If I'm still on course, raise both your arms straight up—I'll see you if you keep away from the bushes. If I'm not, wave me back on track."

"Dammit, Max—I'm not going to just stand here practicing my semaphore skills while my daughter's in jeopardy!'' She darted a lightning glance back at the faraway gorge.

He reached out and pushed a stray strand of hair away from her forehead, his gaze locked on hers. ''Honey, waiting here is how you can help her the most.''

He was right, she thought hopelessly. Damn him, he was right. She felt the tears gather behind her eyes, and blinked them away furiously.

''Then *go*,'' she rasped, her throat thick with fear and pain. ''Go to her, Max. Save my little girl for me.''

''You don't have to ask,'' he said softly. ''You never have to ask me, Jules. Remember that.''

Before she could respond he dropped a quick kiss on her parted lips, and then he was gone, running through the underbrush and down the steep slope of the hillside as surefootedly as a wild animal. The trees closed around him and Julia raised the glasses to her eyes again.

Nothing had changed. Her daughter, as motionless as a marionette with its strings cut, still hung on the root, although it seemed to Julia's anxious gaze that the woody protrusion had bowed a fraction more since she'd last looked. The rest of the children were still huddled, white-faced and crying, around the picnic table. And still no one had moved to help her child.

Even through the binoculars it was possible to see the sick terror etching her sister-in-law's features, Julia thought, swallowing dryly. But although some part of her wanted to scream at the top of her lungs at Babs to pull herself together, most of her impotent fury was directed toward the rest of the adults.

Barbara's crippling shyness and reticence were only two facets of her timid personality, but underneath her protective shell of self-consciousness and constraint was a warm and loving heart—and from the first moment she'd laid eyes on her newborn niece, she'd given that heart to Willa. It wasn't Barbara's fault that she was paralysed with fear, Julia thought hopelessly. She just wasn't physically capable of overcoming her terror.

Even as the thought went through her mind she froze. With the ball of her thumb she adjusted the focusing knob on the binoculars, unable to believe what she was seeing.

Barbara had shrugged out of the cashmere cardigan that was part of her twinset, throwing it down carelessly onto the ground beside her. The next moment, her face pale and set, she was reaching around to the back of her tweed skirt and unzipping it.

What was she doing? Julia's eyes widened as she saw her sister-in-law—a woman so painfully shy that she'd never even owned a bathing-suit—shove the bulky tweed skirt past her slim hips and step out of it. She was wearing a pair of chastely white cotton briefs that were less revealing than high-cut shorts, but even so, her bare legs seemed almost shockingly exposed. Before Julia could accept what had just happened, she got another and greater shock.

Picking up her skirt and snatching the nylon dog lead from one of the seemingly frozen bystanders, Babs marched over to the picnic table. She squatted beside it, tied the lead to it and stood up again. Looking down, her hair a soft cloud obscuring her features, she wrapped the tweed skirt in a protective pad around her waist before beginning to cinch the bright yellow rope securely over it. Julia saw her fingers flying as she tied a series of knots, and then Barbara's hands fell to her sides.

Without hesitation, she walked to the break in the fence at the edge of the cliff.

"But—but you're *afraid* of heights, Babs," Julia whispered hoarsely, her heart in her mouth. "You're *terrified* of them—you won't be able to go *through* with this!"

Barbara turned her back to the sheer drop beyond the damaged fence, and now Julia could see her face again. The brown eyes closed briefly and then opened wide. The bloodless lips moved.

Even if she'd shouted the words out she was too far away to have heard her, Julia thought tremulously. But through the binoculars it was perfectly possible to read her lips.

I'm coming, Willa. Don't worry, darling—I'm coming for you.

Barbara grabbed the rope in both hands. Across the distance that separated them, her eyes seemed to look directly into Julia's. Then, her delicate frame as tense as steel wire, she walked backward over the edge of the cliff.

Julia's vision blurred. Shifting the binoculars just enough to dash the tears aside, she kept them focused on the perilous journey of the lionhearted woman who was attempting to save her child.

Babs was wearing sturdy-soled moccasins. As she carefully played out the rope between her hands, her feet searched for and found what little purchase they could on the crumbling cliff-face. She planned to come down a foot or so to the right of Willa, Julia saw, her teeth sinking tensely into her bottom lip. And she just might make it—

Babs shot suddenly downward. She jerked to a halt just as abruptly. Julia saw her eyelids flutter, and her grasp on the rope slip slightly.

Wrenching the glasses upward, Julia saw three women, quicker-witted than their companions, brace themselves against the picnic table to keep it from sliding any farther on the pine-needle-littered earth. Even as they did, the lone male in the group reappeared, running along the path that led to the clearing.

She'd misjudged him, she thought weakly. Coiled around his forearm were lengths of oily rope, obviously hastily retrieved from the trunk of a vehicle. As he lashed the picnic table to the trunk of a tree with one of the ropes she looked back at Barbara.

Her sister-in-law was inching slowly downward again, and now she was close enough to Willa to touch the unconscious child. Julia saw the indecision that played across her fragile features, and knew what was going through her mind.

The nylon rope was tough, but it wouldn't be strong enough to bear the weight of both of them. And the root was already dangerously close to giving way.

The now-scuffed moccasins were toed into deep fissures in the clay soil. Julia held her breath as Babs gouged out a risky handhold at the side of a jagged rock and brought her free hand to the knots at her waist.

It was the supreme sacrifice. She had to know that by releasing the rope from herself and tying it around Willa she was giving her life for her niece's, but she didn't hesitate. Julia choked back a sob as she saw the woman she'd once thought of as weak and ineffectual work desperately at the nylon cord.

"I did almost everything wrong, Babs," she whispered through her tears. "But I did one thing right when I agreed to make you her guardian. You love her too, don't you? You love her so much you'll give your life to keep her from harm."

Just at that moment, a second rope snaked over the cliff. Barbara's gaze flew upward at the same time as Julia's, to take in the shirt-sleeved father standing by the shattered fence. The hemp rope he was holding was knotted every few feet, and behind him at each knot was a mother, ready to start pulling.

Already Barbara had taken in the situation and was securing the new rope around Willa. Looping it like an impromptu seat between the dangling legs and then feeding it through the straps of the overalls before tying it one last time around her waist, she worked quickly and efficiently. Giving one final tug to a knot, she darted a glance up at the man above her and raised her thumb shakily before moving out of the way.

The man shouted a terse command that Julia couldn't hear. Then he and the line of women behind him began slowly walking backward, pulling the rope carefully up and over the edge of the cliff.

The root slipped free from Willa's overalls. Her small body swaying back and forth, she was drawn closer and closer to safety. When she was only a foot away from the edge, the man at the front of the line released his hold on the rope, stretched out full-length on his belly and grabbed her. He swung her up and onto solid ground at the same time as Barbara, her hands bleeding and swollen, hoisted herself over the cliff-face, took a few stumbling steps, and fell bonelessly into a faint.

"You did it, Babs. You *did* it—you *saved* her!"

Julia found herself laughing and sobbing in the same breath. She watched as one of the mothers cradled a now-conscious and wide-eyed Willa against her shoulder, watched as Barbara was gently picked up in a fireman's lift by the unknown man, watched as the whole group, adults and children and puppy alike, left the clearing and headed back the way they'd come only half an hour before. She took the binoculars away from her eyes, slipped the strap over her head and placed them carefully on the ground.

Then she whirled swiftly away, bent over abruptly, and threw up behind the nearest tree.

The funny thing was, she *did* know semaphore, she thought shakily a few minutes later. She'd actually belonged to the Girl Scouts once, when Sylvia had been seeing a Minneapolis businessman and had attempted to play the part of an all-American mom to impress him. Julia saw Max come out of the woods far below, saw him drag his forearm across his brow as he paused, saw him look up to where she stood.

She swung her right arm down and a little in front of her body, at the same time extending her left arm up at a forty-five-degree angle. She held the position for a heartbeat, and then swung her right arm straight across her breasts until it too was on her left side. Again she paused before going on.

He *had* to have been a Boy Scout, she thought. Even if he'd never been a straight arrow, he would have always done what he had to do to give that impression. She kept moving her arms stiffly, spelling out her message.

Even without the binoculars, she thought she could see the slow grin that spread across his features before she was finished. She continued anyway, signalling her joy and relief across the distance that separated them, her face wet with tears.

C-O-M-E B-A-C-K M-A-X S-H-E I-S S-A-F-E W-I-L-L-A I-S S-A-F-E M-Y B-A-B-Y I-S S-A-F-E.

"...WHICH WAS WHY the chemicals found there and all the evidence stemming from them were inadmissible— because the authorities assumed the Cape Ann house was

Kenneth's too, and never bothered to get a search warrant for it.'' Julia finished the last of her apple crumble. ''How many of these He-Man dinners do you have in your freezer, anyway?''

''A month's supply at a time.'' Max removed the aluminum tray from in front of her. ''No dishes, and I don't have to think about what groceries to buy. Yeah, the cops got sloppy there, all right. And without that evidence, the case against you was almost pure circumstance, except for Barbara's testimony.''

Julia had been petting Boomer. She looked up sharply. ''If the cops hadn't gotten *sloppy,* as you put it, I wouldn't be sitting here right now, Max. You might remember that when you get all misty-eyed over how the case you built against me was botched.''

His expression lightened momentarily. ''Sorry. But my point stands—it wasn't simple bad luck that you took the fall for the bombing, you were deliberately framed. That evidence was planted in the one location that wasn't part of the Tennant holdings, to ensure that no one else in the family fell under suspicion.''

''The other members of the Tennant family being Olivia and Noel,'' she said flatly. ''My mother-in-law or my brother-in-law. You're right—I didn't marry into the Waltons, I married into the Borgias.''

''Olivia, Noel and Barbara,'' Max corrected her. ''And Barbara was the one who testified about seeing you hand the package with the bomb in it to Kenneth just before takeoff.''

''She testified to that because it was true,'' Julia retorted. ''But as I said at my trial, I didn't know there was a bomb in it, I thought I was handing him Willa's birthday present. Even the wrapping paper and the ribbon were identical to the package I'd had sitting in my closet for the past month.''

Her expression softened. ''Besides, after today even you can't suspect Babs of having been part of a scheme that involved Willa. You should have seen her, Max.'' She bit her lip and looked down at Boomer beside her. ''She—she saved my daughter's life. She could have been killed herself.''

''But you were the one who sensed Willa was in danger even before the accident happened. I still don't know how you could have known,'' he said quietly.

She looked up at him. ''I'm her mother. Going to prison didn't change that. Babs getting custody of her didn't change that. Willa's part of me, and, for better or worse, I'm part of her too. I realized that today.''

She let her hand drop once more to the dog's satiny ears, averting her eyes from the man standing in front of her. ''Sylvia wasn't big on church-going, unless it was Christmas or Easter or one of her weddings.'' She shrugged, still looking down. ''So that wasn't something I was brought up on. But I believe there's a God, and I have to believe He knows what He's doing. I didn't expect her and I didn't deserve her...but He gave her to me. *Me,* Max. There's got to be a reason for that, don't you think?''

''Yeah, Jules.'' There was a slight huskiness in his voice and she glanced up at him, her eyes suspiciously bright. ''I think there must have been a reason she got you as a mom.''

She kept her gaze on him, sensing that for once the barriers between them seemed to have dropped. ''Do you believe in God, Max?'' she asked tentatively.

His eyes met hers. Then he turned away to the sink, bracing his hands against the steel rim and staring out of the window into the night through the ruffled curtains. "I believe in God," he said after a moment. "I'm just not so sure He believes in Max Ross. Hell, sometimes I don't know if I believe in me."

This conversation had strayed far from its original course, she told herself, suddenly uneasy. She had the feeling that any further probing from her would take them both into uncharted waters, with all the danger that could entail. But some part of her was unwilling to scurry back to safety yet.

"How—how did you lose them, Max?" she said softly. "How did it happen? You know almost everything there is to know about me, but all I know about you is that years ago you had a wife and a child, and they died tragically. What happened?"

"You got your information wrong." His back was still to her, but under his T-shirt she could see his shoulders tense. "My wife died in a car accident ten years ago. I never had a child."

She frowned. "But I heard—"

He turned from the window, his movements brisk. "Like I said, you heard wrong. Anne was killed before we'd even been married a year." He snapped his fingers, and the black Labrador beside her obligingly got to his feet. "Time to give you your meds, buddy," he said, his attention focused on the dog.

Terra incognita indeed, Julia thought, nonplussed. And from his attitude, she'd just been firmly barred from exploring any further. She remained silent while Boomer got his nightly tablet and his treat, her mind working.

She hadn't got her information wrong. At the time he'd been assigned to investigate her case, Max had been working with another agent, an older man who was only a year or two from retirement. Max had been partnered with Carl Stein since he'd joined the Agency, and even to an outsider it was obvious that the two men complemented each other's styles—Max's unemotional and precise questioning counterpointed by his less-formal partner's deceptively avuncular personality. Before she'd become a prime suspect, Stein had reassuringly informed Julia that Max wouldn't rest until he'd caught the killer who'd planted the bomb on her husband's plane—the bomb that had come so frighteningly close to claiming the life of her little girl.

"Anytime there's a child involved, it's not just a job to him, Mrs. Tennant," the older man had said firmly. "Maybe I'm telling tales out of school, but I want you to know that Agent Ross takes this case very personally. He lost his own wife and son, and your case really hits home with him. He'll find the killer, don't worry."

Shortly after that conversation she'd been arrested and charged, and from then onward Stein had treated her with the same chilly courtesy that Max had always shown. But even if he'd eventually regretted his impulsive confidence, the fact remained that, as Max's partner, he would have known the man he worked with better than anyone else. He certainly wouldn't have made a mistake about something as important as whether the man had ever been a father or not.

Which meant that Max had lied to her just now, Julia thought, confused.

"Why the hell did Kenneth have Willa with him that day in the first place?" Pulling out a chair and sitting down at the table across from her, he picked up the thread of their earlier topic as smoothly as if they'd never strayed from it. "Your late husband wasn't the kind of doting father who usually took his daughter on business trips with him, was he?"

She was beginning to understand the ground rules, Julia told herself with a spark of anger. Whatever he'd said to her earlier today, in every way that mattered Agent Ross had no intention of opening himself up to her. He might want her physically, and occasionally he might even forget himself so far as to share a moment or two of closeness with her, but that was as far as it went.

Which suited her just fine, she thought, meeting his eyes unwaveringly. Willa's safety was her first and only concern.

"Taking her with him was his way of reminding me that he held the reins in our relationship, even where my daughter was concerned." Even after all this time the memories were painful, Julia thought. She forced herself to continue. "He knew how much it would hurt me to be away from her on her birthday."

"It probably wasn't what she wanted either," Max commented. "That could be why she was ill—ill enough to be taken off the plane before it started down the runway."

"Maybe, but Babs said she'd had an upset stomach all day. We'd been at some political dinner dance the evening before, and she'd kept her overnight." She shook her head. "Babs was just as upset as I was that Kenneth was taking her. We'd planned to give Willa her first real birthday party, with a clown and a pony and everything, and Barbara had bought her the most gorgeous doll. That must have been on the plane when it exploded too," she added.

Max's gaze sharpened. "What about your present?" he asked slowly. "Did you ever find it and give it to Willa?"

"I'd found a woman who made old-fashioned teddy

bears." She smiled faintly. "The one I got for Willa was wearing a little coat."

"But did she ever get it?" He leaned forward across the table. "You thought the bear was in the package you handed Kenneth, but it wasn't. You didn't know it, but you were giving him a gift-wrapped explosive device, so identical to the present you'd wrapped that even you couldn't tell the difference. That means that the killer either switched packages completely or made up a duplicate one, but either way, he or she had to have gotten rid of Willa's present somehow."

"I never thought of that." She drew her brows together. "I didn't come across the thing afterwards. Is it important?"

"Probably not." He sat back. "But what is important is who saw that present after you'd wrapped it. You said you'd hidden it from Willa on the top shelf of your clothes closet, so if we—" He stopped as she shook her head.

"We're not going to eliminate any suspects that way, Max." Her shoulders slumped despondently. "The whole Tennant clan saw me wrapping it a few weeks before. Barbara and Robert had just returned from their honeymoon in Bermuda, and we had a family dinner at our place to welcome them home. Olivia was there, naturally, and even Noel made a rare appearance—more for Barbara's sake than because he enjoyed being in the same room as Kenneth, I'm sure. After dinner I showed Babs what I'd gotten Willa, and while Kenneth and Robert and Olivia talked Tenn-Chem business I pulled out some paper and ribbon and wrapped the present in the living room. I even remember Noel putting his finger on the bow while I tied it."

"Until Willa reaches her majority, control of Tenn-

Chem's holdings is in Barbara's hands." As if he was suddenly too restless to sit, Max stood, and began pacing the floor. "But Barbara wants nothing to do with the business, so she's given Olivia *carte blanche* to run the company as she sees fit."

Julia nodded. "Don't forget, Olivia was Tenn-Chem's CEO for almost twenty years before her own son forced her into retirement. From what I've heard, when her husband died the company was in danger of being swallowed up by the big conglomerates. Over the next couple of years Olivia made it her business to learn everything she could about the chemical industry, from what a bunsen burner was to how to lobby Washington for tax breaks, and eventually Tenn-Chem went from a minnow to a shark and did some swallowing of its own. Unfortunately for her, she brought her eldest son up to be even more ruthless than she was."

"I've met the lady," Max said briefly. "You're right, she's one tough cookie. But she must be pushing sixty-five or so, and she's already had her first bypass operation. If anything happened to her, wouldn't Barbara be forced into a more active role, whether she wanted it or not?"

"If anything happened to Olivia, Barbara would hand Tenn-Chem over to the person she always felt should have been running it," Julia said dismissively. "Noel was the brother she cared for. She never agreed with his ousting from the company, but she was too intimidated by Kenneth to take a stand at the time."

"So when Olivia's out of the picture, which given her age and her health isn't too far into the future, all that'll be left between your brother-in-law and permanent control of Tenn-Chem will be Willa." Max stopped pacing and looked at her. "I can't recall offhand, but maybe you do, Jules. Where exactly was Noel Tennant on the night in question?"

Chapter Eight

"This can't be where he's living now." Julia flicked a disbelieving glance at the neighborhood they were driving through, an eclectic jumble of tiny stores and hole-in-the-wall eateries, before turning back to Max. "Noel might go slumming in a funky area like this once in a while, but he'd never make it permanent. Even if he's distanced himself from the family as I told you last night, he *is* a Tennant, after all."

"So were you once upon a time," Max said dryly. Julia closed her eyes as he shoehorned the sedan into a parking space more suited to a motorcycle. "So obviously the condition's curable," he added.

"For me, maybe. But he was born into that lifestyle." Following his lead and getting out of the car, her attention was caught by a figure sitting on a wooden crate on the sidewalk. Two figures, she corrected herself with a smile. Amid the stalls of fresh fruit and unfamiliar vegetables that seemed to be the open-air extension of an Asian grocery store sat a young woman, a lazily alert German shepherd lounging at her feet. Like her dog, the woman on the crate seemed to be both aware of the flow of humanity streaming past her on the sidewalk, and uncaring of it. As she pulled something from the back pocket of her jeans it was possible to see that her wrists and forearms were delicately tattooed with what looked to be Oriental calligraphy. She tapped the harmonica she'd retrieved on a denim-clad thigh, leaned forward to brace her elbows on her knees, and the next moment the notes of an old Robert Johnson blues tune cut through the hubbub around her with a raspy growl.

"She's good," Max murmured, joining Julia on the sidewalk in front of the pair as the raw chords of "Crossroads Blues" began to draw the attention of the crowd. Oblivious to her growing audience, the young woman executed a series of melancholy riffs, her none-too-clean hands cupped protectively around the harmonica at her mouth, her eyes closed.

"She's been there," Julia said softly. "No one plays the blues like that unless it comes from the gut. I wonder what she was in for?"

Closing her own eyes, she didn't notice the sharp glance he threw her way. Instead, she let the music flow over her, giving herself up to it and for the first time since her release allowing herself to relive the pain and despair she'd felt when she'd been locked behind bars. She'd come out toughened, she thought. But what part of her had been lost forever during that tempering process? How much of her humanity had been quenched in order to survive, and would Willa sense a difference in her when they were reunited again?

The last few notes sobbed away into silence, but it wasn't until the spatter of light applause and the silvery chink of falling coins broke the hush that she opened her eyes to see Max looking at her.

"One day it'll start to fade, Jules," he said quietly. "One day you won't think of it all the time."

"Maybe." She fumbled in the pocket of her windbreaker, her face averted from his. "But whether I think about it or not, it changed me, Max. Sometimes I wonder who I've become. Sometimes I wonder if I like the woman I see staring back at me from a mirror." Not seeing the flash of pain that crossed his features, she peeled a bill from the meager roll in her hand.

"Don't worry about it. I dropped a twenty on her plate from both of us." As he started to move away she shook her head.

"I want to give her something myself."

Five bucks wasn't much, Julia thought, bending down to place the money on the battered metal plate beside the blues-player's canine companion. There'd been a time when fifty dollars wouldn't have covered her lunch tab when she'd taken a break from a shopping spree and met a few acquaintances midday to compare purchases. But none of the women she'd socialized with during her marriage had ever contacted her after her arrest. Not even the two or three she'd considered friends had come to see her after she'd been sentenced. Brief as it had been, the momentary bond forged by this street musician had been more real than any connection she'd had in her former life.

Maybe some of the things she'd lost over the past two years hadn't been worth keeping, she thought slowly.

"Keep your money, sister. That one was for you anyway."

Before her fingers could release the bill onto the metal plate, Julia found her wrist being gently grasped. Glancing up quickly, she met the gaze of the young woman who'd just been playing the harmonica. Hazel eyes stared steadily back at her.

"This won't ever heal completely. Be glad it won't."

The strong fingers holding her slid almost tenderly

from her wrist to the back of her hand, carefully turning it over. The thumb lightly traced the scar there.

"When you look at it remember you were stronger than you thought you could be, sister." The low voice was husky with pain. "That lesson never comes freely, but nothing valuable ever does. So hang onto it. You earned it." She let go of Julia's hand, her own dropping down to the ruff of the shepherd.

"You said you played that for me. How did you know I'd—" Julia faltered, unable to complete the rest of her question.

"Been in the joint?" Her unlikely companion gave her a small smile. "You knew I had, didn't you? Survivors recognize each other. Tell your man thanks for the donation. I'll treat Warden and me to a steak tonight, on him."

"Throw in a couple of pieces of pie for dessert." Julia dropped the crumpled bill in her hand onto the plate and straightened up. She looked down at the woman. "I know the song was free," she said softly. "But survivors have to stick together, sister."

"When she grabbed your hand I was holding my breath," Max muttered as they fell into step together and walked away. "I was remembering Cherie."

"Who?" She frowned, and then gave a short laugh. "Oh, the waitress at the coffee shop. She was trying to use me to scam you, Max. I was just protecting your interests."

"I'd like to believe that." His tone was dry. "But the nick on my jaw I had to shave around this morning makes me wonder."

She gave him a direct look. "You pushed me. I reacted wrongly. It won't happen again."

"Which part are you talking about, Jules?" He met

her glance with an expressionless one of his own. She didn't answer, and after a moment he looked away. "I did push you. That won't happen again either."

He stepped away from her as an old lady trundling a bundle-buggy stuffed with sacks of groceries bore down upon them, and when he was once again at her side it was obvious he'd decided to change the subject. His frown was touched with curiosity.

"So why didn't you pull away from her back there?"

Still preoccupied with his last cryptic statement, Julia blinked. "Because she knew what I'd gone through," she said quietly. "She'd been there too." She managed a smile. "Her dog's name is Warden, and apparently you helped buy them a steak dinner with your donation."

"She was looking at your scar." Disregarding her attempt to turn the conversation, he went on, his tone uncharacteristically tentative. "Did that bother you?"

"With anyone else it might have. But she seemed to see it as a symbol of courage," she answered slowly. She met his gaze. "Just as you did, the other night," she added.

"Just as anyone would who cared enough to really look." He shrugged. "Everyone's got scars, Julia, whether they show or not. Some people are tough enough to survive their scars and even take strength from them, like you. Some people never had what it takes in the first place."

"And what happens to them?" He wasn't talking about prison anymore, she thought with sudden conviction. Or at least not a physical set of bars.

"Nothing." His tone was flat. "They just go on existing. This must be it."

He stopped suddenly enough that she took a step past him before halting herself. He nodded at a peeling door set into the recessed wall joining a used-clothing store to the small West Indian groceteria beside it. Someone in the past had used thick black paint to mark the numbers of the address directly on the door itself.

"22B. There must be an apartment on the second floor." Max raised an eyebrow. "You're right. It's a long way from Beacon Hill, but this was what came up when I ran his name through the computer at the Agency."

Without further discussion he gave the tarnished door-knob an exploratory twist. It turned, and he pulled it open.

He'd been talking about himself, Julia thought as she followed him up the steep flight of stairs that led immediately up from the street-level entrance, and when he'd realized what he was doing he'd disengaged. And she'd let him. She felt a brief flash of irritation at herself for not probing further, but then her anger faded.

It was an unwritten rule in prison not to ask questions if the answers weren't volunteered. That was a lesson even the newest of inmates learned quickly, and once learned, it was never forgotten. Questions were dangerous. Questions could wound. Questions, and the answers to them, could destroy a prisoner's fragile hold on survival.

And although she was the one who'd been assigned a number and a cell, Max was the real prisoner here, she thought slowly.

He just didn't know it.

"The rent on this place must be higher than it looks." They'd reached the small landing at the top of the stairs, and in front of her Max tapped a discreet brass nameplate beside another, more freshly painted, door. "He can't even afford to pay for it by himself."

"I told you, there's no way Noel lives here." Roused

from her thoughts, Julia shook her head firmly. "Even though it happened long before I married into the family, I know that Kenneth was forced to give him an extremely golden handshake when he ousted him from Tenn-Chem. He could buy and sell this whole block of buildings if he wanted to."

"Noel Tennant. Peter Symington." Max read the neatly printed square of card inserted into the nameplate out loud. "Maybe he's not interested in buying and selling blocks of buildings, or maybe he already tried that and lost his shirt in a bad investment. Whatever the reason, I'd say your ex-brother-in-law's circumstances have changed."

"It looks like you're right," she admitted with a frown. "From what I remember about Noel, that wouldn't sit too well with him. He liked getting the best table in a restaurant. He liked going over to Paris on a whim. And he was always buying expensive gifts for girls he hardly knew. I can't see him accepting this kind of lifestyle."

"Maybe he couldn't see living like this either. Maybe even two years ago he saw the way things were going for him, and decided to do something about it." Pressing the plastic buzzer under the nameplate, he shifted his stance slightly, and suddenly the shoulders under the grey suit jacket he was wearing seemed somehow bulkier and more formidable. "That's what we're here to find out, Jules."

"You're armed, aren't you?" It hadn't occurred to her before, but now she knew why he'd set out on this unofficial errand dressed, not in the sweatshirt and jeans he'd been wearing the day before, but in one of the suits she was more accustomed to seeing him in. A jacket would conceal a shoulder-holster, she realized belatedly.

"It's a precaution, nothing more." From the other side of the door came approaching footsteps, and he kept his voice low. "I'm not really expecting anything to—"

"You forgot your keys again, didn't you?"

At the sound of Noel's words, even spoken as they were through the door while he was unlocking it from his side, a wave of unhappy memories washed over Julia. She'd forgotten how similar the voices of the two Tennant brothers had always been, she thought. And the similarities, although less striking, weren't confined to the way Kenneth and Noel had sounded. As the apartment door opened, she steeled herself to catch glimpses of her late husband in Noel's assessing stare, his habitual air of almost disdainful reserve. She cleared her throat nervously, and beside her she heard Max draw a breath.

"Oh." It was recognizably Noel, she thought, wondering why she'd been so foolishly apprehensive as her eyes met the pair of gray ones staring blankly at her. "I'm sorry, I thought it was my roommate arriving home," he went on, a slight question in his voice. "Can I help you?"

It was recognizably Noel, but it seemed that since she'd last seen him he'd finally grown out of the resemblance to his older brother that had dogged him all his life. Or maybe it was just that, out of the overwhelming shadow of Kenneth at long last, Noel finally felt free to be himself. Gone was the languid mockery in the small smile he gave her and Max. Gone too was the edginess that he'd never seemed able to completely conceal. She liked him better this way, she thought slowly.

Except that the pleasant man standing in front of her could well be a murderer.

She'd changed too, apparently—at least enough so that Noel obviously didn't recognize her. She couldn't blame him for that, she thought, suddenly conscious of her clothing and her pulled-back hair. She mustered an answering smile, wondering how he would react when he realized it was the woman accused and convicted of killing his brother who was standing on his doorstep.

"It's me, Noel—Julia. And this is Max Ross, the agent who investigated the bombing of Kenneth's plane. We wondered if you could spare a few minutes to—"

She didn't finish her sentence. In front of her, Noel's face had gone white, and his eyes, though still fixed on her, seemed to have lost focus. She was aware of Max beside her, his posture tense.

"I'm not here in any official capacity, Mr. Tennant," he said, his voice sounding harsh in the silence that had fallen. "You don't have to invite us in if you'd prefer not to."

"No. No, of course not." Noel's response was less than enthusiastic, but he stood back from the doorway and gestured them inside. "It's just a shock seeing you, Julia. I guess I'm farther out of the family loop than I realized. I thought you were in—" He caught himself, and she saw a faint flush stain the pallor of his face. "I take it your appearance here means your conviction was overturned?" he queried carefully.

"My conviction was overturned, yes. Most people seem to think justice was a little too blind in my case, though," she said evenly.

She'd touched a nerve, she saw. Noel averted his eyes from hers, his posture suddenly stiff as he perfunctorily waved her toward a nearby sofa. One way or another, this had to be a strain for him, Julia thought as she sat down. Either he thought there was a good possibility he was being forced to entertain a killer who'd manipulated the system, or he knew damn well she'd served two years for the crime he himself had committed. Whichever it was, his self-possession returned almost immediately. As Max settled himself in a massive Mission-style chair on the other side of the low oak coffee table, looking momentarily disconcerted as it creaked slightly under his weight, Noel smiled.

"Don't worry, it's sturdier than it looks, Agent Ross," he said dryly. He turned back to her. "Can I offer you some coffee? Tea?"

"Nothing, thanks, Mr. Tennant." Max leaned forward, resting his forearms on his knees as Noel glanced toward him inquiringly. "I may have misled you with what I said a moment ago. It's true I'm not here on behalf of the Agency, but this isn't exactly a social call. I'm one of the few who believe justice *was* done when your sister-in-law was set free. Among other things, that means I let the real killer slip through my fingers." He held Noel's gaze. "I don't intend to make that mistake again. Tell me, just what the hell is it you're trying to hide here?"

I want you to know that whatever I'm saying or doing at any given moment, underneath it all is the man you saw just now... He'd told her that only yesterday, but it couldn't have been true, Julia thought, taking in the hard line of his mouth and the implacable light in his eyes as he stared grimly at Noel. There was no part of that man in him right now. He wasn't even aware of her presence.

He glanced swiftly over at her, as if he knew what was going through her mind. Something flickered behind the green of his gaze, so quickly that she might have been able to tell herself she'd imagined it, if it hadn't been for the sudden heat that spread through her at his glance.

Across from them, Noel lowered himself into a chair. "I'm not hiding anything, Ross." There was an edge of anger in his voice, but his features remained impassive. "Why would you think I was?"

"This place, for starters." Max jerked his chin at the small living room and the minuscule kitchenette just visible around the corner. "You used to be a high roller, by all accounts, but now you're living in a walk-up barely large enough to swing a cat in. What happened?"

"Ask Julia." Noel's nod toward her was tight. "Maybe she was evicted from the Tennant money nest a little more forcefully than I was, but I'm willing to bet her reaction wasn't that much different from mine after she'd had time to think about it. How about it, Julia—do you miss the parties?" There was a challenge in his tone. "Do you miss your so-called friends? What about the family get-togethers, with my darling mother and my late, unlamented brother crossing swords over how to run Tenn-Chem, while Barbara sat silently throughout the whole meal, you drank glass after glass of wine, and I was pointedly ignored?"

He turned to Max. "Remember that old Bible story kids are taught in Sunday school, about Paul on the way to Damascus? Well, it was like that with me, Agent Ross—one day out of the blue, my eyes were opened. I looked around me and realized I didn't like the life I was leading, and I was coming damn close to disliking myself. So I decided to make as radical a change as I could, and since then I've never been happier."

He spread his hands. "This place represents freedom to me. There's no way Olivia will ever deign to visit me here, and that suits me just fine. Once in a while I meet Babs for lunch downtown, with the ground rules being we stay off the topic of that damned company that came so close to destroying both our lives." His flow of words faltered, and he took a steadying breath. "I know she got custody of Willa, Julia. She's taking good care of her."

"We're not here to discuss your sister," Max cut in before she had a chance to respond. "Like I said, I think Julia was framed for the bombing, and I'm looking into who else in the Tennant family stood to gain from Kenneth's death." He shrugged. "You've gone to some lengths to persuade me you don't care about Tenn-Chem and everything that comes with it, but I'd still like to know what your movements were on the night your brother's plane and everyone on it got blown to kingdom come.

"By the way," he added blandly, "I was brought up by my grandparents—strict, church-going Presbyterians, both of them, and they made damn sure I *did* go to Sunday school. Your St. Paul analogy was a little off."

"Maybe so." Noel shook his head. "But that still doesn't alter the fact that I've got no desire to go back to the life I used to live. Besides, from what little I read about it in the papers at the time, that gift-wrapped bomb could have been substituted at any time for the present it was supposed to be. It might have been sitting in Julia's closet for weeks."

"It was." Max nodded agreeably. "But the timer was set sometime in the two hours before it exploded. The press never got hold of that fact, and it didn't even come out at the trial, since all the rest of the evidence against your sister-in-law seemed so airtight. So you can see why I might be interested in knowing where you were in that two-hour window."

Julia had been watching Noel, but now she turned to Max. "You're right—that *didn't* come out at my trial. This is the first I've heard about a two-hour window," she said tightly. "This changes everything, Max. I had that package with me the whole time that evening—and though I couldn't tell you how long it was exactly, I remember it was well over two hours. I was running some errands, and then I had to pick up Willa. It would have been *impossible* for anyone to tamper with it during that time.''

"They didn't have to tamper with it, Jules." Despite her agitation, out of the corner of her eye she saw Noel's head jerk up in interest at the nickname. Max went on quickly, as if to reassure her without delay. "The timer was activated by a remote control, the experts told me. Apparently it worked along the same lines as a television remote—the box didn't have to be opened, and it was operational up to about twenty feet."

"Then I'm your man, Agent." Noel stood up abruptly, his tone holding some of the mockery Julia remembered from the past. He held out his wrists. "Cuff me and take me away. I might as well come clean—I dropped by to see Babs just as Julia was leaving, so I was probably within the magic twenty feet during that crucial two-hour period that night. I zapped the box with my special decoder ring, and a little while later my big brother and his toadying new brother-in-law went boom."

Julia stared at him, aghast. "What's the matter with you? There's nothing funny about this at all, Noel—*nothing!*" Her voice shook. "Kenneth wasn't a good husband or brother, granted, and I never really warmed up to Robert either but they didn't deserve to be *killed*. And in case you've forgotten, there were two other men on that plane—decent men with families still mourning them!"

Sometime during her outburst she'd gotten to her feet, she realized. Her hands clenched at her sides, she confronted her brother-in-law, but for a moment he didn't meet her eyes.

She let out a sharp breath, and he turned to her, his shoulders slumping. "You're right, of course," he said in a low tone. "This isn't a joking matter."

"But you weren't joking." Max was beside her, and a quick glance at his tense stance and grim expression told Julia he was just barely holding back his own anger. "You were trying to divert us, Tennant—divert us from stumbling onto the one thing you're trying to keep hidden, and it's not the fact that you had an opportunity that night to set off the bomb. You're willing to throw that my way, as damning as it is, just to keep me from your real secret. I'm only going to ask you one more time— what is it you're trying to—"

"You left the door unlocked, lover. Feel like Thai for dinner tonight?"

The man standing in the doorway looked to be a few years younger than Noel, and he was good-looking in a pleasant, unspectacular kind of way. The only reason a stranger would give him a second glance, Julia thought, was the white cane in his hand and the dark glasses that obscured his eyes. He was obviously blind.

It didn't seem to be an overwhelming handicap, she realized a moment later.

"Oops, I didn't realize we had guests." His smile, directed in their general direction, was disarmingly friendly. He approached them without hesitation, stopping a couple of feet away and holding out his hand. "I'm Peter, Noel's main squeeze."

Noel looked over at Max, his own expression drawn. "I guess you stumbled on my secret after all, Agent Ross."

Chapter Nine

Peter's smile faltered. Letting his hand drop to his side again, he turned to his partner. "I thought we'd put this kind of thing behind us, Noel," he said quietly. His movements suddenly awkward, he started to make his way back to the open door, brushing against a side table as he did so. Julia caught the bleakness that swept across his features as he unsteadily swung his cane ahead of him.

"*No.*" Noel hurried after his friend, his expression stricken. He put his hand on the other man's arm. "No, you're right, Peter. This kind of thing *is* behind us. Please stay." His voice was gentler than Julia had ever heard it before. "I'd—I'd like to introduce you to my sister-in-law, Julia Tennant, and Max Ross, the agent assigned to investigate my brother's murder."

So this was the reason Noel had cut himself off from his former life, Julia thought in amazement, extending her hand to Symington as the blind man turned back to her and Max. His clasp was firmly friendly, but as he shook Max's hand his mouth tightened.

"Should Noel be calling his lawyer, Mr. Ross?" he asked bluntly.

"Maybe ten minutes ago." Max shook his head. "But

I don't think that's going to be necessary now.'' He turned to Noel almost impatiently. ''For God's sake, man, was this what all the fancy footwork was about? I'm not here to judge anyone's lifestyle, and if I was you'd be justified in telling me to get the hell out of your home.''

''All those years you were living a lie, trying to conform to what your brother and your mother thought was acceptable,'' Julia said impulsively. ''Oh, Noel—how desperately *unhappy* you must have been!''

He turned a startled glance on her, and then he smiled, a little sadly. ''So were you, weren't you, Julia? So was Babs. We were a pretty dysfunctional family all round. I used to think Kenneth was responsible for that, but he couldn't help what he became. Olivia tried to ram each one of us into the Tennant mold as soon as we were old enough to go to boarding school.'' He lifted his shoulders wearily. ''Be glad Willa escaped that. I know my mother intended her to be packed off to the Tennant alma mater when she turns six.''

''She what?'' Julia's eyes widened in outrage. ''Olivia might have intended that, but I never would have gone along with it. I always thought it was barbaric, the way she raised the three of you.''

''Kenneth didn't. Didn't you know he'd put Willa's name down for Hartley House before she was born?'' Noel looked slightly uncomfortable. ''To tell you the truth, Julia, when you were charged with his murder I privately suspected that had been your motive for killing him—to ensure that she didn't have the same unloving childhood the rest of us had gone through. But I realized that didn't really hold water. Olivia would still have insisted on bringing Willa up to be a Tennant. You wouldn't have been a match for her.''

"That's debatable," Max said shortly. "But what's not is that Barbara couldn't take on her mother and win. Is Willa's name still down for boarding school?"

"I presume so. After all, she'll be taking over Tenn-Chem when she grows up, and Olivia would want to make sure her beloved company is run by someone as tough and ruthless as herself when the time comes." Noel's smile was bitter. "My mother abhors weakness in any form."

"Willa's birthday is in two days," Julia said tightly. "Are you trying to tell me that Babs is going to knuckle under to Olivia and send her off to that—that *prison* as soon as she blows out the candles on her cake, dammit?"

"That's how it was for us. Since my birthday's in July, Olivia enrolled me in an accelerated summer course so I'd have an edge over everyone else when regular classes resumed in September." Peter moved closer and put his hand lightly on his friend's shoulder. Noel shot him a grateful smile before continuing. "But even though I don't see Babs that often, I've noticed a change in her since Willa came to live with her. I'm not so sure she does intend to knuckle under to Olivia on this."

Not sure wasn't good enough, Julia thought, feeling sick. Not sure meant there was a possibility that in two days Willa's world would be torn apart for the second time in her short life, and even if she eventually won back custody of her daughter and took Willa out of Hartley House, by then the damage might be irreparable.

A faint echo of the same dread she'd felt just before Willa had plunged over the cliff stirred in her. Her daughter was in danger, she thought. But this time she knew what the danger was.

They were wasting time here—time that she'd just

learned they didn't have. As if he sensed her sudden restlessness, Max nodded brusquely at Noel.

"I appreciate the information you've given us, Tennant." He started to take a step toward the door, but then checked himself. "There is one last question you can answer for me," he said slowly. "How did your father die?"

A corner of Noel's mouth lifted briefly. "I was wondering when you'd get around to that. He was working late in the lab one night, experimenting with some pretty unstable compounds, and, like my brother twenty years later, he went boom." His voice hardened. "He was never a businessman. He was just a damn good chemist, and he'd come up with a soluble base for a certain kind of medication that could have cut the price of it in half. He wanted to publish the formula in the scientific journals, just to make sure that the patent wouldn't be bought up and suppressed by one of the big drug companies with a vested interest in keeping the price high. I wasn't much older than four or five at the time but I still remember the argument he and my mother had over that—probably because it was the only time I ever saw him stand up to her."

"What happened to the formula after his death?" Max's eyes narrowed.

Noel grinned tightly. "Good question. It never made it onto the market, but curiously enough, just a few months later Tenn-Chem went from being a struggling little company barely managing to stay afloat, to having enough cash to finance its first major takeover. Unlike her late husband, my mother proved to have an excellent head for business, Agent Ross."

"You realize what you're telling me." Max wasn't asking a question, but Noel nodded anyway.

"Yes, I realize what I'm telling you. I'm also well aware that we're not just talking about my father's death, and I still stand by what I say. Any one of us Tennants have enough technical knowledge to build a bomb, but only Olivia has the ruthlessness to carry through on a scheme like that."

"It's something to look into, I agree," Max said slowly. For a moment he seemed sunk in thought, but then he roused himself. "Again, thanks for the help. Mr. Symington—good meeting you."

"If you're talking with Noel's family, I'd appreciate it if you didn't mention our relationship." The blind man sighed lightly. "I realize that sounds odd coming from me, but from what Noel's told me about his mother I think a don't-ask, don't-tell policy is wiser with her. Even though they seldom see each other anymore, she would still regard his sexual preference as a slur against the family name—and she wields enough power to make his life a living hell."

"Been there, done that," Noel commented ruefully. "I hope I've given you something to think about, Ross."

It was a dismissal, albeit a courteous one, and moments later Julia and Max were out on the sidewalk again. She glanced over at him as they began heading for the car.

"Do you buy his story about Olivia?"

"I don't know." He frowned thoughtfully. "I can't shake the feeling that I was being manipulated throughout that whole conversation, and even when I realized he'd been trying to conceal the fact he was gay I still felt he was keeping something back."

"So did I." She raked her hair from her forehead in a quickly nervous gesture. "But I believed what he said about Willa being signed up for boarding school, Max, and that's got me terrified. I've heard Babs talk about

Hartley House. It's run along incredibly strict lines, and the children there seem to be punished for the slightest infraction. If Willa thinks I left her because I didn't love her anymore, how will she cope with being taken away from Barbara and put into an environment like Hartley? Max—whatever it takes, I just can't *allow* it.''

Her last few words came out with edgy intensity as they reached the car. Turning to her, he took her by the shoulders.

"Falling apart now isn't going to help her, Jules, and you know it," he said sharply. "And if you mean what I think you mean, forget it. I couldn't let you snatch Willa away a few days ago, and whatever else has changed, that hasn't. It's called kidnapping."

"How can it be kidnapping when I'm her *mother,* dammit?" she retorted furiously.

"Because Barbara has legal custody of her, for crying out loud!" His voice had risen too, and as two or three curious passers-by glanced at them, he bit back an oath and released her. "Let's keep this private, Jules," he said in a lower tone. "We can continue this discussion in the car."

"There's nothing more to discuss." Folding her arms across her chest to disguise the fact that she was trembling, Julia studied him through suddenly sheened eyes. "You know, I was so sure you weren't telling me the truth last night when you said you'd never had a child, Max. I'd heard differently. But now I know my information had to have been wrong, because there's no way you ever had a son or daughter of your own. There's no way you ever felt as if your heart was about to crack in two because you loved them so much, and you were so afraid you wouldn't be able to keep them safe. If what I'd heard was true and you'd lost a child of your own, you'd understand what I'm going through. But you don't. You *can't*.''

"Maybe I understand more than you think I do." His words were toneless, but there was a flicker of compassion in the green eyes meeting hers. "Not out of any personal experience, but because I care what happens to you, Jules—to you and Willa. And that's why I say I couldn't condone taking her from Barbara before we clear your name completely by finding out who really planted that bomb. You agreed with me a couple of days ago that you couldn't put her through a life on the run. What's changed?"

"I'm not sure."

Her fury draining away, she passed a shaky hand across her eyes, already regretting the way she'd lashed out at him. He was right. As unhappy as Willa might be at a school like Hartley House, being stolen from a playground by a woman she only dimly remembered as her mother and forced to live a fugitive existence, never staying in the same place for more than a few nights at a time, would be even more traumatic for her. She knew that. She'd known that two days ago. What *had* changed?

Again the unreasoning fear rose up inside her, settling in the pit of her stomach like some noxious fog.

"I just have this *feeling*," she said inadequately. "I'm afraid something terrible is going to happen to her, Max. I know it sounds crazy, but—"

"You don't sound crazy. You sound like a mother." He rubbed his jaw worriedly. "This feeling you have— do you think she's in immediate danger?"

"No," she admitted slowly. "It's not like yesterday. I'm not worried that she's going to be in a car accident or something like that this very afternoon, I just feel as if something's threatening her—something that's getting closer all the time. Is there any way you can find out if her name's still down for Hartley?''

''Yeah, I can do that. And tomorrow I'll start checking into Olivia's story of what she was doing the night of the bombing.'' As if he had come to some final decision, he took a deep breath and leveled a somber gaze at her. ''But from now on you're out of this, Jules. I never should have brought you into this in the first place, especially knowing what you've been through these last two years. This is tearing you apart—and your involvement in it stops here.''

IT WAS THE FIRST TIME she'd been alone in his house, but she didn't feel as if she was intruding on his private space. Julia opened the refrigerator door and glanced inside. A few feet away from her, on the oval braided rug that seemed to be his favorite resting place, Boomer sighed gustily, as if he knew as well as she did how unlikely it was that the appliance held anything interesting.

She didn't feel as if she was intruding because there was nothing personal to intrude upon, she thought, letting the door swing shut. The contents, or lack of them, of Max's refrigerator were a perfect example—some eggs, lined up as they should be in the built-in egg compartment, a quart of milk and a pristine jar of mustard that looked as if it hadn't been opened.

She'd already checked out the freezer compartment. It was crammed full of He-Man dinners—chicken, beef or Salisbury steak. She had a three-in-one chance of guessing what Max Ross was going to be having for supper eight Wednesdays from now and getting it right, Julia thought, frowning.

The man was an enigma.

But his personality quirks weren't her problem, unless and until they got in the way of her own agenda, she told herself firmly, walking over to the kitchen window and propping her elbows on the sink. This afternoon they had, and it had taken all of her persuasive powers to convince him not to cut her out of the loop where the investigation was concerned. Actually, persuasion had failed, she admitted with reluctant honesty. The argument had continued on the drive home, and it had taken blackmail to finally change his mind.

"Fine," she'd snapped as they'd pulled up in front of the house. "I'll just call on Olivia myself tomorrow and demand some answers from her. If that doesn't work I'll track down Babs and insist on talking with her. If that doesn't work I'll—"

"I can fill in the blanks, Julia." His tone had been as clipped as hers. "You'll just keep muddying the waters until it's impossible to see anything. Don't you get it—I'm trying to keep you out of this for your own *good*, dammit."

His choice of phrase had touched a fuse. "My own good? My own *good*?"

About to get out of the car, she'd turned back to him, her temper boiling over. "I've had two freakin' *years* of other people making decisions for my own good, Max, and I'm not about to let anyone do that again! Two years of lights out at eight sharp for our own *good*, two years of wearing scuffs instead of shoes with laces for our own *good*, two years of being told what to do every minute of every hour until one day you're standing in line in the cafeteria at dinnertime and you start to shake because you know you're going to have to decide whether you want peas or beans with the damned meat loaf, and you realize you're no longer capable of making a choice for yourself anymore!''

By then she'd been only inches away from him, and her voice had risen to a shout. ''She's my *daughter!* This is something *no* one decides for me—not even you!''

She seemed to have lost the knack of discussing things logically with another person, Julia thought wearily, her hand moving to the cold-water tap to tighten it. Or maybe it was just this particular man who managed to derail her, seemingly with no effort on his part at all.

But at least he'd dropped the idea of her sitting on the sidelines while he continued with the investigation. He hadn't been happy about it—the tense set of his mouth as he'd grudgingly given in had been proof of how he really felt—but he'd agreed to take her with him when he interviewed Olivia the next day.

''I'm going to the office to pull her original statement.'' As Julia had gotten out of the car, almost faint with relief and more than a little astonished that she'd gone up against him and won, he'd taken his keys out of the ignition and snapped one off the ring, handing it to her. ''And believe me, Jules, you won't be allowed to accompany me there. Even if you were, if anyone recognized you with me I'd be pulled up on the carpet and asked to explain myself tomorrow morning.'' He'd paused, and the grimness of his expression had eased slightly. ''Can you feed Boomer for me and let him out in the backyard for a while? I'll probably be most of the evening at this, and I don't want to make the old boy wait for his meal until I come home.''

She'd agreed to feed his dog. Heck, Julia thought, straightening up from the sink and rolling her shoulders tiredly, at that point she probably would have agreed to prepare a four-course gourmet dinner with candles and soft music for Boomer if she'd been asked.

She knew he was putting his career on the line for her. What she didn't know was why.

"It's not like I sweet-talked him into it, is it, boy?" she asked Boomer. He thumped his tail heavily on the floor in reply. "And the days of me getting a male to do what I want simply by batting my eyelashes at him are behind me, I'm afraid. So what makes him tick?"

Panting a little, the old dog tried to get to his feet, but after a moment he gave up, wagging his tail at her as if in apology. Boomer himself was a clue, Julia thought, bending to give the soft ears a rub. She looked around the kitchen curiously. This room was a clue, from the frozen dinners in the freezer to the dripping faucet to the frilly curtains at the window.

She walked into the living room, frowning. A woman had lived here once—Max's wife, who'd been killed over a decade ago in a car accident. And nothing in this house had been changed since the last time that woman had walked out the door, never to return. That explained the Priscillas at the kitchen window. That was why the guest-room bed was outfitted with pastel-pink sheets, why the tissue box in the bathroom had a fussy knitted cosy covering it, why the glimpse she'd caught of Max's own bedroom when she'd passed by his open door last night had revealed a beruffled coverlet and flowered wallpaper that she couldn't imagine him choosing himself.

She couldn't imagine choosing them either, she thought uncomfortably. It wasn't that anything was in poor taste, but taken all together the furnishings and decor seemed banal and lacking in individuality. It was as if the late Mrs. Ross, faced with the task of creating a home of her own and too young to be sure of herself, had panicked and ordered everything en masse from the pages of a catalog, right down to the pictures on the walls and the carpet underfoot.

Only Boomer didn't fit. Even as a puppy it must have been obvious he would be a sturdy dog, big enough to knock over a table lamp with that flag of a tail, rambunctious enough to track mud across the pale linoleum in the kitchen. Boomer didn't fit, so Boomer, out of everything in this house, had been Max's choice.

He'd told her that with him, what she saw wasn't necessarily who he was. He'd made the self-evaluation in an entirely different context, but that didn't matter. She tamped down the tiny flicker of heat that had immediately uncurled inside her at the memory of that context, and tried to fit the pieces together.

In this instance he was wrong. He had to be wrong. What she was seeing was his home, the place where he lived, alone with only an old dog for company. There was no reason for him to keep up any kind of facade here. This had to be who he was, if she could only understand what she was looking at.

It wasn't a shrine. There were no photographs of the woman he'd been married to scattered around, and although she was sure her guess had been correct and nothing of any importance had been changed since his wife's death, she didn't believe Max was preserving this house in order to keep his memory of her fresh. She doubted that he even saw these surroundings anymore.

Dead man walking. The impression she'd gotten two days ago came back to her with jarring force. A small chill ran down her spine as she looked around her and finally saw the pattern.

This wasn't a shrine, it was a tomb.

The sofa was behind her. Without looking, she sank down onto it, her knees suddenly weak.

Once there'd been a man named Max Ross. But ten years ago that man had stopped living, and now he just existed. *"Some people never had what it takes in the first place..."* He'd said that this afternoon, and even at the time she'd known he held himself responsible for something that had happened in his past, something he'd never been able to forgive himself for. Now she knew what that something was.

Max blamed himself for his wife's death. And the sentence he'd imposed upon himself had been to wall himself away from all but the barest of human contact, immerse himself in his work and allow himself to fade into invisibility a little more with each day that went by.

He'd put himself on death row. But her theory wasn't quite right—the man he'd once been hadn't been erased completely. The bars that shut him away could be unlocked with two keys, and one of those keys was the old dog she could hear right now in the kitchen, snuffling a little in his sleep as he chased a dream rabbit on dream legs that didn't fail him.

The other key that released Max was herself.

The dog she could understand, Julia thought, getting up from the sofa and walking restlessly over to the too-heavily-carved-and-curlicued entertainment center. She glanced without interest at the small collection of video-taped movies displayed on a shelf above the television. Boomer was a link to Max's past, a link to the wife he'd lost. But what was it about her that had the power to bring him to life, even if only temporarily?

"Damned if I know," she muttered almost angrily, pulling a tape out, looking at its cover, and almost immediately putting it back again. "I'm just a woman who screwed up her life in every way she could, and still didn't know enough to give up. If there's anything sexy about that, I'd sure like to hear what it is.''

The tape next to the one she'd replaced didn't even have a cardboard sleeve. She pulled it out anyway, not even glancing at its title, and shoved it into the VCR.

Anything beat trying to figure out Max Ross.

When the television remained black she started to get impatiently to her feet again, but without warning the screen was suddenly filled with an image. It was hard to make out what it was, the camera was focused so closely, but as the camera pulled away it was possible to see buttons marching down the front of a piece of flowered material. It pulled back farther, and the flowered material became a woman's dress, the buttons obviously straining over a pregnant belly. A pair of woman's hands came into view, resting almost gingerly on the swell of her stomach, and then pushing toward the camera in a nervously pleading gesture.

There was still no sound.

Julia got up from the sofa and started walking toward the television, but even as her thumb felt for the eject button on the remote she froze.

The camera had finally pulled back to a normal distance. The pregnant woman, young and with silky dark hair cut in a Dutch bob, half turned away from whoever was filming her as if to hide the swelling of her figure. The expression on her face, as she looked back at the camera, held a curious mixture of reluctance and need that might have passed unnoticed in real life but that seemed oddly emphasized by being captured on film.

But Julia's gaze was fixed on the small black puppy at the woman's feet and the crisply ironed Priscilla curtains at the window over the sink behind her.

"...think I got the damn sound working now. C'mon Anne, turn around and smile for the camera."

It was Max's voice. And the dark-haired young woman had to be his wife—his very *pregnant* wife. Still holding the remote in her hand, Julia sank to her knees on the carpet in front of the television, her eyes wide with incomprehension.

Chapter Ten

"Please, Max—I'm as big as a house. I look so *ugly*." The woman's protest came out in an upset wail. She was biting her lip, and even despite the mediocre quality of the old videotape it was possible to see the easy tears that filled her eyes.

"Annie, we've been through this before." Max's voice was softer and more indulgent than Julia had ever heard it. "You're beautiful. How could you not be when you're carrying our child? Look, even Boomer thinks so."

The camera swung down again and Julia felt a shaky laugh bubble up inside her. The puppy was sitting on his haunches gazing up at his mistress, his tongue lolling out in a happy grin and his tail beating furiously on the braided oval rug. As if sitting still for even a minute was beyond him, he got unsteadily to his feet. Splaying his front paws out in front of him in mock ferocity, he grabbed the fluffy bobble on one of Anne's slippers and gave it a playful tug.

"Max! Get him off me, Max—he's ruining my slipper!"

There was a sound of snapping fingers, and the puppy immediately let go of the bobble and looked toward the camera. The next moment the angle swung wildly and then steadied, as if it had been set down on a level surface. A split-second later, Julia's guess proved correct as a jeans-clad pair of legs moved into the frame, an arm reached down to one-handedly scoop the puppy up and Max suddenly appeared at his wife's side.

"He's just a pup, hon." With his free arm, Max pulled his wife close. "By the time the baby's born he'll have settled down some. Come on, now, how about we get the four of us in the picture here—you, me, Boomer and Ethan? What do you say, Annie?"

He didn't look much different physically from the Max of today, Julia thought, her throat tightening. But although on the screen in front of her his features were drawn with concern, there was still an air of desperate hope about him that had long since vanished. He turned a protesting Anne toward the camera, and as she reluctantly took the now-sleepy puppy from him he let his hand slide gently to the curve of her belly.

"Sometimes you talk so crazy, Max." The pretty brunette's voice was softer than a moment before, and although tears still shimmered at the corners of her eyes she managed a tremulous smile. "Ethan's not even born yet, so how can he be in the picture with us?"

"He's here. He's part of us already." Max's hand stilled and his eyes widened. Then he gave an excited short laugh. "He kicked, Annie! Did you feel that? Jeez, we've got a regular little football player in there!"

"I felt it. You've felt him kick before too, Max, so I don't know what the big deal is. I just hope he doesn't get much bigger before he gets born, for heaven's sake. I'm going to look like a tub of lard when you take me out for our anniversary next week." The peevish note was back in her voice, but Max didn't appear to notice.

"He and Boomer are going to grow up together. You

hear that, buddy—I got you your very own dog, ready and waiting for you to play with." Oblivious to his wife's again-trembling lower lip, Max grinned and crouched low enough to bring his mouth only inches from the curve beneath his hand. "You hear that, Ethan? Your old man went out today and picked the very best pup he could find, and he's all yours. So hurry up and get here, little guy. We're all waiting for you."

The expression on his *face,* Julia thought, the tears streaming down her cheeks. It was pure love, undiluted joy, so unguarded that now she did feel as if she was intruding. He looked like a man fulfilled, she thought shakily. He looked like a *father.*

She watched in silence as Anne handed the Boomer of so long ago back to her husband, watched as Max absently took the puppy from her, his other hand still pressed to her stomach and his mouth still curved into a small smile. She saw him whisper something, and automatically her finger pressed the remote's volume control.

"...love you, little guy." His words were barely audible. He closed his eyes and pressed his cheek to his wife's belly. "I'm always going to be there for you, Ethan. I'm always going to keep you safe, son. I love you so *much.*"

For a moment the screen was filled with the image—the man, his eyes closed and one strong hand splayed open to feel the movements of his unborn child, the small dog he'd bought for that child tucked into the crook of his arm. Boomer's tiny muzzle stretched open in a yawn, and he sleepily closed his own eyes. Max hitched him closer. The screen went black.

"He was never born." Julia's fist flew to her mouth. She stared at the blank screen, ignoring the tears that were falling, hot and wet, to her lap as she sat there. "He was killed with his mother in the accident, wasn't he? Your Ethan was never *born*."

It would have happened only days after this video had been shot, she thought, fresh sorrow lancing through her. He'd said his wife had been killed before they'd been married a year, and Anne had been talking about their upcoming anniversary, so this would have been one of the last moments Max had shared with the son he'd loved so much. Shortly after this his world would have been smashed to pieces, never to be put back together again.

He'd had a wife. She'd been carrying their child. Now it was ten years later, and a man lived alone here in this empty house, his only link to the past the old dog that had been meant as a companion to the child he'd lost.

He'd told her she was wrong, that he'd never had a son. He'd lied—not to her, but to himself. He'd been lying to himself for ten years now, because that was the only way he could hold the pain at bay.

"Oh, Max—don't you see?" she whispered unsteadily. "You *did* have a son. He *was* alive, and he must have known that he had a father who loved him so very, very much. You *told* him that, Max. But for the last ten years you've pretended he never existed, and—and that's *wrong*. You've shut him out of your heart, and he's been waiting outside in the darkness all this time for you to let him back in. You've been waiting in the darkness too, Max. You'll wait there in the dark forever if you don't let him back in."

She heard the click of claws on the kitchen linoleum, and Boomer appeared in the doorway to the living room, his tail wagging in greeting as he saw her. Stiffly he walked over to her.

"One of these days he's going to have to let you go, old boy." Julia stroked the velvety head with a hand that trembled. "He knows that but he just can't bear the thought of it, because when you're gone it'll only be him who's left. I think he looks at you and sees the puppy you used to be—big paws, floppy ears and a heart full of love for the little boy you were supposed to grow up with. He says he never had a son, but I think he looks at you and sees Ethan at your side. I think he looks at you and sees a little boy throwing sticks for you, a little boy coming home from school to give you a hug, a little boy falling asleep with you watching over him at night, keeping him safe from all harm. And maybe he's right. Maybe when you're lying there on your rug deep asleep, in your dreams you're playing with that little boy he loved so much."

Throwing her arms around Boomer's neck, she buried her face in his fur, her eyes squeezed shut and her shoulders bowed in sorrow. His actions made sense now. He would allow himself to go so far with her, she realized with reluctant insight, because he hadn't been capable of sealing himself off totally. If she said the word he would give her the only part of him he had to give—the edgy, reckless Max Ross who was the dark side of the man she'd seen in the video. But that would be all she would ever get of him.

That was all he would ever allow himself to give. The rest of him was locked away forever.

She felt a moist tongue at the side of her face, and raised her head. Boomer was looking worriedly at her, his fur sleek with her tears. She gave him a crooked smile and felt her heart crack a little.

"And that's not enough, Boomer," she whispered. "God help me, it's not enough. I think I've gone and fallen in love with the man...and I want *all* of him."

IT HAD TAKEN LONGER than Max had thought. Not only had he pulled Olivia's original statement, he'd reread every other report he'd been able to lay his hands on. He'd known even while he was doing it that his primary reason wasn't to go over material he already knew almost by heart. He hadn't wanted to go home.

He pulled up in his driveway, and saw with relief that the house was dark. She'd left the small light on by the front door, presumably so he wouldn't stumble on his way in, but it was obvious she'd gone to bed—which was what he'd been hoping for.

The house was quiet, but it wasn't an empty quiet, Max thought as he walked into the kitchen. He poured himself a glass of milk to counteract the four—no, five, he remembered—cups of bad coffee he'd downed at the office. Taking it to the kitchen table, he pulled out a chair and sat down, loosening his tie as he did. He closed his eyes tiredly, and finally faced the fact he'd been trying to avoid.

This wasn't going to work. Even the way he was acting right now was proof of what an insane idea it had been, thinking he could function with any kind of efficiency while he was slowly going out of his mind with wanting her. She didn't seem to get it, he thought incredulously. He supposed that was one of those small mercies it was considered appropriate to give thanks for, but if so, it was too damned small, and he didn't feel all that thankful anyway.

He felt scared.

But the fact remained that she didn't seem to understand just being around her was dangerous for him. And he couldn't understand *that*. When she talked about the woman she'd once been, she described that woman as beautiful—not arrogantly, not boastfully, but just as a statement of fact. And she saw it as a simple fact, not as a regret or a loss, that that beauty no longer existed. So she didn't get it. She didn't seem to understand how hard it was for him to keep his hands off her.

"Somebody somewhere along the line sure did a freakin' number on you, Jules," Max muttered. He tossed back the last of the milk, which hadn't done a damn thing to calm his nerves, and absently drummed his fingers on the table. The spare bedroom was past his, only a few feet away down the hall. Maybe he should check on her, just to make sure she was all right. He got to his feet, nearly stepping on Boomer as he did, and took three brisk steps before he stopped himself. He stood rigidly in the shadows of the hall, guilt washing over him.

"Stupid," he said flatly. "Stupid, stupid, *stupid*. Go back to the damned office if you have to, Ross. Hell, get blind drunk and fall asleep in your clothes on the sofa, if that's what it takes. But leave the woman alone."

She was right. She had been a beautiful woman two years ago, he thought a few minutes later. He lifted his glass to the light, and idly swirled the amber liquid inside it a little before taking a swallow. She'd been beautiful the way models were beautiful.

Hell, he'd harbored a twinge or two of lust for her at the time, he admitted. He got up and poured himself another shot, bringing the bottle back to the sofa. He could feel himself flushing. Okay, maybe more than a twinge. And maybe more than once or twice.

But he hadn't felt anything comparable to the sledge-hammer impact he'd experienced the night he'd met her in the coffee shop.

There'd been purple smudges shadowing those fabulous sapphire eyes, emphasizing the dark sweep of her un-mascaraed lashes and the delicate ridge of her cheekbones. Her mouth, even as she'd been telling him to go to hell, had been nakedly lush, her lips looking like the palest of pink velvet. He'd told himself over and over again as he'd sat there, playing the heavy with her, that she wasn't his type, she could never be his type, and he'd kept telling himself that in the days that had followed.

She wasn't his type. But that was only because she wasn't a type at all anymore. There was only one Julia Tennant, and he was sitting here getting quietly and completely drunk because he wanted her so bad he could almost taste her.

He took another hefty swallow of the Scotch in his glass. He lifted his eyes to the doorway, and saw her standing there. He felt an electric *aliveness* jolt through his body, and knew the Scotch hadn't numbed a thing.

The first night she'd stayed here he'd given her a couple of his old shirts to sleep in, and she was wearing one of them now. She hadn't bothered to roll back the cuffs, so only the tips of her fingers showed past the ends of the sleeves, but if it was skin he was hoping to see, Max thought dryly, he didn't have to look too much further in either direction.

Her legs were creamy pale. The tails of the shirt skimmed the front of her thighs, curved up at the sides of her hips, and then presumably dipped back down again at the back to just cover her rump, although he couldn't say for sure unless she turned around and he got a back view of her. She'd left the top four or five buttons of the shirt undone, and as she crossed her arms and looked at him her breasts were almost completely visible. For once her hair wasn't pulled back into an elastic. Still darkly damp from her evening shower, it swung in separate chunks that just skimmed her shoulders.

"Is that decent Scotch?" There was a husky note in

her voice, and her attitude was confrontational. Desire shot through him.

"Single malt. Decent enough."

His own voice was steady, he noted, so perhaps the liquor had done something. She turned on her bare heel, afforded him a glimpse of her shirttail-covered rump and went into the kitchen. She was back in a minute with a heavy tumbler, and as she held it out she slipped onto the sofa a foot or so away from him, curling a leg under her as she sat.

"So why don't you tell me why you're in here getting drunk all by yourself, Max?" she said coolly, her eyes on her tumbler as he tilted the bottle toward it. Glass clattered against glass, and a few amber drops spilled onto her exposed knee.

"Sorry." With more care than the action warranted, he set the bottle back onto the coffee table. "I only intended to get drunk enough to fall asleep," he said briefly, trying and failing to keep his gaze from lingering on the dark gold droplets running together on her skin.

She saw him looking. Thoughtfully she wiped the palm of her hand across the spilled liquid, her eyes never leaving his face. "Then here's to falling asleep," she said, taking a small sip of her drink. "I couldn't either. Funny, huh?"

He looked at her over the rim of his glass. "What are you trying to tell me, Jules?" he asked guardedly. Draining the last of his Scotch, he let the smoky undertaste roll around his tongue before he swallowed. He set his glass on the table in front of him. Not leaning back against the sofa again, he rested his forearms on his thighs, his hands hanging loosely down between his knees, and slanted a glance at her across his shoulder.

"You mean am I trying to give you the word, Max?"

She shook her head, and a strand of hair curved damply to her cheek. She let it stay there. "No, not yet. Maybe not ever. I just wanted to talk." He wasn't conscious of any change in his expression, but she must have seen something in his face. Her smile was faintly ironic. "A phrase guaranteed to make strong men quail, right?"

Despite himself, he felt a corner of his mouth lift in an answering smile, but he responded seriously enough. "So what do you want to talk about?"

She didn't answer him immediately. Instead, she brought her glass to her lips, closed her eyes, and tipped the last half inch of liquid into her mouth as if it were a medicine she'd steeled herself to take. She set the glass on the table with a small thud, and suddenly he saw that beneath the unruffled pose she was as nervous as he was.

"Okay, here's the deal, Max," she said, her voice a little louder than it had been a moment ago. He saw color touch the pale cheeks, and, as if she'd only just realized it was there, with a quick gesture she brushed away the strand of hair that was still clinging damply to the line of her jaw. She cleared her throat. "I think I told you I'd lost the knack of small talk, so I'm not even going to try. You want me in your bed, don't you?"

His head jerked up a fraction, and he was glad that he wasn't holding anything breakable at the moment. He met her eyes. "I told you I did, Jules. I also told you the final decision would be yours," he said, struggling to keep his tone even.

"So we've got that straight." She hesitated, and then went on. "Does it go any further than that?"

He frowned, more in order to buy a second of time than because he didn't know what she was talking about. "Further?"

The velvet lips pursed in irritation, and those strong

slim fingers flicked impatiently at him, as if waving away his stalling tactics. "Cut the crap, Max. This is cards-on-the-table time, and you know damn well what I mean. God knows why, but you've got the hots for me, and badly. I can understand that, because the condition's mutual." She shrugged—for all the world, Max thought, as if she'd just told him she didn't take cream in her coffee. "But I need to know if that's all it is for you. Because I've got this sinking feeling that it might not be all it is for me."

She sank back against the sofa pillows abruptly, keeping her gaze on him. This time when she folded her arms across her chest the white cotton of the shirt bunched up protectively, concealing what it had so obligingly revealed before, and he found himself feeling obscurely grateful for that.

The Scotch had been a mistake. He needed a clear head for this conversation.

"I didn't ask you what the meaning of life was, for heaven's sake." There was an edge to her tone. "Come on, Max—hit me with your best shot. I'm tough. I can take it. This is all there is, isn't it? For you it doesn't go any further, does it?"

Maybe she *was* tough, he thought in sudden weariness. She'd been trying to persuade both him and herself of that since the night in the coffee shop. But she'd taken more than a few shots since that night, and tough or not, she had to have a breaking point.

Except Julia Tennant's breaking point wouldn't be him, he told himself. He leaned back, and met her eyes directly.

"I'm pretty good at my job, Jules, and I guess if you asked them, the people I work with would tell you that

I'm a decent enough guy. But like I told you before, they don't really know me.''

He saw her lashes flick down and then up again, the movement so tiny and swift as to be almost unnoticeable, and even though he knew his reaction was completely and totally inappropriate he didn't bother to fight the hot rush of desire that washed over him. What was the use? he asked himself tightly. If he tried to put out every fire that Julia Tennant lit in him he'd be running around all the time with a mental extinguisher, and he still wouldn't be able to keep them under control.

But that didn't mean she had to get singed as well.

''I don't think you know me either,'' he said flatly. ''If you did you wouldn't ask that question. It doesn't go any further because that's my limit, Jules. There's nothing else in me to give.''

''Was there ever?'' She held his gaze steadily, and all of a sudden Max didn't want to continue the conversation.

He got to his feet. ''No, Jules, there never was. There was always something missing.'' He looked down at her, still motionless on the sofa, and found he couldn't leave it at that. ''For what it's worth, the rest still stands. But I guess I won't be getting the word from you anytime soon after this, will I?''

She didn't answer, and he raked a hand through his hair tiredly. ''We've got a full day ahead of us tomorrow,'' he said, shrugging off his jacket and throwing it onto a nearby chair. He pulled his tie down farther, until it was a loose noose around his neck, and unbuttoned his shirt cuffs. ''We'd better get to bed.''

She looked up at him and blinked, as if he'd interrupted her thoughts. ''What? Oh.'' Uncurling the leg that had been tucked underneath her, she rose too, her bare toes sinking slightly into the pile of the carpet. "I guess we'd better. Good night, Max."

He'd been right, he thought as he saw her walk down the short hall, the shirt she was wearing glimmering whitely in the shadows. Julia Tennant wasn't about to crack over Max Ross. She hadn't cracked when she'd been accused of murder, she hadn't cracked in prison, and the steel inside her was still holding. What had she meant when she'd said she didn't think that was all it was for her? Was it possible that she was—

He was a goddamn fool, he thought, suddenly angry with himself. She'd already endured one bastard in her life, and if and when she decided she was ready to take a chance with another man, she'd take her time about it. She'd be cautious. She'd be smart. She'd look for someone who could give her what she deserved this time, and she wouldn't settle for anything less.

He still wanted her. He couldn't have her. He would get her daughter back for her and then get out of her life.

"Max."

He looked up, startled. She was standing in the doorway of the guest room, and although she'd folded her arms across her chest again, this time there was nothing defensive about the pose.

"The thing is, you never told me what the damn word *was*." She sounded impatient. "How the hell am I supposed to give you the word when I don't even know what it is?"

Chapter Eleven

This was the point of no return, Julia thought faintly. She unfolded her arms and pushed herself away from the door frame. "So what's the word, Max?" she asked once more.

"I guess the word is yes," he said slowly. He was still standing in front of the sofa, and the light from the lamp on the table beside it didn't reach his eyes. She could feel his gaze on her anyway.

"Yes," she said. She turned and walked into the bedroom. She sat down on the edge of the bed.

She'd made a lot of ill-advised decisions in her life, she thought, pressing her knees together to keep them from shaking. This one probably transcended that category. This one was probably just plain stupid. He'd played straight with her all the way down the line, so if she ever looked back on this moment in the future there would be no way she could blame anyone else but herself for what she'd just done.

She'd come right out and asked him, and he'd given her the answer she'd known he was going to give. He wanted her. He wanted to make love to her—no, scratch that, he wanted to have sex with her. And that was as far as it went, according to him.

So he hadn't played games, and he hadn't tried to tell her what she wanted, and she'd still given him the word he'd been waiting for since yesterday.

Why?

There was enough dim light coming from the hall to see him appear in the doorway. He stopped on the threshold, pressing his palms flat against either side of the frame as if to physically prevent himself from coming any farther.

"You sure, Jules?" Except for the use of that damned nickname he'd given her, he could have been asking a witness to verify a previous statement.

But he did use his nickname for her. And the nickname was part of it, Julia thought helplessly.

She'd been born Julia Weston, a blond, blue-eyed, adorably miniature version of a mother who trotted her out when it was convenient and whisked her away when having a daughter might have cramped her flirtatious style. She'd become Julia Tennant, the ice-queen wife of a man who'd seen her as a possession. She'd been dubbed The Porcelain Doll by the media, and in prison she'd been assigned a number.

He called her Jules. He didn't see her as any of those other women she'd once been. By the time she'd met him on the night of her release she hadn't had anything left to hide behind, and that in itself had been a release.

So he'd gotten the real her. And it was the real her he wanted.

If that was all Max Ross had to give, she still wanted it, Julia thought.

"You're the FBI agent," she said edgily. "I walk in on your bout of solitary drinking wearing only a shirt and panties, I toss off a slug myself for courage, and then I do everything but leave a trail of bread crumbs to the door of my bedroom. Aren't those enough clues for you? Of course I'm sure, Max. Stop propping up the door frame.''

A brief grin broke the hard angles of his face. He let his hands drop to his sides and walked into the room, not stopping until he was standing in front of her. ''Let's get the first kiss over with right away,'' he said lightly. '''Cause everyone's nerves are way too strung up here, Jules—mine included.''

''My nerves aren't strung up.'' Still on the bed, she had to crane her neck back to look at him. ''Dammit, Max, you make me sound like some fragile flower. A week ago I was behind bars, and believe me, fragile gets toughened up pretty fast in—''

''Shut up, Jules.'' He moved that last inch closer, and she felt his knee beside her on the bed. She closed her mouth with a snap, her heart suddenly pounding. ''No, keep that open, you're gonna need it,'' he said hoarsely, bending to her and cupping her chin in his hand, his thumb going to her bottom lip and parting it again. ''Let's do this thing,'' he whispered.

She'd expected him to lower himself to her. Instead his arms went around her waist and she felt him lifting her effortlessly to her feet, straightening up himself as he did so. But by then his mouth was already on hers. At that point the mechanics of what they were doing suddenly seemed supremely unimportant.

He tasted of the Scotch he'd drunk, and at first that taste was deceptively smooth, lulling her into letting her lips open more fully as his tongue moved farther into her. But beneath the smoothness was the raw jolt of pure alcohol. Even as Julia's own tongue flicked against his, discovered that rawness and instinctively retreated, it was too late.

It felt as if all the nerve endings in her body had been charged by the contact, had turned into dangerously live wires that no longer transmitted the signals they were supposed to, but instead shot off showers of erratic sparks that scrambled her senses, her reactions, her intentions. Without conscious thought, she allowed her hands to slide up between his body and hers, allowed them to curl into fists, felt them clutching twin handfuls of his shirt and pulling him even closer.

She didn't need to pull him closer. The arms around her tensed with muscle. He took his kiss deeper.

You can do any damn thing you want to do to me…

It had been a rash promise. Only a rash man would have made it, she thought disjointedly. Or had he known that she would have been beyond demanding anything, beyond being able even to string a coherent thought together, when he was doing what he was doing right now with her?

There was an aggressiveness in his kiss, as if he couldn't rein himself in, or didn't want to. His tongue stroked the softness of her inner lips, pushed past hers to the dark well of her throat, slipped tantalizingly back again, velvet-rough, along the sensitive wetness of her cheek. She felt a small shock as his teeth closed firmly over her bottom lip, but before the sensation could translate itself into pain he was licking the tenderness away, soothing it with the tip of his tongue, coaxing her mouth into fullness again.

She felt herself melting.

He wanted her to melt, she thought hazily. He knew liquid heat was beginning to cascade through her, spilling over like burning wax and running slowly down her breasts, her hips, her thighs.

His mouth took hers again, his jaw scraping against

her skin like diamond grit. When this finally came down to what it ultimately, inevitably was leading toward, she thought, she would already be over the edge. She would be as limp as wet silk, unhesitatingly ready for him.

He lifted his head. Slowly she opened her eyes and met his gaze.

The half light from the hall shadowed one side of his face, and for a moment she found it impossible to read his expression. Then she saw the corded muscles in his neck, the hard color high on his cheekbones, the effort it was costing him to remain motionless. He exhaled slowly.

"What was I saying about getting the first kiss over with so we could both relax?" he murmured. "It's not working for me. But you're the tough girl, Jules, honey— did it work for you?"

There'd been nothing calculated about what he'd just done with her, she realized in disconcertion. He'd been melting too. He was *still* melting. Those green eyes were glazed over with heat and his mouth was slightly parted, as if he needed to taste her again.

Even as the thought went through her mind his glance flicked to her temple. He smiled slowly, and just as slowly he ran a light finger along the arch of her eyebrow, past it to her hairline, and softly tucked a wayward strand behind her ear. The tender gesture was so at odds with his actions of a moment ago that she felt her breath catch in her throat.

He was wrong, she thought shakily. She wasn't tough. And she'd been wrong too.

She'd told herself that if this was all she could have from him she would take it, and no harm done. She'd told herself that if the only part of him she could have was the dark side, the side of Max Ross that was the edgy, compelling lover, it would be almost enough.

And it was almost enough. One night with him, or maybe a handful of nights, would be erotic satiation. She would feel those hands on her, and she would bite her lip to hold back her sighs of pleasure. She would have his mouth on hers, and her nails would score his skin. He would be in her, and she would cry out his name until she was beyond making any sound, beyond doing anything but sinking into his arms and letting him catch her as she fell back down to earth.

But he'd just smoothed her hair back, and the man who'd done that, the man who'd stroked her as if she was infinitely precious to him, was the other side of Max Ross. That small gesture was all that was left of the man in the video, Julia knew, because the man in the video was almost completely a ghost.

She wanted that man too. And that meant that whatever happened tonight could never be enough. She saw him looking at her, waiting for her answer. Although his face was only inches from hers, she felt as if he were already turning away, already walking out of her arms. A terrible loneliness swept over her, and she knew that the pain tearing through her heart wasn't for herself, but for him.

"Come on, Jules, you can tell me—*did* it work, even a little?"

The husky, teasing note in his voice came close to undoing her. He traced the line of her bottom lip with his finger, and she found herself swaying infinitesimally toward him, her legs barely able to support her.

"Whatever else we are we're two straight shooters, you and me, honey. Give it to me right between the eyes." His mouth lifted wryly, and the still slightly glazed green of his eyes seemed suddenly darker.

He felt it too, Julia thought. He might not acknowledge it, but he felt that cold wind cutting through him on nights like this. It was part of the reason for what he wanted from her, but like her, he needed a more solid, if still only temporary, shelter from that lonely cold.

She knew how she could give him that. She knew how she could come close to giving them both what they needed, and would never truly have.

"We *are* straight shooters, Max," she said unevenly, meeting his eyes. "Neither one of us believes in fairy tales anymore, and we haven't sugarcoated anything between the two of us, have we?"

As if something in her tone had alerted him, his gaze sharpened and focused. Slowly he shook his head, the movement so controlled that she almost missed it. "No, Jules," he said steadily. "We haven't done that."

"Then that's what I want." She drew back from him. Taking a shallow breath, she continued, her voice a little higher than normal. "You told me yesterday I could have whatever I wanted from you, Max, and that's what I want. Just for tonight let's not be straight shooters. Just for tonight I want you to lie to me."

Even before she had finished he was shaking his head again, and this time the movement was impossible to miss. "You can't want that, honey—"

She cut him off, her tone shakily determined. "I *do* want that, Max. I've had two years of grim reality, and I *want* the fairy tale, dammit!"

She pushed her hair back from her face with a suddenly trembling hand. "I'll know it's a fairy tale. I won't expect it to last, because that's how these things work, isn't it—when the night is over Cinderella goes back to the real world. But she goes back with a few memories of magic and illusion, and that's what I want. I *want* the illusion. I want you to lie to me, Max.''

His gaze searched her face, as if he was hoping to find some reassuring sign there that she'd been joking. But he wouldn't, Julia thought, holding on to the last of her determination and not allowing her eyes to waver. No matter how insane her request had sounded, she'd never been more serious in her life. He sighed heavily, and took a step away from her.

''I can't do that, honey. Ask me anything else you want, but not that.'' He turned slightly, wearily rubbing the side of his face with his hand.

She'd thrown the dice, she thought hollowly. It looked as if she was leaving the table empty-handed. She'd lost.

''See, Jules, when I held you in my arms two days ago after you'd walked out in front of that bus, I found myself wondering why I always seemed to be the one who had to give you the bad news—why I always ended up telling you the hard truths and making you hate me.''

She looked up, a denial on her lips, but he forestalled her with a shrug.

''Maybe you didn't hate me. Maybe it was just that I hated myself for having to do that to you. But I held you there on the street and I wondered if there was some way I could soften things for you, Jules. And then you opened your eyes and I knew I couldn't.''

''*Why?*'' The one-word question was desolate.

''Because no one else had ever cared enough about you to play straight with you, honey,'' Max said hoarsely. ''And when I looked into those incredible eyes of yours my heart turned over and I knew I couldn't give you any less.'' He met her gaze directly. ''That's when I had to face the fact that I was already half in love with you, Jules.''

"That's when you—"

Julia stopped. He was watching her, and though his face was in shadow she could see the tenseness in his expression. He was so still he gave the impression that even his breathing had been suspended. She felt a sudden, foolish moisture behind her eyes, and blinked it away.

Lie to me...

"Tell me more, Max," she said shakily. "Tell me more about when you knew you were falling in love with me."

He let his breath out softly. Turning back to her, he brought both his palms up to frame her face, his touch as light as a whisper. "It started the night I met you in the coffee shop. I couldn't admit it to myself, of course, but even while I was playing the bad guy with you I kept finding myself looking at your mouth. When I grabbed your wrist, some part of me knew that it had only been an excuse to touch you."

His breath was warm on her lips. She gave him a small smile. "And then I walked out on you."

"You walked out on me," he agreed. He let his hands slide slowly back into her hair. "I told myself that was a good thing. Then I went back to the office and pulled every damn photo I could find of you, and stared at your face all night."

A little laugh bubbled up inside of her. "*Really,* Max?" She looked at him with feigned innocence.

"*Really,* Jules." His grin flashed white in the shadows. Before she knew what he intended to do, he bent down swiftly and scooped her up in his arms. She gasped. "Except looking at your face in a picture wasn't enough," he said quietly. "Reading about you in your file wasn't enough. I kept feeling that I was missing the *essence* of you. I felt like maybe I'd been missing that from the start."

He looked down at her, cradled in his arms. "It wasn't until you'd walked away from me the second time that I allowed myself to see who you really were, and then I knew that I'd just let the woman I loved slip out of my hands."

Tell me lies, Max. Just for tonight, lie to me. Julia traced the line of his mouth with a light finger. "But you came after me." She wouldn't think of it as a lie, she thought. She would let herself believe it was all true, from the words he was saying to the tenderness in those green eyes only inches from hers. She let her lashes drift down to her cheeks. "You came after me, because by then you knew you loved me. I think I knew I loved you by then too."

"*Really,* Jules?"

Even with her eyes closed, she could tell that he was smiling. She smiled back, and felt him lower his mouth to hers. She opened her eyes.

"Really, Max," she said softly.

This time there was nothing aggressive about his kiss. He entered her slowly, his tongue touching hers, circling it, and then lightly flicking against the roof of her mouth. She reached up and let her fingertips touch his temples, move into the coarse silk of his hair, like a blind woman relying solely on her sense of touch to discover the face of her lover. She could feel one arm, solid and hard, under her thighs, the other holding her securely around her waist. A dreamy warmth spread through her limbs. She felt like purring, she thought, feeling his mouth come down more firmly on hers. She felt as if he were stroking her with his tongue.

"I want to see all of you, Jules." He whispered the words against her lips. "You're so beautiful, honey."

Instinctively she pulled the edges of her shirt together

as he lowered her to the bed. She looked up at him and
shook her head in automatic denial, for the moment forgetting their agreement.

"I'm too thin, Max." She bit her lip. "The last time
my hair was trimmed it was by a prison barber. And
there's this."

She was clasping her hands against her chest. Not
looking at them, she slid them apart, and held up her left
palm to his gaze. She lowered it again, covering it once
more with her right and averting her gaze from his.

"That? Hell, Jules, that's nothing."

He'd been bending over her. Now he straightened to
his full height and stood at the side of the bed. Her eyes
widened in confusion as he impatiently pulled his shirt
out of the waistband of his pants and unbuttoned it.

"Now this—this is a *scar,* dammit." Opening his shirt
and lifting his right arm slightly, he pointed to a faded
red line running along an upper rib. "Bullet wound," he
said complacently. "It ploughed along the bone and then
hit a wall beside me. Sorry, honey, you'll have to do
better than that."

He grinned sympathetically down at her, and she
blinked, her throat suddenly tight. Her vision blurred as
she looked up at him and the last bar around her heart
shattered and fell. He wouldn't have to know it, but nothing she would tell him tonight would be a lie. She gave
an unsteady snort and abruptly sat up.

"Then what about this?" She pushed her sleeve back
and raised her elbow at him, her tone challenging. "See
that? I was four years old. I fell off my trike on the
sidewalk. It needed *stitches,* for God's sake."

He peered at the almost-invisible mark and raised a
skeptical eyebrow. "A trike accident? That's just pitiful,
Jules. Picture this—a skinny thirteen-year-old on his way

home from the municipal pool with only his bathing
trunks on, riding his ten-speed full tilt down a hill and
wiping out in front of a bunch of girls.'' He unbuckled
his belt and unzipped his trousers, his movements swiftly
efficient. Impatiently he hooked his thumb under the edge
of his briefs and pulled them aside just enough to expose
one leanly muscled hip. ''Bled like a stuck pig. Mary
O'Sullivan laughed at me and broke my heart.''

His tie had come undone, the two ends hanging loosely
down over his chest. He'd shrugged halfway out of his
shirt, its seams straining over his shoulders, and Julia felt
her breath catch as she looked at him. Under those concealing suits he always seemed to wear was nothing but
hard muscle, she thought faintly. There was a scattering
of fine hair V-ing its way down his chest to his navel,
but except for that silky dark arrow his torso looked like
a roughly carved slab of wood in the shadowy light.

She let her gaze go lower and felt sudden heat suffusing her face. She swallowed dryly.

''Poor baby.'' She forced a note of unconcern into her
voice. ''Okay, Max, even you're going to admit defeat
with this one.''

She sat up on her haunches, her legs tucked beneath
her. Briskly she slid the waistband of her panties past her
hips, wriggling a little more than she had to but being
careful to keep her shirttails concealingly in place. Out
of the corner of her eye she saw him freeze to stillness.
She went on as if she hadn't noticed his reaction.

''Camp Minnetowanka. I was fourteen. I had the
world's biggest crush on my leathercraft instructor.'' Her
panties were halfway down her thighs. She looked at him
solemnly. ''The day we were supposed to be finishing up
our punched-leather change purses he walked into recreation
hall and told us he'd just gotten engaged. I was so devastated

I sat down on my work-stool and and right smack-dab onto my newly sharpened awl. Cry uncle, Max.''

Leaning forward onto her elbows and lifting her rump high into the air, she looked innocently at him over her shoulder. She heard him draw in a tight breath. Very slowly, he shrugged out of his shirt, not taking his gaze from her upraised derriere. Even more slowly he stripped off his now-useless tie. He placed one knee on the bed behind her, bracing his arms on either side of her legs. Julia felt her panties moving down to her knees, and then coming off completely.

"Uncle,'' he said hoarsely.

The next moment she felt his open mouth on the top of her thigh, and hot, immediate pleasure cascaded through her in a liquid rush. Her teeth sunk into her bottom lip, but not soon enough to stifle a small moan. She felt his tongue trace a wet, slow circle upward, and weakly she closed her eyes, almost unable to bear the swirl of sensations he was stirring in her with every teasing lick of his tongue, every rasp of his unshaven cheek against the tenderness of her inner thighs. Desperately she clutched the sheet she was lying on, and drew it convulsively toward her, her neck arching back in ecstasy. She felt him part her legs a little wider, and then his tongue went deeper.

"Oh, *no*, Max.'' Her voice was a thread. "Please, Max—it's too *much*.'' His tongue flicked once more against the tautly secret bud between her thighs, and the world dissolved dizzily around her.

"You taste like a flower.'' His own voice was little more than a rasp. "Jules, I want more of you. I want all of you now.''

She was dimly aware of him getting off the bed and stepping out of his pants. How did he *know?* she thought dazedly, feeling the tiny aftershocks rippling through her and bunching her fist, still clutching its handful of sheet, to her mouth. How did he know so unerringly just how to bring her to this, and how did he know that she couldn't delay her need to have him in her any longer either? It was as if his body could read hers, she thought, lifting her head and looking at him through her lashes. He pushed his briefs over his hips to the floor and returned her gaze steadily. She could see a pulse beating at the side of his throat.

"I want it too, Max," she whispered unevenly.

She lifted herself up slightly from the bed, letting her shirt fall away from her as she did. Now she could see that the dark V of hair travelled down past his navel, thickening and coarsening into a shadowy tangle at the top of those tautly muscled legs. Very slowly she brought her palm close enough to brush against the tangle, and felt it curling against her fingers like fine wire. She opened her hand and let her fingers push past the rough hair to the shaft that rose from it.

She closed her hand gently around the solid column, and softly slid her fingers upward.

A shudder ran through him. Looking up at his face, she saw his eyes had closed, and the muscles in his neck were rigidly corded.

She let her hand slide downward again, farther this time, and opened her palm to cup the tautness nestled between his legs. Very carefully, she drew the tip of her finger along the tight fullness there, and heard him exhale with a gasp.

"I already cried uncle, Jules," he said hoarsely.

Stepping away, he bent down to the floor, and fumbled in his pants pocket for something. He stood up, his grin crooked as he flashed the small square of foil at her.

Her eyes widened, and she was surprised into a soft amusement. "You've been carrying that around in your pocket, Max? Don't tell me it dates from the days of Mary what's-her-name."

He shrugged, but she could see the quick gleam of his teeth in the shadows. "Naw, honey, I bought some yesterday when we stopped on the way home. Just on the off-chance." He ripped the foil square open and pulled out the condom, but before he could put it on she stopped him impulsively.

"Let me." Sitting up on the bed, she met his eyes, her lips curving. "I promise to be careful, Max. Lie down."

He raised an eyebrow, but he handed the latex circle to her. Julia shifted over as he lowered himself to the bed, and when he moved toward her she swung one leg over his and straddled him, kneeling. Holding the condom delicately, she fitted it over him.

"I think I know where this is going, Jules."

There was a raw note in his voice. Looking up from what she was doing, she saw him watching her through his lashes, and she felt suddenly weak with desire. Carefully she rolled the thin latex down with her palms until it was snugly fitted.

"*Really,* Max?" she teased. She bit her lip in sudden uncertainty. "I've never done it this way. You don't mind?"

"Being on the bottom, honey?"

In answer he sat up just enough that his outstretched hands could wrap around the flare of her hips. His grip firm, he raised her from her haunches to her knees and pulled her closer, until she was poised in position over him.

"I'm going to be able to see everything you feel," he said huskily. "I'm going to be able to have my hands on you, feel your hair brushing against me when you bend over me. No, honey, I don't mind you riding me at all.''

Slowly he began to lower her, his eyes never leaving her face. She felt a slight pressure as she began to press against him, and his grip tightened minutely, moving her a little forward. He continued guiding her downward, and this time she felt herself receiving him. Her eyes widened, and she stared at him in doubtful consternation.

"Don't worry, Jules. We'll take it slow and easy here.'' His whisper was uneven, and the eyes meeting hers were half closed. The heavy muscles in his arms stood out. "If you want to stop, just tell me.''

"I don't want to stop.'' Gripping his wrists where they held her at her waist, she shook her head, feeling him going deeper inside her. "But Max, what if we don't— what if we don't fit?''

Despite the shadows, she saw the quick flash of amusement that crossed his face. "I think we'll manage,'' he said dryly.

He'd said she tasted of flowers, Julia thought, and she felt as if she *was* one, slowly opening into some secret and night-dark bloom as he continued entering her. The pressure inside her increased and she tightened her grip on the solid wrists at her hips.

Gingerly she let herself be eased farther downward, feeling a flutter of panic as he began to fill her more completely. Desperately locking her gaze on his, she saw his teeth sink into his bottom lip, saw his lashes, thick and dark, brush against the hard ridges of his cheekbones, heard him inhale softly.

He was inside her. She was enveloping him, surrounding him, wrapping around him, and suddenly that dark bloom was edged with desire, was no longer tightly furled but had opened fully to him. A wave of molten pleasure poured through her, and a tiny tremor ran along her limbs.

"Ride me, Jules." His words were no more than a sigh. "I want to see you riding me, honey."

He released her hips. His hands spread wide, he slid them upward, past her waist, past her ribcage, finally reaching her breasts and covering them. Cupping their weight in his palms, his thumbs traced lazy circles around each pink areola as tentatively she began to rock slowly forward along his length. As she sank back on him again he rose to meet her return, his thrust solid and powerful inside her, and all of a sudden it felt as if her whole body was suffusing with heat. She moved forward once more, the soft skin of her upper thighs and her rump chafing lightly against the coarse tangle of hair beneath her. He withdrew slightly, and then filled her again, withdrew and then filled her, his half-closed eyes never leaving her face and those hard hands of his covering her breasts.

Somewhere deep inside her, liquid fire began to spread. She let her own lashes drift down as she felt him slide into her and out of her, into her and out again, and blindly she reached out. She gripped his rigidly muscled arms, and sensed rather than saw him looking at her.

"I wanted to see you like this, Jules." His words were slurred. "Your hair around your face, your head thrown back, your lips parted. You're so beautiful, honey."

It wasn't a lie, she thought dazedly. He really believed it. The room swam dizzily around her. She saw the green of his eyes begin to lose focus, saw the corded muscles in his neck tighten, felt him plunge deeper into her as he dragged in a shallow breath. The heat inside her became all-consuming, and she felt herself spiralling into a maelstrom of pure sensations—wanton need, erotic urgency, hot, wet desire. She couldn't last any longer, Julia thought. She had to let him know that she—

"Ride me all the way home, Jules." His voice was a hoarse rasp. "Let's bring this all the way home *now,* honey."

His hands had slid down to her hips again, and as he spoke his grip tightened. He pulled her convulsively to him and she felt him move even deeper inside her than before. Arching her back and moving onto him again she heard herself crying out his name, heard him gasp out hers, and then he was filling her one final, overwhelming time, and it was as if the black world behind her closed eyelids was dissolving into glittering explosions of heat and light. Now his arms were around her and her breasts were crushed to his chest, and still the shattering sensations poured through her, like a whole night sky blazing with fireworks.

And then she was tumbling through space, falling as weightlessly as a feather back through the velvety night. She could feel the heavy beat of his heart under her palm, the warmth of his breath against the dampness of her hairline.

Slowly she opened her eyes. His were still closed, the thick lashes a dark fan against the hard angles of his face, but even as she watched he opened them and met her gaze.

He brought a hand up to push back the hair from her eyes. "So beautiful..." His whisper was little more than a sigh. "...love you, Jules," he murmured almost inaudibly as his eyes closed again.

Tell me lies...

Tightly she shut her own suddenly tear-spangled eyes. She felt his hand on her hair, and laid her cheek gently down on his chest to hear his heartbeat.

"I know you do, Max," she lied back.

Chapter Twelve

"If you could cut the tags off this blue sweater and the jeans I've got on, I'll wear them out, thanks." Julia looked at the brand-new Timex on her wrist. "I'm running a little late."

"Did you want me to put this windbreaker and your old jeans in the bag with the rest of your purchases?" The young salesclerk sounded dubious. Julia shook her head.

"No. You can throw them—" She paused, and then gave the clerk an abashed smile. "Yes, put them in with the rest. They've got sentimental value."

She was being foolish, she thought as she sped through the mall with her two bulging bags of clothing. But the jeans and windbreaker had been the clothes she'd been wearing the night in the coffee shop, when Max Ross had come back into her life.

She'd left just enough time to have her hair trimmed before she was supposed to meet him outside. Feeling ridiculously self-indulgent as she sat back a few minutes later in the perfumed atmosphere of the mall hair salon and felt warm water spraying down her scalp, she closed her eyes and sighed blissfully.

They would have slept in even later this morning if

Boomer hadn't awakened them. The old dog had simply circled the bed, nudging a cold nose at whatever out-sprawled limb he could reach, and Julia had opened her eyes to see a wagging tail just past the solid bulge of Max's shoulder. Max had opened one sleepy eye at the same time, pulled her closer into his arms, and spoken in a low growl.

"Pretend you don't see him. Sometimes he gives up."

"I'm going to put some intensive conditioner on." She glanced up to see the hairdresser looking down at her in consternation. "Girl, you've got gorgeous hair. What have you been doing with it lately?"

"You wouldn't believe me if I told you," Julia smiled.

"Go ahead. I'm sure it needs it."

Max's ploy with Boomer hadn't worked, but after the dog had performed his urgent errand outside, he'd settled down once more on his rug in the kitchen, and Max had stumbled back to the bedroom looking for her. By then she'd been in the shower, Julia remembered, but that hadn't mattered. He'd joined her there.

They'd made love in clouds of billowing steam. Afterward he'd scrubbed her back and she'd returned the favor, and it hadn't been until they were towelling each other off that Max had told her he had to drop by the office to pick up some information he'd put in a request for the previous night. In other circumstances she might have tried to get him to change his mind and come back to bed with her, Julia thought wistfully. In other circumstances he probably wouldn't have needed persuading. But between both of them was the unspoken knowledge that the night they'd just shared had been an interlude, and that interlude, as sweet as it had been, couldn't interfere with the task still ahead of them.

Which didn't mean she couldn't allow herself to relive

it a little in her mind, she told herself as her hairdresser came bustling back. Her neck arched again into the deep sink behind her, she let a small, secret smile play around her lips.

They'd made love three times after that first time—four if you counted the shower scene, Julia told herself, and she definitely *was* counting the shower scene. And despite the erotic heights they had brought each other to, it hadn't been just sex. It had been lovemaking. Even though he hadn't come right out and said the words again, even though when he *had* said them that once his words had been slurred with languid after-climax incoherence, what they'd had together hadn't been just a series of physical acts, she thought stubbornly.

But you asked him to lie to you. He told you he couldn't give you what you wanted because it wasn't in him to give, and then you asked him to lie to you. You even promised that you wouldn't do the very thing you're doing now—persuade yourself in the morning that it hadn't been a lie, persuade yourself that by some miracle, you'd brought the other half of Max Ross back to life.

"Just a trim, right? Maybe some layers near the bottom to give it movement?" With brisk efficiency the stylist wrapped a thick cotton towel around her head like a turban. "I'll have you looking like Cinderella at the ball before you leave here, girlfriend."

The woman's words were almost an exact echo of her own thoughts. Staring unseeingly at her reflection in the mirror in front of her while the stylist began snipping, Julia clasped her hands tightly together under the plastic coverall she was wearing.

Okay, she'd asked him to lie to her. But had *everything* been a lie? She shook her head in automatic denial, and beside her the hairdresser shot her an admonishing look before resuming her task.

She didn't think it had been, Julia thought, keeping obediently still. The man in the video had been capable of so much love that even in a grainy ten-year-old tape she'd seen it in his gaze. That man had been devastated by a loss so wrenching that even now he hadn't been able to bring himself to acknowledge his pain, but he hadn't disappeared completely.

He was still there. She'd seen him last night. She was in love with him.

"Whoever he is, tell him to take you to lunch at the most expensive place in town. You definitely should make him show off the new you a little before he messes up my handiwork in bed, girlfriend." The stylist whipped away the plastic cape in satisfaction. "Like it?"

Slightly disconcerted that her thoughts had been so visible, Julia focused her attention on her reflection in front of her. Her hastily knitted brows arched in surprised pleasure, ruining her pretence of detachment immediately.

"I love it," she said happily. "It looks...*free,* somehow."

"I didn't take off a lot, I just got rid of the damaged bits. You gotta do that every so often, girlfriend."

Maybe it was Hair Philosophy 101, Julia thought wryly as she stood by the entrance to the mall and waited for Max to arrive, but the woman had made a point worth keeping in mind—and especially today, of all days. In a while she would be confronting her mother-in-law, if Max had managed to arrange an appointment with Olivia as he'd planned. She would have to discard that part of her that had always been so intimidated by her husband's formidable mother, if she wanted this interview to be of any benefit at all.

As she saw his car pull up she hurried over to it, suddenly a little self-conscious of her transformation and
nervously wondering what his reaction to it would be.
Even though he'd given her the money he'd forced Melvin Dobbs to return to her, she shouldn't have spent any
of it on herself, she thought with belated guilt. That
money could set her and Willa up in an apartment while
she looked for a job. That money might be needed as a
safety net until she got back on her feet again. Even the
few hundred dollars she'd spent might better have been—

"God, Jules, you look gorgeous."

He'd gotten out of the car and had taken her bags from
her, but instead of putting them in the trunk he simply
stood there, looking at her. Her guilt lessened.

"I do, don't I?" Smiling, she looked down at the blue
sweater and the hipster jeans, and then reached up to
touch her hair. "No more tough babe, Max. Are you
going to miss her?"

"Oh, I think you're probably still pretty tough,
honey." He lifted an eyebrow. "Just twice as dangerous
now, looking like that."

"I bought something else too." As they got into the
car and Max began heading for the mall exit, she looked
at him, her smile suddenly crooked. "I got Willa a birthday present, Max. Do you think you'd be able to get it
to Barbara to give to her?"

They were merging with a stream of traffic, and it was
a moment before he replied. He glanced over at her, his
expression unreadable. "That's not going to be necessary, Jules. I was about to tell you anyway—while I was
at the office a call came in for me. It was Barbara. She
wants to meet with you." He shrugged tightly. "Apparently Noel contacted her yesterday and told her we were
looking into the bombing. I would have been out of line

suggesting it myself, but since the request came from her we won't be violating the terms of her protection program. I said we'd meet on neutral ground, and she gave me the name of a restaurant.''

''Babs wants to meet with me?'' Everything else forgotten, Julia stared at him in shock. ''Why? She brokered a deal with the government to stay *hidden* from me, for God's sake. She thinks I killed her husband and her brother, Max—why would she suddenly want to see me?''

A thought struck her, and she caught her breath in sudden hope. ''Does she think I didn't do it? Does—does she want to give Willa *back* to me, Max?''

''I don't think so, Jules.''

They came to a stoplight, and he turned to her. ''I tried to get her to soften her position, Jules, but it was no go. She's still just as convinced that you're guilty as she was the day she testified against you.''

The light changed to green, but he ignored the impatient honk of the car behind him and went on, his tone heavy. ''I think she wants to make it clear to you that she's never giving up Willa. I think she wants you to know that it's useless even to try.''

BARBARA HADN'T CHOSEN neutral ground for their meeting, Julia thought stonily as she and Max entered the restaurant. It was one she'd lunched at often when she'd been the aimless and bored Mrs. Kenneth Tennant, and even though she kept her gaze fixed straight ahead of her she was sure she recognized more than a few of the female faces looking up in quickly concealed interest at her. The new outfit that had bolstered her confidence only an hour earlier looked ridiculously out of place amid the designer suits and cashmere twinsets of the women around her, and she was suddenly convinced that her haircut looked exactly like what it was—a budget creation from a mall stylist. She curled the fingers of her left hand into her palm as she and Max followed the maître d' past a table of chattering matrons.

"Remind me again what decade we're in?" Max frowned at the almost exclusively female lunch crowd. "Doesn't anybody in this room hold down an honest job, for crying out loud?"

He sounded so disgruntled that she was surprised into a smile. "Not hardly, Max," she drawled. "Oh, I think Victoria Charles over there might hold a soirée once a year for the symphony, and Peggy Shoemaker calls herself an interior designer because she's constantly redecorating her Boston home and the lodge in Aspen, but work? They married rich so they wouldn't have to." She added with raw honesty, "I should know. I used to be one of them."

"Do you wish you still were?"

His question was blunt, but she didn't even hesitate before giving him her equally blunt answer. "Hell, no!" The table they were just passing fell silent as the exclamation burst from her, and Julia caught the eye of an immaculately groomed brunette before the woman could turn away. "Hi, Sheryl," she purred without missing a stride. "Long time no see."

"That was childish." Max gave her a reproving look as they left the stunned table behind, and then broke into a grin. "Feel better?"

She grinned back at him. "Hell, yes." She sobered. "It was my way of whistling past the graveyard, Max. I'm nervous."

"Don't be." The green gaze holding hers darkened. "Unlike the rest of this crowd, Barbara Van Hale used to be a friend of yours. But she's spent two years building you up into the bogeyman, Jules. Maybe once she sees you haven't sprouted horns and a tail she'll listen to your side of the story.''

''And if she doesn't, what do we—''

Julia broke off as the maître d' stopped just ahead of them and with a flourish pulled out one of the delicate gilt chairs that surrounded the pink-linened table. She stood as if rooted to the spot as the dark-haired woman already seated at the table met her eyes.

''Hello, Julia.'' Babs flushed, but didn't look away. ''I—I'm glad you came. Thank you for arranging this, Agent Ross.''

Her heart thumping painfully in her chest, Julia shakily lowered herself into the chair that the maître d' had been holding out for her. She was vaguely aware of Max taking his place at the table with them.

Babs was as apprehensive as she was, she thought wonderingly, taking in her former sister-in-law's trembling hands and the pallor that had replaced that first flood of color in her cheeks. The soft brown eyes were shadowed and wary. Julia found her voice.

''Hello, Babs.'' It had come out as more of a croak, she thought, but maybe it wasn't such a bad idea to let Barbara know she was on tenterhooks here too. She swallowed dryly, and tried again. ''You—you're looking well.''

''I've put on some weight since you saw me last.''

Babs stopped, and once again her face flamed. Their waiter chose that moment to take their orders for drinks, and it was with a sense of relief that Julia opened her menu in front of her and studied it while the man hovered beside them.

"Just a mineral water," she mumbled up at him as he came to her. "With lots of ice, please."

"I'll have the same." Babs's voice was barely audible.

Julia knew what was going through her mind. The last time they'd seen each other had been on the final day of her trial. Babs had been frighteningly thin by then. She'd been widowed and had lost her brother all in the same day, and after attending two funeral services, one after the other, with her late brother's wife at her side for both of them, she'd been informed only hours later that the woman she'd thought of as her closest friend was the prime suspect in those deaths. By the time she'd had to give her evidence a few months later, she'd been close to having a complete physical and emotional breakdown.

But Babs was like her, Julia thought—tougher than she looked. Her valor and determination on the cliff the day before yesterday had been proof of that.

She saved my daughter. She saved Willa, and she's given her a loving home for the last two years, she reminded herself shakily. *No matter what, I can never repay her for that.*

She closed her menu and laid it aside. "I've lost some weight since we last met too," she said quietly. "Maybe neither one of us is the same woman we were back then, Barbara. For what it's worth, I never blamed you for telling the truth at my trial. I—I always wanted you to know that."

"I thought you would hate me." Barbara's voice was low. "Not just for having to tell everyone I saw you hand the bomb to Kenneth before takeoff, but because I got custody of Willa. If I'd had a child and lost her, I would never have forgiven the woman who'd taken her from me."

Julia was saved from having to reply by their waiter

coming back with their drinks. She cast a beseeching glance at Max as her turn came to place her order, and he interpreted her silent plea.

"Jules, the sole for you as well?" he interjected smoothly, handing both their menus to the waiter. She nodded mutely. A moment later she felt his hand reach for hers under the table, grip it with brief tightness and withdraw.

The small gesture helped. "You didn't take her from me, Babs. I never even thought of it like that—well, not when I was thinking logically," she added. "While I was in prison I *couldn't* take care of Willa. I wouldn't have been able to survive if I hadn't known she was safe with you."

"But now you're out." Behind the brown eyes Julia thought she saw a flash of pain. "Now you're out and you want her back, don't you?"

Barbara *had* changed, she thought. The one Tennant who'd always shrunk from speaking out, the meekly compliant daughter of Olivia and the overlooked sister of Kenneth and Noel, in the past she would never have brought an unpleasant subject out into the open. But that was why she'd requested this meeting, Julia reminded herself unhappily. It was obvious Babs was determined to make her position clear, however nervous she was.

"Did Noel tell you that we talked with him yesterday?"

Max's tone was professionally detached, and for once she was grateful for the lack of emotion he was displaying. She saw Barbara take a deep breath.

"Noel phoned me, yes," she admitted, her voice trembling only slightly. "I knew that Julia was out, of course. But Noel said you seemed to think she was innocent, Agent Ross. He said you'd reopened the investigation."

"Not officially." Max frowned and leaned back in his chair. "But your brother got the rest of it right, Ms. Van Hale. I made a mistake, and I'm trying to undo that mistake now."

"So you do believe she's innocent." Babs's brown eyes widened as she looked from Max to Julia. "You got out on a technicality, Julia. For heaven's sake, I saw you do it. You handed that wrapped package to Kenneth— you *know* you did!"

"I handed Kenneth Willa's *birthday* present!" Stunned by the sudden attack, Julia gripped the table edge with both hands. "I had no idea there was a bomb inside, and *you* know *that,* Babs!"

"I know that's what your defence was. But a jury found you guilty anyway, Julia, because that story just never held water." Twin spots of hectic color stood out on Barbara's cheekbones. She went on, her voice more intense than Julia had ever heard it. "They found scraps of that same wrapping paper at your cottage on Cape Ann, and they found chemicals too—chemicals that proved you'd assembled the bomb that killed my husband and my brother and two other victims, right there on your kitchen table."

"But we never could prove how Julia had learned to construct a bomb," Max interjected, again keeping his voice tonelessly calm. "That was always a flaw in the prosecutor's case."

"She was a Tennant, for heaven's sake!" Babs snapped. "My mother's cook could probably rig one up if she had to. We're in the chemical business, Agent Ross."

"Not all of you. Not anymore." Max sounded unimpressed. "You're not—you're content to let Olivia run things for the next fifteen or sixteen years. Your brother

Noel wouldn't have Tenn-Chem now if it was handed to him.''

"It *was* handed to him. *I* handed it to him. I asked him to be Willa's business trustee, not my mother." For a moment Barbara seemed more surprised than angry. "Olivia takes care of the day-to-day running of the company, but she has to submit reports to Noel on a regular basis." The soft eyes hardened. "My mother gets to see her granddaughter once a month, with me present, but that's as far as I allow her influence over Willa to go. She had three children of her own and she damaged all of us. I won't allow her to damage Willa."

"So she's not enrolled for Hartley House?" Disregarding everything else Barbara had said, Julia focused on her last statement. "Noel seemed to think that Olivia intended—"

"I'd die before I let Willa be shut away there," Barbara said. "My mother may want her to go to Hartley, but it's not going to happen. Willa's going to have a happy childhood—a *perfect* childhood. She's not going to go through what I went through."

Her voice shook on the last few words and she fell silent. As if he'd been waiting for his cue, their waiter appeared, and Julia busied herself with her linen napkin while her lunch was placed before her.

Babs's conviction that she was guilty was obviously near-unshakeable, and that meant that her hopes of getting Willa back without a court battle were probably dim—unless and until she and Max learned who the real killer had been, she thought. Carefully she smoothed the pink linen on her lap, blinking back her tears. But the terrible fear that had dogged her since yesterday had just been proven unfounded. Meek and mild Babs, who in the past had never stood up against her mother in any situation, was ferociously determined to keep Willa out of the boarding school that had been such hell for herself and her brothers.

A wave of shaky relief washed over her. She lifted her gaze and found Max looking at her, his features drawn with concern. She gave him a watery smile and saw him flash her a quick half grin in return before he turned to Barbara.

"As I said, I made a mistake, Ms. Van Hale—a mistake that sent your sister-in-law to prison. You don't agree, I know, but can you play devil's advocate with me for a minute?"

Babs had been looking down at her lap too, Julia saw with compassion. Even if she'd somehow found the strength to stand up to her mother, even if some of her former meekness had changed to an independent toughness, she was still finding this conversation a strain. She looked up, and Julia realized that unlike her, Babs hadn't been able to hold back the tears.

"Devil's advocate?" She reached for her purse on the chair beside her. She touched the handkerchief she took from it to the corners of her eyes and the reddened tip of her nose before tucking it away again in the handbag. "Go along with your assumption that someone else planted that bomb?"

"Just for the sake of argument."

Barbara picked up a wedge of lemon and frowningly squeezed it on her salad. "All right," she said reluctantly. "I suppose you want to know who else wanted my brother dead, Agent Ross. The answer is, take your pick."

She speared a curly leaf of endive and looked at Julia. "You could have told him that. Noel turned against Kenneth when he lost any say in the company. It wasn't the money that meant so much to him—he received a seven-figure severance check, so he certainly wasn't hurting financially—but he knew from that day forward Olivia would see him as the weaker of her two sons, and that shattered him. We all grew up trying to win her love, and only Kenneth succeeded.''

She popped the endive in her mouth and chewed carefully. She swallowed. ''Kenneth succeeded, but then he turned against her. I don't know how much Olivia cared about that, but I know her first heart attack wasn't brought on by stress. It was brought on by rage—pure, towering rage that Kenneth had managed to out-maneuver her with Tenn-Chem's board and had forced *her* from the company.'' She shrugged. ''She shouldn't have been so surprised. She was the one who'd taught him to go for the jugular in the first place.''

''And you?'' Max's question sounded almost offhand, but at it, Julia saw Barbara's lips tighten.

''My brother saw me as a nonentity, Agent Ross.'' Her voice shook and then steadied. ''He wouldn't have given a moment's thought to my opinion of him.''

''What about me, Babs?'' Julia set her knife and fork neatly on one side of her plate, unable to keep up the pretence of eating any longer. ''The official theory always was that I wanted Kenneth's money without Kenneth. Noel thought I might have killed him to keep Willa from following in the traditional Tennant path of Hartley House, Olivia and Tenn-Chem. But what do you think my motive might have been?''

''I don't think you wanted to kill Kenneth, any more than I think you wanted to kill Robert or the pilot or Kenneth's secretary,'' Barbara said evenly. She held Julia's confused gaze for a moment and then turned her attention back to her salad. She pushed aside a slice of radish before lifting a tiny half of a cherry tomato to her mouth.

"I don't understand. You just said you didn't think I was innocent."

Julia waited as Babs finished chewing. The soft hands plucked at the linen square on her lap, unnecessarily pressed a corner of it to her mouth, and took a sip of water. Only then did the brown eyes turn her way.

"I don't think you're innocent. But I don't think your target was Kenneth, Julia."

Suddenly Barbara was the woman on the cliff again, and everything else fell away—the fussy mannerisms, the easy tears, the hesitant voice. Her eyes blazed with implacable hatred at the woman she'd once called her friend.

"I know about the agreement you signed with Kenneth before Willa was born. I know you never really wanted to be a mother at all. I think when you planted that bomb your real target was your *daughter*—and I'm going to make sure you never see her again."

Chapter Thirteen

"Thanks, Carl, I owe you one."

The phone in Max's kitchen was a rotary-dial mounted on the wall by the refrigerator. Another example of time seeming to stand still in this house, Julia thought dully. As she watched him he went on with a constrained smile.

"No, not the last piece of the puzzle by any means. But it helps." He paused. "Yeah, it sounds like your part-time detective agency's turned into a full-time job."

Julia stopped listening. Boomer came up to her chair and nudged her, and for a moment she felt like throwing her arms around the old dog and letting herself cry for as long and as hard as she could into the silky fur, but she merely stroked the glossy head with a shaky hand, taking comfort in the animal's quiet presence.

This time-standing-still thing sounded good, she thought leadenly. She'd be content to freeze everything a second before Barbara had thrown that terrible accusation at her. Instead, the moment kept repeating in her mind over and over again like some nightmarishly endless film loop.

It was repeating right now.

Her shock at what Babs had just said had been so great that she hadn't even managed to put her protest into words, but at her gasp of horror Barbara had flicked her a cold glance.

"You want her back? You want the money back, you mean. It didn't work out the way you planned, did it, Julia? You thought you'd be sitting pretty—a fabulously wealthy young widow, able to indulge your every whim without any responsibilities at all. That's the kind of life you were hoping for when you married my brother."

She'd picked up the lemon wedge and squeezed it on her salad again as if she couldn't stand looking at Julia anymore, but her words had continued, far more caustic and stinging than the drops of juice falling onto her plate.

"You signed your own daughter away before she was *born*. What kind of mother could you ever be to her after that?" She'd pressed her lips together tightly, and even through her own tears Julia had seen that Babs's eyes were brimming over. "A child isn't a pawn, Julia. A child isn't a bargaining tool. A child is a precious gift— more precious than those obscene pearls you used to be so proud of, more precious than the diamonds and furs and trinkets that Kenneth used to drape you with. But you never saw it that way. Your whole world was ruined when she was born—you can't deny it. Everyone saw the change in you, the way you just withdrew from every-thing. So you decided to wipe out both your husband and your inconvenient daughter at the same time, and then you expected to resume your exciting and glamorous life of parties and men and spur-of-the-moment trips to Paris. Instead, Willa was taken off that plane, you fell under suspicion, and in the end they put you in prison."

Max had broken in at that point, his voice steely. "Someone's been filling your head with poison, Ms. Van Hale. You used to be Julia's friend. Don't tell me you came up with this insane theory all by yourself."

She'd narrowed her gaze at him. "Insane? Ask Julia how insane I'm being. Ask her about the paper she signed, giving away all rights to her daughter."

"He knows about that, Babs." Heartsick, Julia had raised her eyes to the woman accusing her. "I made a terrible mistake, but believe me, I've regretted it ever—"

"The only thing you regret is that Willa gets Tenn-Chem, and now you need her back so you can dip into the company coffers whenever you want," Babs had said. She'd turned back to Max. "No, Agent Ross, I didn't put this together all by myself. My mother and I don't see eye to eye on most things, but when she told me what she suspected it all fell into place for me."

"She's my *daughter,* Barbara. I'm her *mother.*" The words had felt as if they were being torn from Julia's throat. "How can you believe I'd—"

"*I'm* Willa's mother now!" Her movements jerky, Barbara had reached for her handbag and abruptly pushed back her chair. "And I'm a better mother to her than you ever were—than you ever *could* be! Even if you'd never planted that bomb, Julia, do you honestly think you could have provided her with the happy childhood I'm giving her? You would have given in on sending her to Hartley House. You would have let Olivia take over her upbringing. It's ironic in a way." She'd stood, her slim frame shaking with emotion. "I wanted children more than anything else in the world. You had a child you didn't deserve. Maybe justice *was* done in the end."

Julia felt a moist warmth on her hand. She blinked, and saw Boomer's pink tongue come out again to lick her reassuringly. The dog had an almost human expression of worry on his face, and as she looked down at him he gave a puppy-like little whine and placed his silver-flecked muzzle on her knee.

Time didn't stand still, she thought, vaguely aware of Max hanging up the phone. Even the dog in front of her was proof of that. Tomorrow her daughter would celebrate her sixth birthday, and she wouldn't be there with her to watch her open her presents, to see her playing with her friends, to hold her close and tell her how much she loved her. It was another milestone in Willa's life she wouldn't be sharing with her, and once gone, it would be as irretrievable as all the rest she'd missed.

But as Barbara had said, maybe that was simple justice.

"Noel lied about his role in Tenn-Chem." Max pulled out a chair. "I just found out he lied about something else too."

"What?" Julia's voice was toneless. He frowned.

"Do you remember Carl Stein?" At her slight nod he continued. "About six months after he retired he realized he was going out of his mind with boredom, so he started picking up the odd investigating job here and there, and somehow the whole thing just snowballed." He shrugged. "Anyway, after we talked with Noel yesterday I asked Carl to nose around Cape Ann, maybe flash your brother-in-law's photo at the locals and ask if anyone remembered ever seeing him."

"Noel was never at the Cape Ann house," she said without interest. "No one in the family was. Once in a while I'd take a run up the coast to check on things there, but it's not much more than a cottage, Max, and rustic wasn't Noel's style. There's nothing in a place like Cape Ann to interest him."

"Which makes it all the more curious that he went up several weekends in a row around the time of the bombing." He looked at her, obviously expecting a reaction. She shifted her shoulders slightly.

"Maybe it wasn't him. Maybe it was someone who looked like him." Her tone was flat. "Or maybe I'm wrong and Noel thought he'd give the simple life a shot for a while. It obviously didn't last."

"No, it didn't last. But perhaps it only had to last long enough for him to use your cottage as a base of operations to construct a bomb," Max said impatiently. "For God's sake, Jules—don't you see this could be the lead we've been looking for?"

She stood up abruptly. "No, Max, I don't see that. There's only one thing I can see right now. Do you want to know what it is?"

Not waiting for his reply, she walked stiffly over to the corner of the room, where she'd deposited her two bags of purchases when they'd arrived home. She reached inside one and pulled something from it, holding the object out to him as she came back to the table.

"*This* is what I see, Max!" She gave the teddy bear in her hand a violent shake. "I see a woman who thought she could just pick up the threads of a relationship with a daughter who probably doesn't even remember what her mother looks like anymore. I see a woman who thought if she bought her child a stupid *bear* that looked a little like the one she never got to give her two years ago, she could pretend that everything in between had never happened. I searched that damned mall high and low for this—this *thing,* Max!"

She let the bear fall from her hand to the table, her vision blurring. "I don't even know if she *plays* with stuffed toys anymore," she said, her voice dropping to an agonized whisper. "Babs was right. I'll never get Willa back. I don't *deserve* to get her back!"

He was on his feet and pulling her roughly to him. "Stop that," he commanded unsteadily. "Stop it right now, Jules—do you hear me? We went through all this, and you *know* Willa needs to come home to you, whatever your sister-in-law said today. How can you give any weight to her opinion in the first place, dammit? She doesn't know you at all—she never could have! If she did, no one would have convinced her that you could have put your child in jeopardy."

She looked up at him. Slowly she shook her head.

"No, Babs doesn't know me anymore. But she knows Willa better than I do now, Max. What if she's right, and she can give her a happier childhood than I can?"

"She can't, Jules. I don't think Willa will ever be completely happy without you, and that's not just my opinion." Releasing her, he raked his hand through his hair indecisively and then sighed. "Since Willa's a minor the Agency bears some responsibility for her. She's under our protection program, after all, and uprooting a child from everything familiar in her life isn't usually our first choice. We insisted on having one of our child psychologists meet with her every couple of months to monitor her emotional wellbeing. Wait here a minute."

He left the room, and a moment later she heard the sound of a metal cabinet being opened in the small anteroom at the end of the hall that Max seemed to have converted into a pocket-size office, judging from the passing glance she'd given it the first night she'd arrived. She sank down on a chair, her gaze fixed on the discarded teddy bear lying on the table in front of her.

They *had* gone through this before, she thought unhappily. She couldn't blame Max for not understanding why her doubts had come flooding back, because she hardly understood why herself. But today when she'd seen herself through Barbara's eyes—Barbara, who'd once been her friend, Barbara, whose timidly soft voice was so seldom raised in anger—she'd felt as if she was once again being judged and found guilty.

Barbara knew about the agreement she'd signed. Julia squeezed her eyes shut and let her head drop into her hands. When Willa had been born she'd made a desperate promise to herself and the newly born baby girl in her arms that Willa would *always* know she was loved— loved so much and so totally that nothing could ever take that away from her.

I thought I'd given her that much, at least, she thought hopelessly. *But what if Babs is right, and Willa is happier with her?*

"Then you'll have to give her up," she whispered to herself, raising her head from her hands and staring sightlessly at the teddy bear in front of her. "If Willa sees Babs as her real mother now, you're going to have to give her up…because sometimes the last gift that love can give is letting go."

Returning from his office, Max saw her tearstained face and his jaw tightened as he laid three sheets of paper down on the table. "Dr. Rowe specializes in art therapy. These are some of the pictures Willa drew for her, and although Dr. Rowe couldn't get her to talk about what they meant she told me she found them disturbing images for a child that age. They probably should have gone in the official file, but I just couldn't bring myself to do it."

Slowly, Julia drew the pictures closer. Even at first glance it was obvious they all were variations on a similar theme, and as she picked the nearest one up and studied it her hands began to tremble. The paper, stiff with dried poster paint, made a faint crackling noise.

"I'm no expert and Rowe admitted there could be any number of ways to interpret what Willa's trying to express with these, but she said if she was forced to guess she would see this as some kind of visualization of terror. The most she could get out of Willa is that the small bird in the black cloud is her.''

He pointed to a tiny crimson shape in the bottom right-hand corner of the paper, almost obscured by the heavily scribbled black circles surrounding it. A chrome-yellow dab that had to be the bird's beak was portrayed as jabbing at the blackness. Julia tried to speak past the thickness in her throat, but nothing came out. Max went on, his tone edged with concern.

''But Rowe says this is the part of the image that really worries her—this threatening symbol trying to break free of its own cloud and get at the Willa-figure. It's hard to tell what it's supposed to represent, but from these jagged rows of teeth Rowe says it's a classic fear hieroglyph.'' He shrugged tensely. ''Rowe assured me this is almost a textbook symbol. The one thing she's sure of is that this is Willa's way of sending out some kind of message.''

The poster paint was daubed on so thickly that Julia could feel its ridges and lumps under her fingertips as she lightly traced the two figures in the picture. *Willa* had painted this, she thought shakily. Her *daughter* had painted this—and she'd painted it knowing that only one person in the whole world would ever be able to look at it and see at once what it meant.

It looked like a picture. But although the good doctor had misread everything else, she'd been right about one thing. It really *was* a message—a message sent by a little girl who didn't know where her mother had gone or if she was ever coming back. And by some miracle the message had found its way to the person it had been meant for.

Me, Julia thought, oblivious to the tears spilling down her cheeks. *This is to tell me she hasn't forgotten me.*

This is to tell me that she knows I haven't forgotten her, that she knows I would never, ever stop trying to find her again. And she's telling me to hurry up and bring her home.

"Tell me something, Max." Carefully she set Willa's picture down on the table and looked up at him, a hiccuping little laugh belying her still-streaming tears. "Dr. Rowe doesn't have any children, does she?"

"She's not married, but what's that got to do with it? She's one of the best in her field." Swearing suddenly under his breath, he hunkered down beside her chair and took her hands in his. "Dammit, I knew showing you these was probably a mistake. Don't cry, Jules. For God's sake—Rowe could be all wrong on what she thinks they mean. She said herself that only Willa really knew what she was trying to say with these drawings."

"Only Willa and her *mom*," Julia corrected him, smiling through her tears. "That red bird is a hen, Max. And that—what did Rowe call it?—that hieroglyph, I'll have you know, is an alligator. It's supposed to be me."

"I don't get it."

His smile was no more than a brief quirking of his lips, as if he was trying to humor her. He probably was, Julia thought, giving up all attempts to wipe away the tears, and simply letting them fall. He probably thought she was crazy. Dr. Rowe would probably think so too if she could see her.

She didn't care. In fact, what she was about to say was going to sound even crazier, until she explained it to him.

"See you later, alligator," she whispered unsteadily. *"See you then, red hen.* That's what we used to say to each other, Max. Those are the last words I ever said to my little girl before I went away."

"SO YOU'RE TRYING to tell me that steak doesn't just naturally come shaped in triangles?" Max frowned in heavy suspicion and pulled her closer to him on the sofa.

"That's right," Julia said dryly. "Of course, the down side, as you saw tonight, is that you have to use real plates and real pots and pans."

"Yeah, I think Boomer was pretty surprised when he didn't get his usual aluminum trays to lick clean." At the mention of his name the dog at their feet looked up. Julia stretched out a bare foot and rubbed the furry haunch. "It was a great meal, Jules."

"I felt like celebrating," she said simply. "Oh—I forgot something."

Hopping off the sofa, she padded softly into her bedroom and came back again a moment later. Max squinted at the object in her hand.

"A hot dog?" he asked dubiously.

"A squeaky hot dog," she elaborated, demonstrating. "Here Boomer. This is for you."

The Lab's softly folded ears had pricked up as she'd squeezed the thing. Now as she dropped the rubber chew-toy between his front paws he sniffed cautiously at it. Gently he took it in his still-strong jaws, and as he closed his mouth around it it squeaked again. He dropped it, the expression of surprise on his face almost human.

"I get the feeling we'll be hearing squeaking all night long." With a smile, Max watched the old dog firmly take the toy in his mouth again and clamp down on it. Julia gave him a disapproving look.

"I know my voice gets pretty high when I'm in the throes of passion, Max, but really—squeaking?" She gave him a small jab in the ribs with her elbow. "Just for that you have to bring in the coffee."

It was only silly banter, she thought as he gave her a

mock salute before getting to his feet and going out into the kitchen. But she'd never been able to be silly with anyone before, and it felt good. A picture from the past flashed into her mind: Kenneth and herself being driven home by Thomas from yet another excruciatingly dull Tenn-Chem function. Kenneth had spent most of the drive on his cell phone barking out orders to some hapless minion on the other end of the line, and for the rest of the ride he'd sat silently a full arm's length away from her, his mouth tight with tension and his eyes staring straight ahead.

He'd been a cold and ruthless man. But he hadn't deserved to be killed by a member of his own family, Julia thought as Max set two thick mugs of coffee on the table in front of her.

"I hope you wanted brandy in yours," he said offhandedly as he sat down. "I put a hefty slug in."

"Then if I drop off in the middle of a sentence and start snoring with my mouth open, I hope you'll close it for me. I'm not an amorous drunk, Max, I just fall asleep." She smiled over the rim of her mug at him and took a sip. "You think Noel did it, don't you?"

If her conversational change of gears took him unawares he didn't show it. "I don't know. But he lied to us, Jules—lied twice, and I'd like to know why. Like I said when we left his apartment, the man's definitely keeping secrets."

"One of which is that he's gay." She wrinkled her nose. "In this day and age that strikes me as sad."

"Sad or not, he still had the opportunity and the motive." Max shook his head, frowning. "I phoned the office while you were making dinner and asked them to verify Babs's story about him being the real power behind Tenn-Chem, but I'm sure it'll check out. If it had been set up this way at the time of the initial investigation Noel would have been a suspect from the first, but as it was…'' He let his words trail off. She finished his sentence for him.

''As it was, I seemed to be the only one who benefited from Kenneth's death,'' she said quietly. ''And I was the last person to handle that package. You just collected the evidence, Max—it took a jury to decide that I was guilty. Don't beat yourself up over it.''

''But two *years,* dammit!'' His eyes darkened. Taking a deep breath and leaning forward, he loosely laced his fingers together between his knees. ''You say everyone saw you wrapping that present for Willa?''

''Babs and Robert, the two brothers and Olivia.'' She nodded. ''The usual merry Tennant gathering, with Robert the newest member of the family. But he was so self-effacing around Kenneth and Olivia his presence didn't really change the dynamics much.''

''Van Hale came up through the Tenn-Chem ranks, didn't he? Then he married the boss's sister,'' he said thoughtfully. ''Everyone always describes him as ineffectual, but that sounds pretty damn smooth to me.''

''I thought it was pretty smooth at the time myself,'' she admitted with a shrug. ''But you've got to understand that Barbara wasn't looking for romance when she married him. She just wanted to start having babies, and she was afraid that in a few more years it would be too late.''

She sipped reflectively at her coffee, her smile a little sad. ''She's a pretty woman with a warm and loving heart, and I'm sure the Tenn-Chem millions didn't put too many suitors off. But Babs was so shy, especially around men, that she never even had a boyfriend. So she saw Van Hale as her last chance, and she grabbed at it.''

''Except he was killed before he could give her what

she wanted.'' Max, still leaning forward, looked over his shoulder at her. ''Warm and loving, Jules? Even after today?''

''As you said, she's come to see me as the bogeyman—The Porcelain Doll Bomber.'' She spread her hands in a helpless gesture. ''That's the way I was portrayed at the trial and in the media. It sounds as if Olivia's encouraged that notion too.''

''The grande dame of Tenn-Chem, who now has to submit reports on her management of the company to the son she once turned her back on. That must sting.'' Max gave her a hard grin. ''Are you up to meeting with her tomorrow?''

''After today I'm up to anything,'' Julia said wryly. ''And this time I won't be going into it with any false hopes. Olivia didn't object to me as a daughter-in-law, but we were never close. She approved of the fact that I'd given her a granddaughter, though.''

''Maybe she liked the idea of the next Tenn-Chem generation being female again, despite Kenneth wanting a boy. God, what a convoluted family.'' Max sat back, his arm going along the back of the sofa behind her. ''Look at that crazy old dog,'' he said with rough affection. ''He's gone to sleep with that hot dog between his paws.''

''Is he in much pain, Max?'' She voiced the question tentatively, but still she saw a shadow cross his features. ''The pills are for his heart, aren't they?''

''Yeah, but the pills aren't working the way they used to.'' He lifted his shoulders tightly. ''The vet tells me he's good for another few weeks before it gets too bad to bear. It's—it's going to be hard taking him in that final time.''

He cleared his throat. ''But he's just a dog, right?

Maybe I'll get another one. Anyway, about our meeting with Olivia tomorrow—''

"I saw the video, Max. I know you got him for Ethan. I know Boomer's not just a dog to you."

She hadn't meant to tell him like this, Julia thought, feeling him stiffen beside her and seeing him glance automatically at the shelf of videotapes over the television. But last night their relationship had reached a new level—and she wasn't thinking solely of the physical closeness they'd shared, she told herself. Maybe it was time to let him know that she'd seen the other half of him—the half he swore didn't exist.

"As long as he's alive, a little part of your son is still with you, isn't he?" she said softly, her hand reaching out to rest on his.

Slowly he turned to her, and suddenly she knew she had made a mistake. His eyes, their green dulled almost to hazel, were shuttered and unreadable, and his voice when he spoke was completely toneless.

"I never had a son, Jules. If you saw the video then you know Anne was pregnant when she was killed in that accident, but even if her injuries hadn't been what they were, there was never any possibility of the baby surviving outside her womb. I lost a wife." His tone was final. "I didn't lose a son."

She stared at him in consternation, taking in the grim set of his mouth, the tightness in his jaw. She shouldn't have brought this up, she thought tremulously, but now that she had there was no going back.

"But you *did* lose a son. He *was* alive—very much alive, Max," she insisted with shaky stubbornness. "He had a name. You bought him a puppy. You *talked* to him, and you knew he could hear you, for heaven's sake! Maybe he never had the chance to come into the world, but he was alive in your heart, and you know it. You loved him and he was taken from you, and every time you visit his grave it must tear you apart. Why won't you admit that?''

''I go to the cemetery twice a year, on Anne's birthday and the date of our anniversary.'' He got up abruptly and walked over to the living room's picture window, its heavy drapes closed now against the night. He stood there with his back to her, his posture rigid. ''I put flowers on her grave. Her name's the only one on the headstone, Julia.''

Her eyes widened in appalled disbelief. ''You—you didn't even have his name put on the headstone? There's nothing there to show he even *existed?* But, Max—he was your—''

''I never *had* a son, Jules!'' He swung around to face her, his movements jerky and somehow mechanical. The natural tan of his skin had ebbed to a grayish tone, and only his eyes seemed to have any life in them. ''What the hell do you *want* from me? If you want me to admit Anne's death was tragic, you've got it. It *was* tragic. I *did* grieve for her. We probably never should have gotten married in the first place, and the last thing she really wanted was to be pregnant, but we *did* get married—way too young and for all the wrong reasons. And she did get pregnant.''

The fire in his eyes died as instantly as it had flared up. His ramrod posture seemed suddenly to sag. ''She stopped taking her birth-control pills without telling me, because three months after the wedding I already knew it wasn't going to work out between us. We were never right for each other.''

It was the closest to personal he'd ever allowed himself

to be. Julia chose her words with care. "Then why did you get married?"

His laugh was nothing more than a sound issuing from his throat. "That's just it. I married her because she told me she was pregnant with my child. Two days after the wedding it became obvious she wasn't, but she always insisted it had been an honest mistake."

He shook his head and his voice softened. "I couldn't hold it against her. In a lot of ways Annie wasn't much more than a child herself, and I think she just thought I could give her the security she needed so badly. She wanted to hang on to that so much she let herself get pregnant for real. But she was terrified of becoming a mother."

"Maybe that would have changed," she said hesitantly. "Maybe she just hadn't grown up enough."

"Maybe." Shoving his hands in his pockets, Max looked down at Boomer. "And maybe I let her down. God knows I'm no one's idea of a white knight."

He looked up at her, and at the raw bleakness in his expression Julia felt a lancing pain shaft through her heart. "You know how the accident happened, Jules?" He gave her a tight smile. "I was working late, trying to catch up on some paperwork at the office. I was so new at the Agency I was still on probation, and I was determined I wasn't going to screw up. Anne had been at the movies, and she phoned me to come and pick her up because it was snowing and she didn't want to wait for the bus. I told her to take a taxi home."

"And the taxi got into an accident?"

He nodded, his gaze dark with memory. "Yeah," he said softly. "The taxi was broadsided by a truck. They told me later she was killed instantly."

"And you've never forgiven yourself since." She

looked up at his expressionless face, her own features etched in sorrow. "You think you were somehow responsible for your wife's death."

"I *was* responsible. If she hadn't taken that taxi home—"

In the silence that fell, Julia got to her feet. Stepping carefully over the dog lying between them, she laid her hand lightly on Max's sleeve, feeling the hard muscle tense as she touched him.

"That's why you can't let him live, isn't it?" she whispered unevenly. Tears shimmered at the corners of her vision. "Because if you let yourself accept that Ethan was real, then you'll blame yourself for his death too. But it *wasn't* your fault, Max. It was an accident—a tragic accident—but it wasn't your fault."

For a moment she thought she'd reached him. A tremor ran through his rigidly held frame, and the desolate bleakness in his eyes was replaced for a second by sharp pain. Then the arm under her hand stiffened again, and his gaze became once more shuttered and blank. He took a step away from her and her hand fell away from his arm.

"You're wrong on both counts, Jules. It was my fault that my wife was killed that night." He walked to the doorway and paused. He spoke without looking back at her.

"But I didn't lose a son. Like I told you before, I never had one."

Chapter Fourteen

Gosh, the boy was getting big, Max thought as he lobbed the softball to his son with an easy underhand throw. Ethan hooted in derision and made the catch one-handedly.

"Come on, Dad." He whipped the ball back. "I'm not a baby anymore, you know."

Max grinned and shielded his eyes, squinting. This time he put a slight spin on the throw but even so, a split-second later he heard a solid *thwack* as the ball lodged in Ethan's glove.

"I was just thinking that myself, buddy. Hey, why don't you give your old man a break here and change position? I can hardly see you standing against the sun like that."

He could just make out the movement of Ethan shaking his head before the ball came whizzing back. Max had to scramble to catch it.

"You know I can't do that, Dad." The young voice sounded regretful. "I've got to be getting back soon, anyway."

"I know." Max forced a smile. "But not just yet. We've got time for a few more throws." The ball left his hand and he saw his son's arm shoot up to catch it.

A year ago he would have had to jump for that one, Max told himself with a pang. *Maybe even six months ago. It seems like every time I see him now he's grown another inch. How much longer is he going to want to play catch like this with his old man?*

"How's Boom doing, Dad?" The clear tones held a smile. "Still chewing up slippers?"

Max blinked and caught the ball just before it flew past him. "He got a new toy last night. A squeaky hot dog. But he's not doing so great these days, son. He—he's gotten old."

"I know you don't want to let him go." Seemingly with no effort at all, Ethan opened his glove and the ball dropped into it. He didn't throw it back immediately. "But he won't really be gone. He'll never be lost to you—not as long as you still remember him."

Max saw the ball fly past him. He heard a soft thud as it hit the grass a few feet away. He shielded his eyes again, but the sun was so dazzling that all he could see was a wavering blur where his son was standing.

"But that's not true. I lost *you,*" he said hoarsely. "I lost you, and I never found you again. I love you so much, son—but I *lost* you."

His throat closed completely and he stood there, the tears streaming down his face. He saw the blurry figure start to walk away, but then it stopped and turned back to face him.

"You didn't lose me, Dad. I'll always be here waiting for you. You just lost yourself for a while." The boyish voice began to fade. "You lost your way, Dad. When you find it again you'll find me…"

Max opened his eyes, and for a moment the dream was still so real he could almost smell the golden-green scent of freshly cut grass, feel the solid weight of the softball cradled in his palm. Then his gaze focused on the flowery wallpaper, the fussy furniture of the room around him. His brain still slightly fogged, he felt for Julia beside him but his hand encountered only empty bed.

Maybe it had seemed real, but it hadn't been. He threw back the sheets and got to his feet, reaching for a nearby pair of sweatpants. Reality was getting up and walking the dog. Reality was finding a killer who had gotten away with murder. Reality was putting a little girl's world back together again if he could.

His dream hadn't been real. And the last few days with the woman who was sleeping right now in his guest room hadn't been reality either.

She'd thought she didn't deserve the child she'd been given. She'd thought she hadn't measured up as a mother. He shook his head, his mouth tightening. "Hell, Jules," he muttered as he pulled a T-shirt over his head. "Willa got the best darn mother in the world when they put her into your arms at the hospital. Can't you see that? And you deserve to have more like her one day. You deserve *everything,* dammit."

And everything was exactly what he could never give her. He jammed his feet into a pair of runners, grabbed a jacket from the closet beside him, and then just stood there, his eyes closed and his head bowed.

Still—the dream had been so *real.* He'd been having it, or variations on it for ten years now, and it always had seemed real. But Ethan had never existed. He'd never had a son. All he had was an empty space inside him.

Jules deserved everything, and for a few brief hours the other night he'd fooled himself into thinking that maybe—just maybe—he might be the one to give it to her.

"But you're not." He opened his eyes and stared at

the man reflected in the dresser mirror in front of him. "You wanted her to bring you back to life, and she might even have been able to pull it off for a while. But in the end she'll want a whole man to share her life with, to make a family with. She'll get that man one day. He just won't be you."

He raked a hand through his hair, shrugged into his jacket and took a deep breath. Before he let her walk out of his life for good there was one thing he could do for her. Her child had been taken from her. He was going to bring her child home. He took one last look at the man in the mirror, and gave that man a ruefully lopsided smile.

"She asked you to tell her lies, buddy." Despite the smile, the green eyes reflected back at him darkened in sudden pain.

"But you couldn't even get that right, could you?"

"YESTERDAY YOU SAID Noel had the opportunity and the motive. Why are we on our way to see Olivia instead of him?"

Julia raised an eyebrow in detached inquiry as they drove to Olivia's. Her voice was politely curious, nothing more. Prison was a great finishing school, she thought. What she really wanted to do was to grab the stone-faced man walking beside her by the lapels, shake him until that blank mask he was wearing fell away, and demand some answers from him.

But even that wouldn't do any good, she thought. If men were supposed to be from Mars, then Max Ross had the rest of his sex beat by a couple of galaxies. Since he'd silently walked away from her last night he'd gone so far out of reach that the man who'd held her in his arms, the man who'd laughed with her and made love with her, might as well not exist anymore.

He didn't, she told herself bleakly. The man in the video was once again a ghost. She wouldn't see him again, and part of that had been her fault.

But if she had it all to do over again she wouldn't be able to change anything she'd said to him. Maybe Max was able to pretend that his Ethan had never existed, but she couldn't, she thought sadly. She wouldn't. Going along with him in his conspiracy of silence was as impossible as seeing a child standing outside in the rain, and turning her back on that lost child.

"Olivia's the driving force behind the Tennants. She always has been," Max said evenly. "Getting her perspective on what makes Noel tick might just give me enough leverage to open a crack in the wall of lies he's throwing up, and that could be crucial. If he built that bomb, he's had plenty of time to cover his tracks."

"But Olivia's perspective on Noel is probably as distorted as looking through a fun-house mirror." Julia's lips thinned. "She persuaded Babs that I was capable of getting rid of my own daughter, for God's sake."

"That's right." He glanced at her, his smile humorless. "And the fact that Olivia could accept a mother killing her own child for gain told us a hell of a lot more about her than about you, didn't it? Yeah, her perspective'll probably be distorted. But that doesn't mean it won't be revealing, Jules."

She wished he wouldn't call her that, she thought, her eyes closing briefly. Not now. Not when everything else between them was on such a coolly courteous level. She looked up and saw they were nearing the severely plain federal facade of Olivia's house. Beside her, Max was wearing one of his ubiquitous suits, and she had on a pair of tailored slacks and a thin-knit, neutrally shaded sweater, but all of a sudden she felt they might as well be outfitted in breastplates and leggings and horned Viking helmets. They were the unwelcome marauders at the gates. They were unpleasant reminders of the violent world outside this privileged little sanctuary. From what Max had told her, Olivia had agreed to this meeting with no outward sign of reluctance, but Julia was willing to bet the grande dame of Tenn-Chem Industries had little real desire to reacquaint herself with her daughter-in-law.

But Max was right. Behind the deceptive facade of unostentatious affluence Olivia showed to her neighbors was a woman who had possibly rid herself of her own husband, a woman who had attempted to force her offspring into a rigidly ruthless mold, a woman to whom the idea of doing away with a child wasn't inconceivable. Julia's gaze jerked up at this last thought.

"You think Noel and Olivia could have been in this together, don't you?"

He pushed open the ornamental iron gate fronting the house and held it open for her. "It's possible." His nod was curt. "Under Kenneth she'd lost all power. At least in the current arrangement with Noel she's back at the helm of Tenn-Chem. The animosity between them is probably real enough, but that doesn't mean they don't both prefer this state of affairs to the way things were when Kenneth had absolute control."

He raised the polished pewter knocker affixed to the gleamingly black-painted door in front of them, and let it fall. "Whatever she says, don't let her get to you, Jules," he added softly. "Snap right back at her if you have to, alligator."

She shot him a startled glance, but before she could

say anything the door opened, and she received a second small shock.

"Hello, Mrs. Tennant." The kindly and once-familiar face of her former housekeeper, Maria, wore a tentative smile. "It's so good to see you again." Her smile wobbled and her eyes brightened with what looked suspiciously like tears. "Please—come in. Mrs. Olivia is expecting you."

"Maria!" Ignoring the other woman's halfhearted attempt at reticence, Julia threw her arms around the plump shoulders in a tight hug. "You're working here now?"

Releasing her and standing back, she mustered her own shaky smile. "I got the letter you and Thomas sent me in prison," she said quietly. "You don't know what it meant to realize I had someone on the outside thinking of me."

"We never believed what they said about you, Mrs. Tennant." Maria dabbed at her eyes with a corner of her apron. "Never! But you are out now, yes? You will have little Willa home soon?"

"Any day now, Maria. Agent Ross is looking into the case." Julia forced a note of unconcern into her voice and the older woman nodded happily.

"That is good. The little one should be with her mama." She gave one last sniff and straightened her apron. "Mrs. Olivia is in the small sitting room. She asked me to bring you straight through when you arrived."

She continued talking as she preceded the two of them down the walnut-panelled hallway. "When Mrs. Olivia's housekeeper retired she hired me and Thomas. We preferred being in a house with a child, but not so many people are looking for chauffeurs and household help these days."

She hadn't even laid eyes on her formidable mother-in-law yet, and already she was an emotional basket case, Julia thought wryly as she let Maria's softly accented chatter roll over her. If meeting one of the few people from her past she had fond memories of wasn't enough, Max's disarming reference to Willa's picture a few moments ago had come close to sabotaging her desperate attempts at self-control. It hadn't been anything more than a reminder that he was on her side, she told herself tightly. It certainly didn't negate what he'd told her two days ago and what his reaction last night had sharply underscored—that there was a limit to how far their relationship could go, and that it stopped well short of where she might hope it would lead.

"Mrs. Olivia? Your visitors are here." Maria's tone took on a formal detachment. "Shall I bring the tea in now?"

"Please, Maria."

As Julia, with Max one step behind her, entered the attractive and airy sitting room that she remembered as being Olivia's favorite place to hold court when she received guests, her mother-in-law crossed the silkily carpeted floor to greet them. Wearing unrelieved black and with her hair severely secured in a chignon at the back of her head, with both heavily beringed hands she reached for Julia's.

"My dear, it's been so *long*." She pressed a kiss to the air a quarter-inch from Julia's cheek, and stood back. "And Agent Ross. Do make yourselves comfortable."

With a gracious gesture she indicated a cosy seating area, but even as Julia, struck dumb by the unexpected welcome she'd received, obediently began to move toward the velvet-covered sofa and button-back chairs, she stopped in her tracks.

Above the white marble fireplace hung a beautifully framed photograph. Slowly she walked over to it, her breath catching in her throat.

"Taken last summer." Olivia had come up behind her. "It's my favorite picture of her, and since Barbara has seen fit to limit my granddaughter's visits I like to look up at it while I'm working away here."

Buttery-pale hair gathered in a ponytail high on her head, Willa was sitting motionless on a swing, both chubby fists holding tight to the ropes supporting it and the toes of her sneakers lightly touching the ground. Her gaze seemed serious and faraway, as if she was unaware of whoever was taking the photo. On the ground behind her was a fallen toy, a vivid splash of contrast to the muted colors of the sylvan setting, the spangled sunlight, the dreamy blue of the little girl's gaze.

With an effort, Julia kept her own eyes from tearing up. "Yes, Babs told me she doesn't allow Willa to see you as often as you'd like." She wrenched her gaze from the picture and turned to the sofa. Max followed suit, waiting until Olivia sat before taking his place beside Julia.

"You know why we're here, of course, Mrs. Tennant." His smile was perfunctory. "As I told you on the telephone, now that Julia's conviction's been overturned I've taken it upon myself to revisit my initial investigation into the bombing of your son's plane."

"In an unofficial capacity, I believe," Olivia countered with a thread of steel in her voice, no longer an indulgent grandmother or a welcoming hostess but reverting without difficulty to the persona that Julia was more familiar with—the implacable matriarch of the Tennant family and the brains and will behind the financial empire she'd created.

"Unofficial for the time being, yes," Max conceded. "But not for much longer. I'll be filing a report with my director this week, telling him not only do I now believe the wrong person was convicted, but that I feel there's sufficient new evidence to reopen the case. Officially reopen, that is," he added, his tone suddenly as hard as Olivia's.

Their gazes locked. Olivia broke off eye contact first. "Then I presume you'll be looking more closely into my younger son's whereabouts on the night in question, Agent Ross." She patted back an invisible strand into the elegant silvery chignon. "Means, motive and opportunity—I gather from the detective novels I occasionally indulge in that those are the three components to look for, am I correct?"

"So they say," Max said with a touch of amused dryness. "Are you telling me you suspect Noel of wanting his brother dead, Mrs. Tennant?"

"We'd all grown heartily tired of Kenneth's overbearing manner and bullying tactics. My son wasn't sorely missed after his death—not even, I'd venture to guess, by his wife. Certainly not by his brother," Olivia riposted. "I'm sorry if my attitude seems callous, Agent Ross, but I believe in calling a spade a spade. By the way, I'll thank you not to patronizingly cast me in the role of a doddering Dr. Watson to your Holmes." Her tone was ice. "Better men than you have underestimated me, to their eventual regret."

"I've heard that rumor." Max's smile didn't reach his eyes. "But I didn't put full credence in it until now."

"You have your hands full dealing with a two-year-old crime. I wouldn't advise you to go back twenty years further, Agent," Olivia said softly. "I'm sure the FBI doesn't want to waste valuable hours on ancient history."

"You're right, the Agency probably doesn't." Max sat back expansively. "But I'm on my own time here, as I think I've already mentioned."

To Julia's surprise, Olivia's austere features broke into an almost flirtatious smile and she relaxed her poker-straight posture a trifle. "Touché," she said with a light laugh. "Shall we set aside our foils now and get down to business, Mr. Ross? We *are* on the same side, you know."

Julia narrowed her eyes at the older woman, not taken in by her suddenly relaxed demeanor. Everything Olivia did was calculated, she reminded herself, and, like a snake, it was when she stopped hissing that she was at her most dangerous. She felt sudden uneasiness wash over her.

Maria entered just then with a wheeled tea trolley, and as the housekeeper whisked a linen cloth from a basket of miniature muffins, Julia caught Max's inquiring glance. She lifted a helpless eyebrow at him.

She couldn't figure out Olivia's game either, and their past relationship was no help in guessing what was behind her mother-in-law's puzzling attitude. She'd been expecting a reaction much like the one Babs had displayed. Instead, she thought in confusion, she was getting the strong impression that she had suddenly come into favor with Olivia.

But that made no sense. If what she was saying now was to be believed—*and that's not a given,* Julia told herself sharply—then Olivia's suspicions *had* shifted, and to her own son, of all people.

Which blows our theory of her working together with Noel right out of the water, she thought as she accepted a delicately thin cup and saucer from Olivia. *However convoluted the woman is, she wouldn't offer up Noel as a sacrificial lamb if there was a good chance he could implicate her as his partner.*

"Let me play Holmes for a moment, Mr. Ross. Forgive me—lemon? No?" Olivia raised her own cup and saucer. "Barbara will have told you how the management of Tenn-Chem has been set up, I'm sure. After building the company from the ground up and keeping it at the top of a very competitive field until Kenneth pushed me aside, I now must report to my other son like a none-too-bright child who needs constant monitoring." The rings on her fingers clattered against the bone china and abruptly she set her cup and saucer down on the table in front of her. "That *galls*," she said with soft venom.

"Motive. Noel got control of Tenn-Chem." Max shot her a keen look. "We'd gotten that far, Mrs. Tennant. Means, ditto. Your daughter told us that growing up as a Tennant meant growing up with the rudimentary knowledge of how to construct a bomb."

"Barbara," Olivia sniffed. She'd regained her composure, Julia saw. "She'd be more likely to blow herself up. But yes, Noel had the means. He had the opportunity too. What would you say if I told you he'd been seen in the Cape Ann area, where a good deal of the evidence was later found, in the weeks just prior to the explosion?"

She sat back with the air of a cat that had just caught a canary. Julia had the unworthy impulse to be the one who removed the bird from her before she could enjoy it.

"I'd say, tell us something we don't know," she drawled. "Like what happens to Tenn-Chem if Noel *is* found guilty? Do you get to run the whole show once more? Or does the animosity that Babs has toward you extend to shutting you out of that as well as to curtailing Willa's time with you?''

Olivia had been reaching forward for her tea. Now she paused, and the thin lips curved into a smile as she looked at Julia.

"You've changed, my dear,'' she said with what seemed like genuine admiration. "You never would have spoken up to me like this before. The last two years have toughened you, haven't they?''

"Prison'll do that to a girl,'' Julia said shortly. "But maybe I always was tougher than either of us knew, Olivia. You still haven't answered my question—will Babs take over Noel's role at Tenn-Chem if it's found he was responsible for the bombing?''

"No, at that point she'd have no other recourse but to let me resume my former role. She knows nothing about the running of the business, and I'm sure she wants Willa's inheritance to be kept intact,'' the older woman said definitely. "Of course, there's *your* new status to be considered. I see no reason why you shouldn't come under my wing now that your conviction's been reversed, and if you were already involved with Tenn-Chem when it came time to groom Willa for her ultimate position with the business it might make things more comfortable for the girl.''

Her casual assumption that Willa's career path was already preordained shook Julia. Olivia had sacrificed one generation on the altar of her precious Tenn-Chem, she thought in stupefaction, and the woman was already planning how best to slot her six-year-old granddaughter into the same corporate mold.

"I doubt that Barbara would agree to Julia having any closer contact with Willa.'' Max sounded mildly regret-

ful, and as Julia, alerted by his tone, looked up, she saw
Olivia's nostrils flare in anger.

"I know she puts about some crackbrained story about
Julia intending to kill her own daughter with that bomb.
Barbara's a fool—especially where her niece is concerned. She'd say anything to keep her. I believe she's
persuaded herself Willa's her own child—which is almost ironic, since even if he'd lived, Robert could never
have given her one."

She stopped, biting her thin lower lip as if she'd said
more than she'd intended, but Julia wasn't taken in. This
was what Olivia had wanted to tell them from the start,
she thought, meeting Max's eyes. He gave her the
slightest of nods and leaned forward.

"Robert was unable to give her children?" He
frowned. "From what I gather, Barbara's sole reason for
marriage was to have a family. Why would she marry a
man who couldn't help her fulfill her greatest desire?"

Olivia hesitated before answering, as if she were cal-
culating how best to formulate her reply. She wasn't acting now, Julia thought slowly. Whatever she was about
to tell them was something she would normally have kept
to herself. But like a master chess player, she was willing
to sacrifice even a vital piece for her ultimate goal.

"Barbara didn't know," she said finally. "It was part
of the deal. I'm sure if Robert had lived she would eventually have accepted the situation and adopted."

"Part of the deal? What deal?" It *couldn't* be what
she thought it was, Julia thought faintly. What she was
suspecting was monstrous—*unthinkable*. Surely even
Olivia couldn't have been capable of—

"Oh, it sounds a trifle cold-blooded blurted out like
this," the older woman said testily. "But you have to
understand, Kenneth had just gone through a messy battle

with Noel and the company had nearly been torn apart over it. He and I both agreed that it couldn't happen again—ever.''

"'Ever' as in with the next generation of Tennants?" Julia said carefully. She fixed her eyes on Olivia, and, to her disbelief, saw the faintest color creep up under the woman's expertly powdered cheeks.

"There could be only one Tennant line to inherit," Olivia snapped. "And since Kenneth was the first to have produced a child, we decided it would avert future problems if the man Barbara married took care of that eventuality *before* marriage. Robert saw it as a fair price to pay for a permanent vice-presidency at Tenn-Chem, and we all three decided that Barbara need never know he'd had—"

"Van Hale had a goddamned vasectomy," Max said flatly. "He had a vasectomy *before* he was allowed to marry into the family, didn't he?"

"It seemed the most expedient course." Olivia leveled a hooded gaze over the rim of her teacup, and at that moment she reminded Julia of nothing so much as a hawk. "For God's sake, Van Hale was at best an adequate second-in-command, and *Barbara*—" The beringed fingers holding the cup tightened. "Barbara's always been so infernally *weak*. The girl can't say boo to a goose." She shook her head. "Oh, I know Kenneth hoped to have a son, but Willa's sex never mattered to me. She comes of strong stock—stronger, I see now, than I realized even then."

"You think I did it." Julia stared at her in horror. "You think I did it—and you don't *care*."

Olivia looked momentarily disconcerted. She darted a glance at Max and then switched her attention back to Julia. The hooded eyes widened a little.

"I think you—? Oh, my dear, of *course* I don't. And since you can't be tried twice for the same crime, the official verdict is that you're innocent too." She smiled understandingly at Julia, as if she were trying to convey some silent message to her. "If nothing else, I know you never would have harmed Willa. And Willa wasn't harmed, was she? Thank God she had that little tummy upset just in time to make sure she had to be removed from the plane."

She set her cup and saucer down on the table. Stretching both hands across the elegant silver tea service, she held them out to Julia in the manner of a queen receiving a favorite.

"It's been two years, but now it's over," she said softly. "Welcome back to the family, Julia."

Chapter Fifteen

"I feel *unclean.*"

Julia stared straight ahead as, beside her, Max slid into the driver's seat. Even the few blocks' brisk walk in the spring sunshine to where they'd parked the car hadn't dissipated the nausea that had risen in her at the realization that Olivia saw her as an ally. Fists clenched tightly in her lap, she shuddered again and felt Max's hand on hers.

"She's a horrific old bird, I agree. But I think we have to scrap the idea she was Noel's partner in crime." He frowned thoughtfully. "I wonder how long she's known he's gay?"

"I caught that too." She allowed her hands to unclench a fraction. "When she and Kenneth were ensuring he would be the only Tennant to have children, they didn't even consider Noel. They must have known then. They probably saw it as a weapon they might be able to use against him one day." She shook her head, her eyes darkening in revulsion. "God, Max—they made a deal with Babs's husband-to-be to have a vasectomy! It's—it's unthinkable!"

"Olivia was right about one thing." He gave her hand

a reassuring squeeze. "Willa does come from strong stock. She's all you, Jules. I don't think there's a scrap of Tennant in her."

Looking up, she met his eyes. "Thank you for that," she said softly. "I see myself in her too. But there's an awful lot of Willa that's pure her and no one else, and that's one of the reasons I love her so much."

"Maybe that's also why Babs loves her so much." He exhaled heavily. "And why she's been so adamant about protecting Willa from what she had to endure as a child, like her ogre of a mother and that boarding school she was banished to."

"Hartley House." Julia smiled sadly. "I hope Babs and I can heal the breach between us one day. I'd like her to be part of Willa's life, and even if Olivia gets a lenient sentence because of her age she won't be allowed to—"

"Olivia?" Max had been about to start the car. Now he took his hand slowly away from the ignition. "Noel, you mean. As soon as I drop you off at home I'm heading to the office to request a meeting with my director. I meant what I said at Olivia's—I think there's enough evidence pointing to Noel to reopen the investigation. He'll probably be charged within a day or two."

"Noel? Weren't you listening to anything that murderous old woman *said?*" Julia stared at him disbelievingly. "She says she loves her granddaughter, but what if something had gone wrong with her plan to get Willa off that plane in time? She played dice with my little girl's *life,* dammit—and you're thinking of charging Noel?"

"What plan to get Willa off the plane?" He was staring at her blankly and she felt her already fraying nerves give way.

"I picked Willa up at Barbara's that night—she'd stayed over the night before, and Babs had asked if she could keep her for the day. I told you this already, Max."

"I know you did, but where the hell does Olivia fit in?" he asked tightly.

"Olivia had come by to see Barbara just before I arrived. When I walked in she was getting Willa to drink the last of her juice, damn her!" Julia heard the tremor in her own voice. "That must have been when she did it, Max. That must have been when she gave Willa something to make her sick enough so she wouldn't be able to get on that plane—and it nearly didn't work! That wicked, evil old woman nearly *killed* my daughter with her insane scheme!"

He held her gaze a moment longer. Then he looked away. She saw a muscle jump at the side of his jaw.

"You don't believe it," she said in slow comprehension. "But you were there! You *heard* what she said—she practically came out and told us that Willa's illness had been brought on by her."

"She still thinks *you* planted that bomb. She was telling you she knew how you'd ensured Willa's safety, Jules." Max raked a stray strand of hair back from his forehead. "I'm willing to bet the rings on those hands have been dipped in blood at least once in her life, but not in this instance. For one thing, she didn't get what she wanted from Kenneth's death. If Olivia was the bomber, then it follows she planted that evidence at your cottage. But why would she want to get you out of the way, knowing damn well that Barbara, as Willa's guardian, would unquestioningly choose Noel to have the final say in Tenn-Chem?"

"She'd always controlled Babs before. She thought

she'd be able to again, but she was wrong," Julia said swiftly. "Max, Noel's not the same man I used to know. If he did all this to gain control of the company, what's he getting out of it? He lives in a one-bedroom walk-up. He doesn't hang around with the high-rolling crowd that used to be so important to him. He seems to have made a new life for himself with Peter Symington, and what's more, he seems happy living the way he does. Maybe when Babs asked him to oversee Olivia's running of the business he only agreed because he doesn't trust her either."

"And maybe he figured it wouldn't be so obvious if he eased back into Tenn-Chem this way. Olivia's not a young woman, and she's already had one heart attack. It's just a matter of time before the company falls totally into his grasp." Max shook his head. "He lied about being at Cape Ann and both of us felt he was hiding more than his sexual orientation when we left his apartment the other day. At the very least, Jules, I've got a few hard questions for the man."

"Then let's go and ask him those questions right now." Impulsively she put her hand on his arm. She saw him start to speak, and she continued hurriedly. "I don't know why he lied about being at Cape Ann either, but what if there's a perfectly reasonable explanation for it? If you tell him his situation's a lot more serious than it was two days ago and he's still evasive, then go ahead and have him arrested. But if I'm right and Olivia was behind all this, taking the next few days to build a case against Noel is just a waste of time."

"I want this wrapped up as soon as possible too." A shadow crossed his features, and gently he lifted her hand from his arm. "But we're not exactly in a race against time here. Willa's safe for now with—"

"But that's just it—we *are* in a race against time!" This time when she grabbed his arm she could feel her nails digging into hard muscle. She saw the green eyes watching her widen slightly. "I don't know how to explain it, but from the moment I stepped into Olivia's sitting room today and saw her again I felt uneasy, and that feeling hasn't gone away. So help me, Max, if you won't confront Noel, I'll march right over to his apartment and question him myself—but one way or another, I want some answers today!"

"For God's sake—the man's probably already killed four people." Now he was gripping her. He gave her a little shake. "Do you think I'd allow you to walk in there by yourself and—"

"*Allow* me?" White-faced, Julia released her hold on him and tried unsuccessfully to break free of his grasp. She gave a short bark of angry laughter. "Allow me, Max? I'm a free agent. You and I have no claims on each other—you said that yourself. And maybe *you* can turn your back on your own child, but I can't!"

She heard his sudden indrawn breath even as the unforgivable words left her mouth. The echo of them hung in the silence between them as slowly Max's iron hold on her relaxed. Finally free, her hands crept shakily to her mouth and her fingers pressed tightly against her lips. She stared at him, her gaze wide and appalled, but even as she did he turned away.

"Then we go see Noel, I guess," he said huskily. "You don't leave me much choice."

He turned the key in the ignition. The car's motor caught and started. Looking briefly over his shoulder for oncoming traffic, he began to pull out of the parking space.

Julia let her fingers fall from her lips. "I never meant to say that, Max," she said dully. "I had no *right* to say that."

"Then we're even." Merging with the traffic, he sped up slightly to beat the amber light just ahead. "I've said things to you I had no real right to say, Julia. Let's leave it at that."

Taking his eyes from the road for a second, he gave her a briefly impersonal smile. "One way or another, Willa should be back with you soon. I doubt a judge will bar your custody claim once the Agency charges someone else. You'll be able to throw her a belated birthday party."

There was no hostility in his tone. There was no affection in it either. In fact, she thought bleakly, there was nothing in his voice at all. He could have been making a casual comment about the weather with a stranger, instead of saying goodbye to the woman he'd made love with only two nights before.

Because he was saying goodbye, she told herself. They might spend a few more days together for expediency's sake, but this was goodbye. The man in the video had gone away for good, never to return, and the man who'd said she could bring him to his knees with want for her had gone too. She stared straight ahead, and saw the world around her shimmer and blur.

"Yes, I'll be able to give her her present," she said softly. "We'll be able to get to know each other again. I've waited a long time for this, Max. Thank you."

His voice held an edge of harshness. "I destroyed your life, Julia. I don't deserve thanks for trying to patch it up again. It was because of me you got that damned scar on your hand. Yeah, I'm a hero, all right.''

In faint surprise she lifted her left hand and turned it, first one way and then the other. She touched the ugly piercings with the index finger of her right. ''You know, it doesn't bother me anymore,'' she said evenly, letting her hands fall again to her lap. ''And you didn't put me in prison, Max. It wasn't until they hung a number on me that I finally broke free of the bars that had always been around me. I—I wish I could have given you that much,'' she added almost inaudibly.

''Don't worry about me.'' He shrugged, his gaze focused on the traffic ahead of them. ''I get by okay, Julia. I always have.''

He was lying all by himself now, she thought, blinking rapidly and willing her tears not to fall. The man didn't need any prompting from her anymore. He wasn't okay. Max Ross hadn't been okay for a long time, and he would never be okay again. His scar might be invisible, but it was deeper and more wounding than hers had ever been.

But he would never acknowledge it. And until he did it would never heal.

''We're in luck.'' As he jockeyed the vehicle into a curb parking space and inclined his head toward the sidewalk, Julia saw that they were only about a block away from Noel's apartment. ''Isn't that Tennant and his friend across the street? They must be doing their grocery shopping.''

''Yes, that's Peter with the cane. And that's Noel with the trendy shades on.''

Pushing her unhappy thoughts aside, she followed Max's glance just as the blind man, a string bag full of vegetables over one arm and a long French baguette tucked under the other, took a seat on a sidewalk bench and said something to Noel. Grinning, Noel deposited a paper grocery sack beside Peter on the bench and entered the nearest store. Julia frowned.

"Let's get this over with." Max, his shoulders stiffly set, was already halfway out of the car. Hastily she unfastened her seat belt and scrambled out herself.

"Wait a minute," she said, her heart pounding. "Max, I think—"

"You wanted answers today. We're getting them," he said without breaking stride. "I'll go in and give Tennant the choice between going back to his apartment or having this discussion on the public sidewalk. You wait outside with Symington."

"But Max—"

He was already at the other curb. She waited to let a couple of cars go by, and got to the sidewalk just in time to see him enter the store. Folding her arms across her chest, she exhaled in sharp frustration.

"He's a headstrong guy, isn't he?" Peter Symington's pleasant voice held a touch of amusement. Julia glanced over and saw him looking in her general direction. She crossed the distance between them.

"You recognized my voice?"

"Like you recognize what I look like after only seeing me once." Peter nodded. "I've been blind since birth. My sense of hearing's as vital to me as your eyes are to you."

She sighed, and pushed the baguette closer to him as she took a seat on the bench. "Yeah, he's a headstrong guy," she said. The store's windows were piled high with merchandise. It was impossible to see inside. "But you'd know what that's like. Noel's as stubborn as they come too, isn't he? How long has he been blind, Peter?''

He gave no sign that her question was unexpected. Tapping the cane he was holding lightly on the pavement in front of him, he gave her a small smile. "He'd tell you he's been blind most of his life. But if you're asking when his vision started to go, I'd say about five years ago. It was gradual."

"And two years ago? How well could he see then?" Not well enough to assemble and plant a bomb and arm a timing device, Julia surmised. Peter confirmed her guess with his next words.

"Shapes and movement." He shrugged. "Just well enough to hide it from his family, if he was in a familiar environment and no one left a chair pulled out in his path. He used to pass off his occasional stumbles as the result of too much wine at dinner or a few too many martinis at lunch, and with his reputation as a party boy, people accepted that. But in the end he knew he either had to tell his family what was happening to him, or cut off ties with them."

"And being Noel, he chose the latter. He wouldn't have wanted Kenneth or Olivia to know," she said, nodding slowly.

"Do you blame him?" Peter gave a short laugh. "From what I've gathered Mommie Dearest would have shunned him like the plague if she'd known. She has an abhorrence for anything she sees as weakness, and her definition of that would include blindness."

He fell silent for a moment and then gave her a rueful grin. "But you and the fed aren't here to listen to the story of the great love of my life, right? You're here because of the Cape Ann connection."

"Max thought he'd found his man. I had my doubts," Julia said simply. "An explanation of what Noel was doing there two years ago would tidy things up so we could concentrate on someone else."

"Someone else like Olivia?" Peter asked shrewdly. "When you left the other day Noel told me what little I didn't already know about how your husband died, and that you'd gone to prison for the bombing. I told him he should have come clean with the two of you then, but he's still not ready to let that old harridan learn of his blindness and he thought it might get back to her. But I've got the feeling your Agent Ross is doing some detecting right now and putting two and two together, whether he's actually spoken to Noel or not. Echolocation's pretty intriguing to a sighted person when they witness it for the first time."

"Echo-what?"

"Echolocation." Peter grinned. "I grew up using the cane so I just never got the knack of acting like a bat, but Noel can zip around the city using it. It's based on the way bats send out sonar to keep from flying into things in the dark—by making a little clicking sound with your tongue you can tell a lot about your surroundings by listening to the tiny echo that comes back to you. Noel heard of a woman in the Cape Ann area who was willing to teach him how to use it. I can give you her name."

"I don't think that's going to be necessary." Julia saw Max appear in the doorway to the store, looking bemused. She got to her feet. "I believe Max is doing that addition you were speaking of right this minute, and finding he can't make two and two add up to five no matter how he tries. Thanks, Peter. I'll let him know what you told me."

She started to turn away, and then paused. "Noel said he'd been blind most of his life? What does he mean by that?"

Peter's smile in her direction was gentle. "He says he never saw what was really important until he lost his vision. Maybe one day he'll take on a bigger role at Tenn-Chem, but he'll never let that company rule his life the way he did before. He's a happy man, Julia."

Max's face was unreadable as the two of them crossed the road to his car, but when he unlocked the passenger-side door for her he didn't open it right away. He looked at her quizzically.

"You knew he was blind even before I went into that store. What alerted you?"

"I'm not sure." She made a helpless gesture. "I think my subconscious had already guessed what he was really hiding that day in his apartment. Don't forget, Max, I knew him quite well once. I saw a difference in the way he was interacting with us. Did you speak to him?"

He shook his head. "No. The store was crowded and the aisles were packed with boxes and displays. I saw at once he wasn't using his eyes to negotiate his way around everything, though I'll be damned if I know what he *was* doing."

"Peter called it echolocation. We had quite a little chat—about that and Cape Ann and a few other things."

Briefly she explained what she'd learned, and Max's frown slowly faded. "You said he wasn't the man he'd once been. I guess you were right, and not only about that. He couldn't have been capable of the delicate work involved in arming an explosive device." His eyes darkened. "But I'll bet Olivia could build a bomb with one arm tied behind her back. It's going to take a couple of days and a team of agents, but she strikes me as just arrogant enough not to have covered her tracks completely. I'll get the Agency to reopen the investigation right away, with her as the prime suspect."

His wording struck her as odd, and she realized her confusion must have shown in her face when he went on. "I'm taking myself off the case, Julia. My involvement with you doesn't make me a completely unbiased investigator, and I won't risk another tainted trial. If Olivia did this, she's going down for good."

"Those pesky constitutional rights." She smiled faintly, recalling their conversation on her first night of freedom. It seemed like a lifetime ago now, she thought sadly. Or maybe it only seemed like yesterday. A wave of pain washed over her, but as Max opened the car door she managed to lift her chin steadily enough and shake her head at him.

"No, Max. This is probably as good a time and place as any to say our goodbyes. I can send a taxi to collect my things and I'll contact the Agency later this afternoon to tell them where I'm staying so someone can let me know when Willa's coming home to me."

He was standing in bright sunlight. The flicker of anguish she thought she saw flash across his features had to be a trick of the light, Julia told herself. It had gone already.

He gazed steadily at her, his expression closed. His nod was no more than a curt inclination of his head. "That's probably best. You'll want to find a place and get settled in before we bring her back to you. I'll tell the investigator who takes over the case to keep you posted."

He let the door he'd been holding open for her swing

closed. As if he didn't know what to do with his hands, he jammed them into his pants pockets and looked past her to the street, his jaw tight.

He wasn't going to say anything more, she thought hollowly. He'd reverted completely to the man she'd encountered two years ago, the man she'd thought of as almost invisible, the rigidly professional agent whom she'd seen as devoid of any human emotion.

She'd been wrong about him then. But it didn't make any difference. Whatever he felt for her, he would never show it. He couldn't risk showing it. She gave him a too-brilliant smile, and hoped the bright sunlight would explain the shimmer in her eyes as well.

"Take care of yourself, Max," she said unevenly. Without waiting for his reply, she turned on her heel and started to walk away. She'd taken half a dozen steps before she heard him call her name.

"Jules." His tone was uninflected. She looked back to see him still standing where she'd left him, his hands in his pockets, his shoulders slightly hunched as if against a chill wind. He met her eyes, and even from a few feet away she saw desperate hope flare behind that green gaze.

Then it died. He shrugged. "Willa's a lucky little girl, Jules," he said quietly. "You're a good mother."

It wasn't what he'd started to say, she knew. And she also knew why what he'd started to say would never be said. The sunlight couldn't account for the tears that were streaming down her face now, she thought, but she was beyond caring anymore.

"And you were a good father, Max." She smiled at him through her tears. "You loved your Ethan very much, didn't you? That's why you won't let yourself begin to live again—because somewhere deep inside you think you'd be abandoning him if you did.'' She shook her head. ''You say you never had a son. I think you know that's a lie.''

For a moment he said nothing. Then a corner of his mouth lifted, but there was no humor in his expression. ''If it is, it was the only one I ever told you, Jules,'' he said tonelessly.

''I already knew that.''

Her throat was so tight she wasn't sure if her whisper had reached him or not. She saw him draw in a deep breath, felt his gaze linger on her a second longer, saw him take his hands irresolutely from his pockets. Those thick dark lashes dipped briefly to his cheekbones and then up again. He strode to the driver's side of the car, unlocked the door and got in.

But even as she heard him start the engine and drive off she was hurrying away, her shoulders set as stiffly as his had been, her attention focused on the cracks in the sidewalk, the feet of passers-by, the pieces of paper and carelessly discarded scraps of waste that were mute evidence of the hasty and urban world around her. How many of the people around her were in their own prisons? she wondered achingly. It was impossible to tell. Max was proof of—

A crushing weight seemed to slam into her chest with the force of a blow, stopping her in her tracks. She fought to get her breath, oblivious to the stream of humanity parting with irritation and impatience around her on the sidewalk.

Willa was in danger. *Willa was in danger!*

''Dear God, *no.*'' She wasn't even conscious of forming the words that pushed past her numbed lips. Frozen with dread, she swayed and nearly fell as she jostled her way to the edge of the sidewalk and leaned dizzily against a store window.

It didn't make sense. Within a few days Olivia would likely be arrested and charged, and any chance she'd hoped for to shape Willa's life as she'd shaped her own children's would be gone forever. Even now she was kept at arm's length from the child, thanks to Babs's vigilance. It wasn't as if the woman had plans to *harm* her grand-daughter, Julia told herself shakily.

She closed her eyes, frantically willing herself to think, but instead all that filled her mind was the photo of Willa she had seen only an hour or so ago—the serious, dreamy expression, the little hands clutching at the ropes of the swing, the fallen teddy bear behind her in its patchworked coat—

The teddy bear that had been bought for Willa's birth-day two years ago, the teddy bear that had been replaced in its beautifully wrapped package by a bomb, the hand-made, one-of-a-kind teddy bear that Barbara hadn't thrown away, but instead had given to the child she loved so much...

Suddenly the puzzle pieces flew into their rightful po-sition, and Julia knew she'd been looking at it the wrong way from the start. She felt what little blood there was left in her face drain away.

"She knew she couldn't stand up to Olivia," she whis-pered out loud, not seeing the curious glances coming her way. "But she made up her mind she wasn't going to let Willa go through the same hellish childhood she'd had. She decided she was going to give her every last minute of happiness she could, and when the day came that Willa was to be taken away from her and put into

Hartley House she was going to do the only thing she could think of to save her from that.''

She whirled around, ran into the store, and reached across the cashier's counter for the phone sitting there. With trembling fingers she punched out a number, and as the woman behind the counter grabbed angrily for the phone, Julia straight-armed her away.

Her fist tightened around the receiver as it rang a second time, and then a third, and she found she was biting down on her bottom lip so hard she'd drawn blood.

''Hello? This is the Tennant residence.''

The words were softly accented. Julia sagged against the store counter in relief, and choked back a sob.

''Maria?'' she said hoarsely. ''Maria, it's Julia. I—I need your help badly, and I need Thomas to let me have Olivia's car.''

Chapter Sixteen

The first thing he noticed when he let himself into the house was how quiet it was—which was crazy, Max told himself, since he'd been letting himself into a quiet house for over ten years now. He tossed his keys onto the hall table, and walked through the living room into the kitchen.

"Hey, boy." Without raising his head, Boomer thumped his tail in greeting as Max bent down and patted him. The brown eyes gazed up at him, following his every movement. "Getting pretty lazy there, aren't you, old guy?" Max said, standing.

He opened the refrigerator, looked blankly at the nearly empty shelves, and shut it again. He walked over to the sink and tightened the taps. He started to shrug out of his jacket and then stopped, instead pulling out a chair and sitting heavily down at the kitchen table.

Julia Tennant had been in his house with him. And now she wasn't.

He heard a muffled little squeaking sound. He looked down just as the dog closed his jaws over the foolish rubber hot dog Julia had bought him.

He leaned his forehead against his fist and squeezed his eyes shut, but it didn't do any good. She was still there, a dozen images of her flying through his mind—petting Boomer, washing up the dishes with him last night, standing in the hallway wearing his shirt and waiting for him to come to her.

His Jules, laughing up at him. His Jules, crying over Willa's pictures. His Jules, beside him in the half dark after they'd made love, her hair across his mouth, her head in the hollow of his shoulder, her heart in her eyes as she'd looked at him.

He'd stood on that damned sidewalk and let her go. He'd driven to the office and had asked to see the director right away. After giving him a quick outline of the situation he'd been grimly assured that the investigation would be reopened immediately. Then he'd left and come straight here. He'd had to come straight here. In the back of his mind he'd had the insane hope that by being here where she'd been only this morning he'd be able to hold on to some lingering trace of her, but as soon as he'd walked in the door he'd known it wasn't going to work.

He didn't want the memory of her. He wanted her *back.* The rawness of his longing flayed across his soul like the lash of a whip, and with a jerk he lifted his head and opened his eyes.

"You could have had her," he said out loud. "But in the end you would have driven her away. You never could have given her what she needed—what she deserved. There's a big piece of you missing, and you know it."

It was true, but not for the reason she'd given him. Impatiently he rubbed the heel of his hand over his face. Maybe the job had taken its toll on him over the years, maybe it went back further than that. He'd been raised by his grandparents, and after his grandmother had died, it had been just him and his grandfather. The old man had loved him, Max knew, but he hadn't been one to display or even admit to affection.

But why didn't matter. All that mattered was that he'd known he'd loved her, and still something inside him had held back whenever he'd contemplated making a life with her.

His feelings for Anne had been different. He'd cared for her, yes, but his love for her had been composed of equal parts of compassion and worry and regret. She'd made her need for him so obvious, Max thought tiredly, and sometimes he'd wondered whether it was really him she'd needed or whether any father figure would have done. But that didn't matter either, because in the end he'd failed her too.

So Jules had been wrong. There were a handful of alternative reasons he could come up with as to why he was the way he was. None of them had anything to do with betraying Ethan.

He caught himself a moment after the thought went through his mind. "For God's sake, how could it have?" he muttered impatiently. "I never *had* a son, dammit. There never *was* an Ethan."

The dog at his feet made a small snuffling noise in his sleep. Max looked down at him.

Something inside him cracked slightly.

You hear that, buddy—I got you your very own dog, ready and waiting for you to play with...

He frowned. He could dimly remember a man saying those very words a long time ago, but for the life of him he couldn't recall who the man had been. It hadn't been his grandfather, because his grandfather had never had much use for pets.

So hurry up and get here, little guy. We're all waiting for you...

This time it was an actual, sharp pain. This time he thought he could *hear* it—a fissure widening, breaking slowly open, somewhere deep inside him. He shook his head in quick denial.

"He never existed. I never lost a son, because he never existed." He tried to stand, but he found he couldn't. The pain was all-encompassing, a cold, searing sensation, as if he had come all too close to having frostbite and now was only inches from a roaring fire. He felt his heart crashing in his chest as if it were trying to burst free.

I'm always going to be there for you, Ethan. I'm always going to keep you safe, son. I love you so much...

Clutching the edge of the table with both hands, Max lurched to his feet, the pain so unendurable he could hardly breathe. He swayed unsteadily and nearly fell.

"But I didn't," he rasped hoarsely. "I didn't keep him safe, dammit. He was my son and I loved him and I didn't keep him *safe!*"

The pain had been unendurable before. Now it rose up in a towering wave, blotting out everything else, and he felt as if he was being torn asunder as finally—*finally*—the decade-old casing of ice and stone and sorrow that had surrounded the man inside him broke completely and fell away. Still holding on to the tabletop, he opened his eyes, his face wet with tears that had been waiting ten long years to fall.

"I had a son." He dragged in a slicing breath. "I had a son and I lost him. His name was Ethan and I loved him and I *lost* him." His vision wavered and blurred. He blinked. His vision cleared.

"And I wanted to die too," he said unevenly. "But I didn't, and in the end that was the hardest thing of all to accept. I love you, son. I've missed you so."

His heart rate steadied and slowed, and gradually the

trembling left his limbs. Max took a deep breath and let it out, a bittersweet sense of peace stealing over him. "I'll always keep you safe in my heart, Ethan," he whispered softly. "You know I always will, son."

Feeling almost dizzily light, he started to lower himself into the chair again, his palms still braced against the table. He stopped suddenly, every muscle in his body stiffening.

He'd let her go. He'd stood there on that sidewalk and let her *go*. He needed to find her, needed to tell her what a goddamn fool he'd been, needed to tell her he was completely and totally in love with her. He needed to ask her for a second chance.

Maybe she'd already left a number where she could be reached at his office. He grabbed up the receiver from the phone on the wall, but even as he lifted it he heard it give a small *ping*.

"Mr. Ross? Agent Maxwell Ross?" The voice on the other end of the line was brusquely impatient. Max pulled himself together, realizing that he'd picked up the phone just as a call had been coming in.

"This is Max Ross, yes." He tried to keep the impatience out of his own tone. "Who's this?"

"Agent Ross, it's Gerald Beeman, the headmaster at Hartley House." There was a touch of arrogance in the announcement. "You left a message with my secretary yesterday, asking if I could get back to you on whether or not young Willa Tennant had been enrolled in our institution. You understand, we don't normally give out information about our students, but I called your office and they confirmed you are who you say you are." Beeman sounded disgruntled.

"Willa Tennant's name was put down for Hartley at birth, Agent Ross, and when I spoke with her aunt and guardian yesterday, Ms. Van Hale assured me she would be bringing the child here today. As Ms. Van Hale attended our institution herself, I would have thought she'd realize that any tardiness in Willa's arrival would automatically result in a black mark against her niece, and that's certainly not the way we approve of our students starting off their years at Hartley—''

This time it was Max who interrupted. ''Ms. Van Hale told you she was bringing Willa to Hartley today? *Barbara* Van Hale?''

''That's what I'm trying to tell you.'' Beeman's tone was clipped. ''But when she didn't arrive here an hour ago as scheduled, I had my secretary telephone her home and I actually spoke to Ms. Van Hale myself. She was— she was quite *rude*.''

For the first time in the conversation his self-possession seemed to leave him. His voice shook in remembered outrage. ''She told me that as soon as Willa's birthday party was over, she intended to take her out on a nature walk, of all things, and that no one was ever going to force her to put the child into Hartley House. Then the woman actually hung *up* on me.''

Max was no longer listening. Letting the receiver drop from his suddenly nerveless fingers, he tore from the kitchen, grabbing up his keys from the hall table as he reached the front door. Behind him, Boomer scrambled to his feet with an alacrity he hadn't displayed for years and raced after him. Even as Max opened the door and ran outside, the old dog slipped out behind him.

''That's been her plan all along.'' Cold fear tore through him as he sprinted to the car. ''She thinks she's saving Willa—she always intended to save Willa from growing up the way she had to. The woman must be *insane*.''

And that was probably the simple truth of it, he thought grimly, wrenching open the sedan's door. With a mother like Olivia, all it would have taken was one final straw to break Barbara's tenuous grip on sanity. That straw might well have been finding out that her husband had connived with her brother and her mother to deprive her of the children she'd always wanted so badly.

"*No,* Boomer!"

But it was too late. The dog had already jumped into the car and was sitting in the passenger seat, his tail wagging as if in apology. Max stared at him in frustration, and then got into the car himself, slamming the door closed behind him.

"You always did like coming with me, didn't you, old boy?" he said under his breath. "Well, brace yourself for the ride of your life, Boomer, because we've got a little girl to save—and we don't have a second to waste."

WILLA'S SIXTH birthday party had come and gone. The mute and somehow forlorn evidence of the festivities had been strewn all over the lawn in the sprawling half acre or so of Barbara's backyard. Julia had left the Mercedes running in the drive outside the house and had run around to the rear of the rambling and old-fashioned home when her frantic pounding on the door hadn't been answered. She'd stared at the balloons tied to the backs of child-size chairs, at the crumbled remains of a chocolate cake sitting in the middle of the pretty mauve cloth covering the long trestle table, at the party-favor gold clip-on tiara lying discarded beside a plate of melting ice cream.

Despair had washed over her, and she'd closed her eyes, trying frantically to figure out where Barbara would have taken Willa.

Then she'd remembered the little clearing by the cliffs. Instantly she'd known with icy certainty that her daughter was there.

It wasn't a hunch, Julia told herself desperately as the Mercedes's suspension crashed over a pothole in the rutted road she and Max had driven only a few days ago. Hunches could be wrong, so she wouldn't allow herself to think of it as a hunch. It hadn't been a hunch when she'd known earlier that Willa was in danger, and it wasn't one now. It was as if there was a finely-woven silver cord stretching between her daughter and herself, a cord that had been there since the physical one between them had been removed at the little girl's birth, and she was so acutely attuned to Willa that even the slightest disturbance in her daughter's life ran down that cord to alert her.

Max wouldn't think that was crazy, Julia told herself. Max would think that was perfectly reasonable.

He'd been about to ask her not to go, she thought in anguish. But in the end he hadn't been able to say the words that would have meant he'd finally come to terms with his past and the child he swore he'd never had.

She'd had her daughter taken away from her. He'd lost a son. Maybe that had been why they'd understood each other's pain so well.

And maybe that was also how she knew what Barbara was planning to do, she thought. The children Babs had dreamed of having had been taken from her just as brutally, and in her own unbalanced way she was trying to ensure that she never lost another child again.

But she is unbalanced. Julia's mouth firmed implacably. *And it's my daughter she's planning to take with her. Whatever it takes to stop her, I'll do it.*

The small parking area came suddenly into view. Almost unable to see past the roiling dust cloud that had flown up around her vehicle, she wrenched the wheel hard over and turned into the lot.

As the dust dissipated she saw she'd narrowly missed hitting the only other car parked there. Barely waiting for the Mercedes to rock to a stop, she jumped out and ran over to the small blue sedan.

On the back seat was a teddy bear. It wore a patch-worked jacket. Its boot-button eyes stared blankly up at her, and she felt her blood turn to ice.

A moment later she was sprinting.

Twenty minutes into her run Julia found herself having to stop and wipe away the blood that was trickling down from a cut above her eye and obscuring her vision. She caught her breath and plunged on, almost immediately stepping on a loose rock and twisting her ankle painfully, but she didn't allow herself to break stride.

She shot around one last corner and skidded to a halt, her heart in her mouth.

Since the near-tragedy only a few days ago, the railing at the edge of the cliff had obviously been repaired and strengthened. Just as obviously, Barbara had spent some considerable time and effort in tearing it down again. She had what looked like a tire iron in her hand. She whirled around and met Julia's frozen stare.

"You." Her voice was dull. "I didn't expect you, Julia. But it doesn't matter anyway—you're too late."

Very slowly, Julia allowed her gaze to travel downward, to the huddled shape of the child at Barbara's moccasin-shod feet. Her heart beat slower and slower, until finally it hardly seemed to pump at all.

Willa stirred slightly. One curled fist crept up to her mouth. Julia felt hope jolt through her like an electric shock.

"She's *alive!*" she said tremulously. She took a quick step forward. "Dear God, Babs—I thought you'd—"

"Stay where you are, Julia." Barbara's voice cut through the silence of the little clearing like a whip-crack. She bent down and grasped Willa's limp wrist as Julia halted. "One more step and you'll see your daughter die. We'll both be over that cliff before you can stop me."

"But Babs, *why?*" Her question came out in an agonized whisper. "You don't have to *do* this! I know you want to save her from what you went through, but this isn't the way! You *love* her—how can you even think of ending her life like this?"

"That's right, Julia. I love her." Again there was a hopeless note in Barbara's soft voice. "I love her more than anyone possibly could, but Olivia's stronger than me—strong and ruthless. Even you never could stand up to her, could you?"

The brown eyes filled with tears. The slim shoulders shook. Julia took a cautious step closer.

"I made a lot of mistakes when I was married to Kenneth," she said evenly. "But I wouldn't have allowed Olivia to take over Willa's upbring—"

"I couldn't take that *chance!*" Barbara's eyes blazed furiously at her. "I knew about the agreement you'd signed, and all I could see was another human being—a *child*—about to be destroyed by my monster of a mother. She did it to me. She did it to Noel and to Kenneth. Dear God—she made sure my husband couldn't give me any *children,* Julia! Did you know that?"

"I knew that. And you're right, she is a wicked woman." Barbara's face was contorted in a rictus of pain, and Julia edged forward a few more steps. "You planted that bomb, didn't you, Babs? You planted that bomb, and you made sure all the evidence pointed at me."

"I found out about Robert's operation. I wasn't in love with him, but I'd thought he would make a good father—and I *knew* I would be a good mother. I wanted that more than anything in the world." Her voice wavered, and then hardened. "But when I found out what he'd done, and that Olivia and Kenneth had made it a condition of his marrying into Tenn-Chem, I decided to destroy them the way they'd destroyed me. So I blew up that plane with my husband and my brother on it, and I made sure that you went to prison for it by leaving the evidence at the Cape Ann house. That meant that I got Willa—and that meant that Olivia was robbed of any chance of influencing her only grandchild."

She straightened and threw her shoulders back, letting go of Willa's wrist. Her chin lifted. "It was worth it," she said simply. "These last few years have been heaven. I kept her safe from all harm right up until the end, Julia."

"I know you did, Babs." Julia kept her voice soft and non-threatening. "I know you would have given your own life for her. And that's why I can't believe you'd harm her now."

"I haven't harmed her." Barbara shook her head and gazed lovingly down at the child at her feet. "We had a wonderful time today, and then she fell asleep. I gave her something in her milk, like I did before," she added softly. "Nothing dangerous, just a mild sedative. I didn't want her to be afraid."

Barbara still looked like the shy, sweet-natured sister-in-law she'd once known, Julia told herself shakily. But that woman had gone forever. The Barbara standing in front of her was totally insane, and no amount of reasoning would reach her.

Even as the thought went through her mind she saw

something shift behind Barbara's gaze. The slim shoulders bent swiftly. The delicate-looking hand reached down to grab Willa.

"Stay away from my daughter!"

Covering the space between them in a leap, furiously Julia threw herself at Barbara, almost knocking the other woman off her feet and pushing her several yards past Willa's huddled body.

"She's my *daughter*—and I won't let you have her!" she gasped as Babs, with surprising strength, grappled with her. Julia felt a numbing pain glance off her shoulder, and looked up just in time to avoid the tire iron as Barbara one-handedly brought it swinging down at her head. With a mighty effort, she rammed the other woman a few feet farther back along the path, and then she saw Babs's eyes widen.

Still gripping Barbara by the shoulders, Julia turned, half suspecting a trick. A wave of cold dread washed over her. Even as she released her grip and started to run she felt Barbara's hand grab at her, holding her back.

Willa, groggy and dizzy, but on her feet, was only a foot or so from the edge of the cliff and tottering closer to it with each unsteady step. She didn't even look up as Julia screamed out her name.

"*Willa!* Willa, *no!*"

"It's better this way." Barbara's hoarse whisper was cracked and broken. "Let her go, Julia. This is the best way."

"For God's sake, let me *save* her!" Julia struggled frantically to get away, but even as she did she felt the tire iron smash down on her wrist. Barbara raised it again, her face an unrecognizable mask of madness. Julia twisted around, her eyes fixed desperately on the tiny figure at the edge of the cliff.

From the trees at the edge of the clearing burst a compact black shape, moving so fast it was almost a blur. It raced at top speed toward the little girl swaying on the edge of the cliff, and launched itself like a missile at the child.

The heavy black body crashed into Willa, knocking her backward and away from the crumbling drop. The dog—it was a dog, Julia saw now—took a few more stumbling steps and then dropped like a stone on the dirt path.

"Boomer!" It *was* Boomer, Julia thought in shock. But how—

"Julia!" Max tore into the clearing, and even as he raced toward her she saw him take in the small body still lying only feet away from the cliff. Bending down at a run, he scooped Willa up in his arms and sprinted toward the line of sheltering pine trees behind the picnic table. Gently he deposited his small burden on the ground, safely away from the dangerous cliff edge, and then he turned back.

"She was mine! She was supposed to be mine *forever!*" Barbara's words were ragged with shock and hatred. "If I can't have her, then you can't either!"

Gripping Julia's throbbing wrist with insanely superhuman strength, she darted back to the break in the fence. Julia saw Max's eyes darken in horror, saw him racing toward her, saw the desperation in his face as he reached out for her.

She felt the earth beneath her feet shift. In front of her, Babs stepped off the cliff into thin air.

And Julia felt herself falling with her.

"Jules!"

Max's hand shot out as she lost her balance, and as he grabbed her, Julia felt Barbara's grasp on her loosen and slip. In shock, she saw the slim body fall past the jagged edges of granite and land brokenly on the rocks far below.

She felt herself being pulled into a crushing embrace, felt Max's hand pushing her hair back, looked up and met his eyes, still clouded with fear. He was shaking, she realized. No, they were *both* shaking.

"Let's get away from the edge," he muttered, not taking his gaze from her face. "God, Jules—I thought I was going to be too late. I *was* too late. If it hadn't been for Boomer—"

He broke off, and Julia saw him glance over at the still body of the old dog. Her eyes filled with tears, and, slipping from his embrace, she ran to the animal. Kneeling, she stroked the velvety ears one last time. As she did, Max squatted down beside her. With gentle fingers he closed the still-open eyes.

"He—he saved her life, Max." She got awkwardly to her feet, her gaze flying to the small blond figure curled up at the base of one of the pine trees. "He gave his life for her."

"I told Ethan I got him the best dog in the world for his very own." Max's smile was unsteady, the green eyes brilliant with unshed tears. "I told my son his old man had gotten him the best puppy he could find. I guess I was right, wasn't I?"

"I guess you were," Julia said softly. Her eyes held his questioningly, and her next words were hesitant. "You had a son, Max?"

The green eyes smiling down at her shimmered and closed. He pulled her into his arms, and she could feel his breath against her hair as he spoke.

"Yes, I had a son, Jules. His name was Ethan, and I loved him very much."

He lifted his head and looked down at her, and Julia knew she was looking at the man in the video and that the man in the video would never disappear again.

"But I'd like to have a daughter as well," he said huskily. "And I'd like to have her mom, if she'll have me."

"Her mom says yes." She felt the tears spill over and run down her cheeks even as she gave the man she loved a trembling and joyous smile. "Let's get our little girl home, Max. I'm pretty sure that when we ask her later tonight she'll say yes too."

Holding her useless wrist close to her body for support, Julia watched as Max bent down and effortlessly lifted her little girl in his arms. Willa's eyes opened sleepily, and then drifted closed again.

"Trillions and jillions, kitten-paws," she whispered. "And forever and ever, Max."

And walking side by side with Willa cradled in Max's arms, Julia Tennant and the two people she loved most in all the world left the clearing to go home.

Epilogue

"Is this a park, Mom?" Willa looked around her with interest. Julia smiled and ruffled the flyaway blond hair.

"Not a park for playing in. It's more a park where you come to remember the people you love." She shielded her eyes from the bright June sun and gazed across the smooth swath of green grass. As if he sensed she was watching him, Max turned and started walking back to her and Willa.

The simple marble headstone had previously been inscribed only with Anne's name and the dates of her birth and death. Now there was a second inscription carved into the marble. Julia hadn't seen it, and she'd decided Willa was still too young to fully comprehend that her new daddy had once had a little boy who hadn't been born, so she and Willa had stayed here by the gates of the quiet cemetery while Max had walked over to the grave.

But she knew what it said. She'd seen Max write out the words he'd wanted the stonemason to add.

"Mom, we'd better get back to the car soon. Buffy's going to be wondering where we are." Willa tugged at her hand, and impulsively Julia scooped her into her arms. The little girl wriggled, laughing.

"I'm too big to be picked up now," she protested.

"I know." Julia bent over and rubbed the tip-tilted nose with her own. "But I don't care. I like cuddling you just like you like cuddling Buffy. And sometimes I like tickling your tummy like you tickle his."

She demonstrated, and Willa dissolved into giggles. "But Buffy's a puppy! I'm not a puppy, Mom."

Julia set her firmly onto her feet as she saw Max pause and look back at the gently rolling hills and the graceful old willow trees that seemed to accentuate the peace of this place.

"I know you're not a puppy, kitten-paws," she said softly. "You're my daughter. You're my darling, darling daughter."

THE SUMMER SUNLIGHT shafted between the branches of the trees. Max saw Jules and Willa waiting for him, and he smiled to himself. He was a lucky man, he thought. He had a brand-new daughter and a wife he loved with all his heart. And he'd had a son once—a son he'd lost for a while, but would never lose again.

Ethan, Beloved Son of Maxwell Ross. Max blinked. He jammed his hands in his pockets and turned back for one last look. It was written there for all the world to see, he thought, and that was the way it should be. He cleared his throat and started to turn away again, but then he stopped.

It had to be the sunlight, he thought shakily. It was dazzlingly bright, but just for a moment he'd thought he could see—

At the top of one of the gently rolling hills he saw the figure of a young boy. Close by his side was a blockier silhouette—a silhouette of a dog, with a happily wagging tail. Even as Max watched, the boy threw the softball in his hand and the dog bounded exuberantly after it.

The next moment the brow of the hill was empty again.

His heart overflowing, Max Ross turned away and walked back to the woman and the little girl he loved.

HARLEQUIN®
INTRIGUE®

brings you an exciting new 3-in-1 collection from three of your favorite authors.

Gypsy Magic

by

REBECCA YORK,
ANN VOSS PETERSON
and PATRICIA ROSEMOOR

Ten years ago, scandal rocked small-town
Les Baux, Louisiana: the mayor's wife was murdered,
her Gypsy lover convicted of the crime.
With her son sentenced to death, the Gypsy's
mother cursed the sons of the three people
who wrongly accused him.

For Wyatt, justice is blind.

For Garner, love is death.

For Andrei, the law is impotent.

Now these men are in a race against time to find the real
killer, before death revisits the bayou. And only true love
will break the evil spell they are under....

*Available OCTOBER 2002
at your favorite retail outlet.*

HARLEQUIN®
Makes any time special ®